Rogerson at Bay

By the same author

Jolly Rogerson
A Narrow Time
The Priest
Gate of Heaven

ROGERSON
AT BAY

A NOVEL by
RALPH McINERNY

HARPER & ROW, PUBLISHERS
New York, Hagerstown, San Francisco, London

ROGERSON AT BAY. Copyright © 1976 by Ralph McInerny. All rights reserved. Printed in the United States of America. No part of this book may be used or reproduced in any manner whatsoever without written permission except in the case of brief quotations embodied in critical articles and reviews. For information address Harper & Row, Publishers, Inc., 10 East 53rd Street, New York, N.Y. 10022. Published simultaneously in Canada by Fitzhenry & Whiteside Limited, Toronto.

FIRST EDITION

Designed by Stephanie Krasnow

Library of Congress Cataloging in Publication Data

McInerny, Ralph M
   Rogerson at bay.
   I. Title.
PZ4.M1514Ro   [PS3563.A31166]   813'.5'4   76–5108
ISBN 0–06–012944–1

76 77 78 79 80 10 9 8 7 6 5 4 3 2 1

For
my brother Dennis Q.
and for
Dave Solomon
too

Marriage is no real excuse for not loving.

—*The Art of Courtly Love*

ROGERSON AT BAY

1

In the third season of his life, wearing mortality as he might a smile with a cheek numbed by Novocaine, Matthew Rogerson, forty-seven, beyond the dreams of avarice and professional success, though not of good and evil, wheeled into his driveway one spring afternoon to find his wife, Marge, standing on the front steps of the house, a frown on her face, a book in her hand, impatience in the thin line of her lovely mouth. She came quickly to the car when he stopped.

"Don't turn off the motor, Matt."

"Where are you going?" That Marge had obviously been waiting for him surprised Rogerson. He had thought of his afternoon return as a surprise. The telephone call from Bastable had filled him with warm uxorious thoughts; his blood was aboil with fidelity and love for his now impatient wife.

"I've been calling your office every five minutes."

Rogerson got out of the car and Marge, eluding his embrace, slipped by him into the driver's seat.

"Bastable phoned." To hell with the demands of drama. He went straight to the punch line. Marge seemed not to have heard his explanation of the busy signal she had been getting. She put the car into reverse.

"I'm late."

"Where are you going?" he asked again.

Her words flew back to him from the departing car, a bodiless voice behind a windshield opaque with reflected trees and sky.

"To class," she cried.

Groaning aloud, Rogerson turned toward the house, widowed for the nonce by Marge's late-blooming interest in the life of the mind, allegedly pursued on the campus from which he himself had just returned.

Marge's water pistol, filled with ammonia, lay on a bench just inside the front door. Rogerson picked it up to try its heft. It was Marge's weapon against a large gray cat who prowled the borders of the yard and questioned with vertical eye Marge's questioning of the law of predator and prey. Rogerson's mind went foraging too. Marge now stalked a cat who hunted birds whose own heads cocked for the squirm of worms. His wife with a plastic pistol was an ineffectual posse of one. *Ab posse ad esse non valet illatio.* It endeared her to him. Lost causes were a link between them. He returned the pistol to the bench.

The bench was of wrought iron and had been picked up at a garage sale, painted, its seat recovered with red velvet. Of uncertain age, it was classed with other dubious items in the house as an antique. And what is an antique but the embodiment of memories not our own? Nailed to the wall over the workbench in the basement was a four-inch stick stripped of bark, with "Valley Forge" penciled on it. It had been there when they bought the house. That and other signs of a time antedating their purchase of the house gave Rogerson the sense of being an intruder still. But this bench, repainted and recovered by Marge, was theirs. Its renovation, not its prehistory, claimed Rogerson's affection.

He squinted back at himself from the hallway mirror. His face was fuller, his hair thinned, his half-assed sideburns were puffs of gray. He would have said that he was aging well, but that is a questionable feat, like being a good thief. This day thou shalt be with me in paradise. Perfidious Bastable: did he not find in his mirror similar signs of age? If anything, Bastable looked older than Rogerson. Rogerson remembered him at the convention in Detroit a month before, Bastable in an old-fashioned seersucker suit and shoes whose white polish, daubed imperfectly on, had reminded Rogerson of a first communicant's footwear, or stale divinity, these similes prompted by Bastable's improbable justification for leaving his wife and five children.

Rogerson got a can of beer from the kitchen and continued into the back yard. A dogwood flowered at the corner of the garage and there was a scent of lilac in the air. Rogerson sat at the picnic table that had been left outside all winter, its redwood gone gray, its benches wobbly. In a month classes would be over and he could sit in the yard and read, a whole vast summer before him. His refusal of the request that he teach summer school seemed strangely irresponsible now. Why? Self-indulgence of any kind likened him to the despicable bastard Bastable.

He should not have been surprised by his old friend's confidence. He was at the age when the bulk of his contemporaries had fallen apart in different ways: into drink or casual affairs, into campus politics, into the many and various dishonesties of the academic trade, out of marriage. But he had been surprised. He had been shocked. Seldom as he had seen Bastable over the years since graduate school, they had kept in touch. There was the bond of academe, the bond of memories shared in hopeful penury, the parallel of their courtships and marriages. Now Bastable too was going the fleshy way of the world, down the drain with all the others. And Bastable was a Catholic.

Forget the twenty years of marriage and those five dependent mouths which chorused in whatever words the echo of Bastable's promise to Theresa one rainy Saturday in Milwaukee, forget them if he could, but remember the promise that had been made and where, under what auspices. Did he have to remind Bastable that marriage is a sacrament, not just an impetuous pact made with an eye to a shared bed and more easeful nights?

"I don't even remember the ceremony," Bastable had incredibly said.

"What the hell do you mean, you don't remember? Look at your wedding album. Get out your goddam license. Call up that church and have them check the records."

"I remember sitting in the tub that morning and wondering what I was doing. I remember that I didn't really want to get married."

"You don't remember the ceremony?"

3

"I said *words,* Matt. But did I mean them? Did I really honest to God mean them?"

"With five kids, how can you ask?"

Around them in the hotel bar other MLA conventioners were being drunkenly assertive over their drinks. Rogerson whispered hoarsely across the table to Bastable, actually worried that they would be overheard. Bastable listened, the message clear as the Baltimore Catechism, all the while wearing a smirk of a smile which suggested that he had himself rehearsed a hundred times any argument Rogerson might make, tried it and found it wanting. In his heart of hearts —this was his position—he was still an unmarried man.

Rogerson got Bastable out of the bar and up to his room and the more economical bottle he had in his briefcase. In the elevator he was aware of the cage in which they were pulled up the shaft in a whoosh of efficiency; his mind was on the manmade cable, the manufactured floor beneath their feet, the distant machines and motors with their too many parts, any one of which could give way under the stress of its appointed task. Bastable's story filled him with vertigo, Bastable with his kinky gray hair, manic smile and ten-year-old suit, who might have been himself announcing that he was leaving Marge.

Of course there was a girl, an ex-student. Worse, far worse, Rogerson had met her. She was the lass with the haystack of brown hair and the wide green watchful eyes to whom Bastable had introduced him at breakfast. Rogerson had the wounded retrospective certainty that they had slept together. The gall of Bastable to bring his girl to the breakfast table of the man who had been witness of his wedding long ago, to share his syrup, to smile wondrously at tales of Madison back in the ice age when they were young. Rogerson ground his teeth at the memory. Had Bastable sought an unwitting benediction on his shack-up? Bastable frowned at the word.

"I'm going to marry her, Matt."

"You're already married. Only one to a customer."

In the room, Bastable took off his suit jacket and laid it carefully on the bed. Rogerson watched the bastard posture before the mirror: darting eyes, nervous narrow nose twitchingly on the *qui vive* for a future better than the past. Didn't Bastable realize how ridiculous he was, a swain at his age?

4

"I've started annulment proceedings in Chicago."

"You're as married as I am."

Bastable grew serious. "Matt, do you remember, in the sacristy, when I told you I didn't want to go out there and marry Theresa?"

"No."

"I told you it was all wrong, too fast, I didn't want to."

Had Bastable said that? What difference did it make? It was the sort of remark the occasion called for. The reluctant bridegroom is the stuff of folklore. And Bastable had drunk his fill at the stag party the night before.

"Is that your story—a shotgun wedding?"

"Do you remember?"

"Remember what?"

"That I expressed on the very day, minutes before the ceremony, my reluctance to go through with it."

"I remember you promising to love Theresa till the day you die."

"The canon lawyer will put you under oath for the deposition."

"What deposition!"

"The annulment proceedings. It's important that they know I didn't want to do it at the time, that it isn't just now, an afterthought."

"Forget it, Jimmy. Do you think I would do that to Theresa?"

"Matt, it's God's will."

Bastable apparently meant this. He had convinced himself that God wanted him to desert his wife and family. His putative wife. Were the kids only putative too, bastards for the kingdom of hea-ven's sake? God wanted Bastable to marry Dolores. Dolores was the girl.

"And this time you'll really mean it?"

"I don't expect you to understand this, Matt. My God, I hardly understand it myself. Do you think I wanted this to happen? I didn't. It's not just another affair with a student, Matt."

"Have there been those too?"

"Don't be a maiden aunt." Bastable's expression was fleetingly that of the worldly man, but then he was back to the divine will, to annulment, to Dolores. Dolores was Catholic too.

"Have you convinced her of all this shit?"

"I'm not doing anything illegal, Matt. Dolores has a brother who was a priest. He got out of it, perfectly legitimately. Now he's a married man in Skokie. She knows mistakes are made, tragic mistakes, but nowadays they can be rectified. The church is learning compassion."

"Tell it to Theresa and the kids."

He lectured Bastable, he preached, he was a poet of monogamy, he was drunk. They were both drunk. Bastable cried. Rogerson settled for prophetic wrath. If Bastable had said he was ditching Theresa and the kids, that he knew it was wrong but he had the hots for Dolores and couldn't live without her, Rogerson might have understood. At least he said he would have understood. What he could not take was Bastable's unctuous way of describing his planned desertion as a dutiful trodding of the path God had laid out for him. Bastable would not leave. He seemed determined to stay until he had received Rogerson's blessing on his decision. Over my dead body. When Rogerson passed out, his harangue continued in his head. He argued and reargued the case for keeping promises, honoring vows, hanging in there through thick and thin despite the passing attraction of the campus's yearly bounty of virginity on the make.

He came to at three in the morning. Bastable was no longer there. Gone to his paramour? Rogerson went downstairs. Furtive types came through the revolving doors, returned from who knew what Detroit debauch. Outside, Rogerson stood on the sidewalk, where he decided against a sobering stroll. The empty streets seemed full of menace. The world was a goddam jungle.

He did not see Bastable again. Rogerson left Detroit at the crack of dawn, eager to get back to Fort Elbow. Sitting unshaven in the airport coffee shop, he surprised in his heart a spiteful pleasure at Bastable's fall. I alone have escaped to tell thee? But when he got home he could not bring himself to tell Marge what Jimmy Bastable meant to do. To mention it would have been to voice a dreaded impossibility, to foul his own nest, to stir memories best left dormant. It would have been like confessing his own infidelity.

Today the phone call and Bastable cheery as a kid announcing that Theresa had agreed to a divorce. A divorce and not an annulment. That could still come, later. Meanwhile he and Dolores would live in legal sin together.

"Don't do it, Jimmy."

"It's done."

"Undo it."

"It's too late."

"That's what I mean. Twenty years too late."

A pause and then, reproachfully, "I thought you'd understand."

It was that more than anything else that had brought him home to Marge, Bastable's words an accusation. Why the hell should Rogerson understand? What had Jimmy meant? To cleanse himself of the implication, he had meant to share the tragicomic news with Marge, trade incredulity with her, savor Bastable's fall, exult in it. And he had forgotten that Marge was waiting for him and the car.

His watch said two o'clock. He had to get back to campus himself. If he had been thinking straight, he would have returned with Marge. The prospect of walking did not appeal. Marge should have a car of her own. Why should she be stranded here? It was un-American not to have two cars; their two-car garage was an affluent rebuke to their solitary Ford. Summer school could provide the wherewithal for another car. Something to think of there.

Tommy's ten-speed was in the garage. Did he dare ride it? He had tried it once last summer, sailing down the driveway and returning a harrowing fifteen minutes later. He had not been told of the hand brakes and, back-pedaling furiously and to no avail, had come to a scratchy halt in a forsythia bush. Rogerson went to the garage for the bike. Its tires looked flat. The seat was jacked up as high as it would go. Rogerson looked doubtfully at the bike, conscious of the aches and pains that had made the Merck manual his breviary since his return from Detroit. Bastable's youthful exuberance on the phone had brought back his undiagnosed symptoms, as if a reminder of mortality might quell such antics as Jimmy was engaged in. Inside the house the phone began to ring. Bastable again? Had he pursued him here, importunate Jacob still intent on a blessing? Rogerson hesitated, then went to answer it.

"Mrs. Matthew Rogerson?"

"She isn't here."

"This is Western Union."

"I'm her husband. What is it?"

Expecting a plea from Theresa or a carefree announcement from Jimmy that he had eloped, Rogerson was not wholly unprepared for what he heard.

7

" 'Father dead. Please come. Mother.' "

From where he stood, Rogerson could see the bicycle in the driveway. The cracks in the concrete had been repaired with tar. Olson had been a cement contractor in Milwaukee. Rogerson thought of his father-in-law, short, stocky, deaf. Of late the bows of his glasses had been burdened with huge hearing aids, but years of blessed silence had ingrained the habit of asking that everything said to him be repeated. Rogerson often just moved his lips to get Olson's attention and then to the old man's "What?" said once what he wished to say.

"Would you like the message sent to the house?"

"Yes." It seemed a chance of not having to tell Marge himself. Olson had been nearly eighty, but Rogerson was stunned by the news. He went out onto the front porch. Late April sun lay on the grass. He felt a tug within as if his reins, in the psalmist's sense, were being pulled. Olson dead. Olsonofabitch gone to that great cement mixer in the sky, no more Svenskarnas Dag for him, the bunting yellow and blue, a reminder of the Sweden he had never seen. Marge had urged her parents to travel, to see Europe, to go to Sweden. A light, half atavistic, half romantic, glowed in her eyes, the traditional dream of the grand tour, a Henry James heroine longing for culture and a king across the water. Mrs. Olson had no desire to move among the foreign and her husband shook his bullet head at the thought of boarding a plane. He was content to sit before the tube, smoke his pipe and sip beer from quart bottles. Portrait of a cement contractor preparing for death. Had he ever given his impending end a passing thought? Olson had always regarded abstract thought, like grammatical correctness, as an affectation. Rogerson imagined the old man propelled from the inanity of daytime television into the world beyond. God rest his soul.

The words formed in his heart with tenderness. The poor old sonofabitch. Fifty years with Mrs. Olson should count as a plenary indulgence. Rogerson's hand now lay on the uncomfortable curve of the bicycle seat. Should he leave, carrying the knowledge of Olson's death about with him? Marge had to be told. But how? No way to reach her by phone. He was more likely to run into her on campus. He kicked up the stand of the bike, raised his leg over the seat against the protest of his muscles, an exercise bar, Rogerson as Nijinsky, his balls bulging in a skintight tutu or whatever the masculine number is called. The bike began to roll, he got his seat on the seat, felt that he was offering it defenselessly to air, got the bike under control, steered down the driveway, his little fingers hooked prudently on the hand brakes. How could he just go up to Marge, if he found her, and tell her that her father was dead?

The Fort Elbow campus of the state university was half a dozen buildings more than it had been a few years before, its feeble torch of learning beckoning into port the malcontent illiterates who preferred the boredom of infrequent lectures to the grim realities of military life or the more grueling routine of a job. Wooley, once called its president, had, in the inflated nomenclature of the profession, become its chancellor. Herb Laplace had surrounded himself with four assistant deans and withdrawn into Oriental isolation, from which too frequently he addressed lengthy letters to his faculty, encyclicals of a minor metropolitan. The place had become a college of artifice and letters. Herb was currently concerned about grades. He would not, of course, presume to intrude on the professional autonomy of the staff, but he felt he should bring their attention to the fact that the average grade in the college was B+. Some might regard this average as high; Laplace himself did not express an opinion, except to say that there seemed to be a national trend toward a higher assessment of student performance. As a result, however, transcripts of student grades were an unsure guide to future employers and graduate schools. Faculty were going to have to show a greater willingness to write letters of recommendation to provide a finer-grained analysis than the grade point average.

Rogerson had smiled and put the letter in his file. He kept the dean's correspondence as if he were gathering evidence. Rogerson had himself devised a form letter which he used in response to requests for recommendations.

Dear _____,

(Mr., Mrs., Miss, Ms.) _____ has asked me to write on his (her) behalf, though I am mystified why I should be the object of such a request, given the performance of _____ in my class. The transcript of _____'s grades, which no doubt you have received, gives no true indication of the quality of performance which has marked his (her) college work. These are of course special times and allowances must be made; nonetheless, I know that you will agree that _____ has achieved a remarkable record. I hope that these few remarks will be helpful as you make your decision. If I can be of any further assistance, do not hesitate to call on,

Your obedient servant,

Matthew Rogerson
Professor of Humanities

His further assistance had never been required though, oddly, three or four former students had thanked him for his help. Of course, no one reads either transcripts or letters of recommendation. They are noted when they arrive, but weightless when the heavy decisions are made to the feathered whir of thrown darts, the spin of milk bottles, the eenie-meenie-minie-mo whereby the elite are elected.

Laplace, shown Rogerson's form letter by a fink in the typing pool, asked to be allowed to provide it to the faculty at large. Rogerson refused.

Approaching the campus this April afternoon, his center of gravity somewhere between the Mont Blanc of his rear and the prow of his chin, thrust forward in such a way that he had the sensation of looking up to see straight ahead, Rogerson the five-day racer wheeled onto a walk and shot among knots of pedestrians with a finesse that came as a pleasant surprise. Agility and speed belying his years, the sting of stirred air in his eyes and flushing his cheeks, he was filled with a springtime zest. He braked to a stop behind the new faculty office building and filed the bike away in the stand, rolling its front wheel into a slot. There was a chain and lock looped around the seat post, but the lock was a combination whose numbers Rogerson did not know. The rack was all but full, each bicycle lashed in place; a hurried thief would argue from analogy and not notice that Tommy's bike was free for the taking. Rogerson rolled with a sailor's gait to the door of the building, not quite repressing a seasonal whistle. April and Rogerson icumen in.

He stopped at the English office to ask where Keane's class met and was greeted by Sylvia Wood, a forward redhead in her first year on the faculty. A white pleated skirt concealed her concupiscent thighs, she wore a blazer with brass buttons, her eyes sparkled with disarming camaraderie. Sylvia answered the question Rogerson had addressed to the secretary, a small starling-like creature who simpered mournfully behind her desk.

"He took his class out onto the lawn. Your wife among them. To get the lay of the land."

Keane was one reason for his almost friendship with Sylvia, a shared odium drawing middle-aged academic and fledgling instructrix into the intimacy of uncharitableness. Keane was trying to peddle a book, whittled from his dissertation, entitled "Pound Devalued: Economic Theory in the Cantos." Sylvia and Rogerson vied with one another to convince Keane of its insightfulness and relevance.

"I wish some editor would see that," Keane whined. "It has been rejected by dozens of publishers."

Keane's sparse hair curled greasy and unwashed over his ample ears and might have lain on his shoulders if he did not toss his head while he talked. His pale pocked face expressed a longing for recognition, a commodity he received from a minority of students who, finding a match for their own inarticulateness in Keane, mistook it for profundity. Like Plummet-Finch, Keane professed to share Sylvia's hopes for the liberation of womankind, but she, with the perversity of the true believer, preferred the unabashed chauvinism of Rogerson.

"Do you know where they went?"

"We could look."

Rogerson glanced at his watch. "I have a class."

"Don't forget the taping."

Reminded, Rogerson felt more annoyance than guilt at his failure to remember. "What time do we do it?"

"Well, we tape at four-thirty."

Sylvia followed him into the hall and came along to his office, a functional cube one wall of which was windows, their glare subdued by Venetian blinds. Desk, swivel chair and bookcases were of pale green steel. Rogerson missed his old office in the basement of the library, which had been dignified by shadows and crammed with memorabilia. Haunted by memories too, so the change was for the better. Sylvia put a testing fingertip to the coffeepot. Cold.

"I've got coffee made," she said.

"I'd like a cup."

They adjourned to her office, identical to Rogerson's, so much for the perquisites of rank. There was a massive blow up of Janis Joplin affixed to the inside of the door. Rogerson accepted a styrofoam cup of coffee. The Western Union message formed in his mind and he felt suddenly old.

"My father-in-law died today."

"Oh!"

"Marge doesn't know yet." It seemed a species of infidelity to tell Sylvia first. Death was a rumor she could not yet make out, a destiny for others, for strangers. Still in the grip of the pride of life, poor girl. She told him about Keane's cat.

"He buried it in a pet cemetery. With a headstone."

"Did you attend?"

"Gilbert and I were pallbearers." Gilbert was Plummet-Finch, a fey Englishman who had fluttered to rest in Fort Elbow, to his own unrelieved amazement. At the feline funeral, Gilbert had read from the *Book of Common Prayer.* Ashes to ashes, dust to dust. Both he and Keane had cried.

Rogerson, against his grain, found the described scene touching. His contempt for Keane gave way to pity, almost to affection. He doubted that Sylvia would understand. She was a post-Christian, her dislikes undiluted by the hope of mercy. Rogerson found her fascinating, horrible, beautiful, an alien who belonged while he did not, not anymore, if he ever had. One man's exile is another's home. His vale of tears was Sylvia's motherland. How odd that he had kept his acquired faith while Marge had lost her native religion. Would news of her father's death bring her to church again?

"He's keen on your wife."

"Who?"

"Keane."

It was an old story. Marge had gone through life as the target of lusting eyes. Her single lapse had all but undone them both. He did not fear a repetition, least of all with Keane. But Sylvia, bored, aboil with youth, demanded that the faculty exhibit the same untrammeled sexuality the students did and, in default of fault, invented liaisons. Keane and Marge was a favorite suspicion.

12

"Woman as sex object," Rogerson sighed insincerely. "The same old story."

Sylvia studied him as if from some eminence. "Are you really that sure of her?"

"*Cogito ergo sum.*"

"She wants a life of her own."

"Does she?"

"Why do you think she is taking that class? It's symbolic. God knows she can't be learning anything from Keane."

"Hang it all, Robert Browning."

"No Pound at all. He is currently blathering about Sainte-Beuve and his history of Port-Royal."

"In a course in modern poetry?"

"Keane has become bored by it. He lectures on his current whimsical reading. Just now he is chock-full of nineteenth-century French literature, so that is what he teaches."

How important it is not to know too much of those we despise. Sylvia was turning Keane into a sympathetic character. Had Keane learned already at thirty-five that a teacher should amuse only himself? Rogerson knew that no student remembered five months, let alone five years, after the fact what a given course had been about. Better then to perform in class, entertain, create the possibility of a pleasant if empty memory. Good old Professor Whatshisname. A bell rang.

"It tolls for thee."

Rogerson was already on his feet. Telling Marge of her father would have to wait.

"What are you teaching?" Sylvia asked.

"Students."

He closed the door on her puckered expression. The hall swelled with noise, but he heard her call.

"Don't forget the taping."

He took his own class outside, a reluctant flock following him over the still khaki-colored lawn. Rogerson had half a hope that he might catch Keane and his class still pursuing Pascal among the hedgerows of the mall. Such benches as there were had already been claimed by Rodin couples, embracing with abandon, the exhibitionism of

13

youthful love. Rogerson paused before a couple grappling as if in the grip of the life force itself. There was an appreciative murmur from his class. Rogerson's refutation of hedonism, his lecture for the day, evanesced and slipped up and away among the burgeoning branches of the trees. He turned to get their attention. Among them unisex reigned. Their gender could no longer be visually described: long hair, slovenly dress, no curve or brawn pressing the fabric to give a clue. "I, Teresias, an old man," Rogerson announced.

His babble stopped theirs. Something like attention formed in their spaced-out eyes.

"Who wants class today?"

Consternation. Mumbling. Confusion.

"All those who want to cancel class, raise your hand."

Their arms shot up like a corps of Hitler Youth. Rogerson bade them begone and retraced his steps to the faculty office building. Freed to find Marge, he hoped he would not. It was a bad day for bad news. The twitter of birds, the glint and warmth of sun, the odor of humus and early blossoms blended pleasantly. Marge, your father is dead. No. Inside the building, Rogerson stopped. If only Marge had answered the phone so some stranger could have conferred orphan-hood upon her.

"Matthew."

Rogerson turned to face Fallor, tenured just two years ago, the new chairman of the humanities department. Laplace had made only a *pro forma* gesture in Rogerson's direction with the dubious plum. Once Rogerson had been given reason to hope that he would have the position that had gone, in the event, to Herb Laplace. Dean Matthew Rogerson? Thank God, he was not among the swift of the race. Fallor's face was afrown with the burdens of his office.

"Why don't you want to teach summer school?"

"I defer to the young." Summer work brought an extra stipend, well earned, God knows: classes every day, sixty-minute meetings, no chance to while away the first quarter hour summarizing the nuggets of the previous session; memories were too fresh. Vast amounts of material were covered, the faculty bathed in honest sweat as they crammed to keep ahead of returned secondary school teachers in quest of an M.A. and a higher rung on the pay scale.

"But that's just it," Fallor complained. He shifted his books to the

14

cradle of his left arm and put his now free right hand under Rogerson's arm to guide him toward the stairs. "Everyone seems to have a grant or some other source of money."

Everyone but Matthew Rogerson, the dead wood among the green shoots on the staff? "That's too bad."

"It would really help if you would take a class or two. Two would make it worthwhile, financially."

"I plan to do some work of my own."

Fallor's brow rose in skepticism. On the spot, Rogerson conceived the resolution to spend the summer writing doggerel. Of the several poems he had published, in badly printed quarterlies which had appeared for the typical five issues then disappeared, only one had lines he could bear to recall. The weather, his prostate, the death of Olson, had combined to tempt him into verse.

"Some creative work," he explained.

The adjective had its desired effect on Fallor. Nonetheless, puffing with the ascent, his pudgy body putting his heart through its paces though he was in his early thirties, Fallor expressed the wish that Rogerson would give the matter more thought. It seemed a shame to bring in outside teachers for summer school. Rogerson said nothing.

"Don't you have a class?" Fallor asked when they reached the third floor. No doubt the younger man had the schedules of the staff emblazoned on his memory. It was becoming more and more difficult to retain a gentleman's approach to the meeting of one's classes. In the bad old days, as the young men doubtless imagined them, not having been the beneficiaries of the once unashamed and acknowledged mediocrity of the place as a community college, it had been understood that one skipped at least six meetings a semester. The quantification of learning, reducing such pearls as they might secrete to credit hours, had been regarded disdainfully by the infecund oysters of the day. Rogerson felt the wash of nostalgia. How bitter to have survived into the apotheosis of this backwater place. Now there were seventeen thousand students, a chancellor, a nursing school, the sciences ensconced, Laplace with four assistant deans. And Fallor.

"We had a short session. I'm due to make a tape for *Focus on Faculty.*"

Undisguised envy took possession of Fallor. He longed to appear on *FOF,* but Plummet-Finch, the moderator, kept putting him off.

"Let him blush unseen," Gilbert had explained to Rogerson. "My apparent cruelty is true kindness. Fallor must learn to cherish the obscurity he so richly deserves."

"You don't think he would be impressive," Rogerson said, egging Gilbert on.

Plummet-Finch's eyebrows rose like hairy horizons over the frames of his glasses. "Quite the contrary."

"He wrote his dissertation on Emily Dickinson."

"With an electric needle, no doubt."

Focus on Faculty, taped in the studio the journalism department had bullied Wooley into building for them, was broadcast by a commercial station in town. As a public service, in the equivocal phrase. The station, torn between the desire to give the appearance of dabbling in educational television and disbelief at the tapes they were sent, ran them on Saturday nights, Sunday mornings really, after the night-owl movie, at an hour when only the participants were sure to watch, crouched before their sets, enthralled by their own well-honed remarks while the camera brooded on another's face. Rogerson knew. After his first appearance, he had sat up to watch, alone, Marge having yawned through the movie and fallen asleep on the couch before *FOF* was shown. Rogerson had felt his pulse quicken, his hearing sharpen, his attention become total. There he was on the same screen where earlier Howard K. Smith and Howard Duff had been visible. He imagined the world watching. No one had ever mentioned the program.

"Who's on with you?" Fallor asked breathlessly now.

"Sylvia."

"Anyone else?"

"I don't think so."

"Just the two of you! What's the topic?"

" 'The Role of Women in the Modern World.' "

Rogerson no longer minded the banality of Plummet-Finch's selections. Whatever the topic, a televised discussion sank swiftly to a mindless level. Gilbert had somehow achieved the status of the Alistair Cooke of the Midlands, his British mumble conveying the arch viewpoint of the landed aristocracy, although his father had

16

been a chemist and his mother was matron of a home for wayward youth. The journalism department grumbled. Their defeat became honorable when they persuaded the rival station to broadcast their insipid weekly *tour du monde* in which they aped the wrong-headed omniscience of network newsmen. Plummet-Finch had tried arcane subjects: "The Role of the Liffey in *Finnegans Wake,*" "Goedel's Theorem." Time had lowered his sights until the role of women in the modern world was about as adventurous as he was likely to get.

"You'll oppose Sylvia?" Fallor was impressed.

"I shall be the embodiment of reason."

"Wouldn't it be wise to have a middle point of view represented?"

"I suppose Gilbert considers that to be his job."

"But that's not the same thing." Fallor's expression sought some dignity in desire. Rogerson found himself taking culpable pleasure in the thinness of the younger man's crinkled hair. At Rogerson's age, Fallor would be fat and bald and old. Had he ever looked young?

"Why don't you talk to Gilbert?"

"Yes." Despondency shone in Fallor's eyes. "You wouldn't mention it to him, would you?"

"Mention what?"

Fallor could not look at Rogerson. "The desirability of having a third participant."

"Would *you* be willing to take part?"

The question was cruel. Dawn broke on Fallor's face, rosy-fingered, the world's first morning. Hope is a heartless taskmaster. Did Fallor really regard that ridiculous program as a stage? And what *were* his views on the role of women in the modern world? He had been heard to complain of the necessity to interview as many women candidates as possible for the new position that would be opened if the state legislature was seduced by the fallacies of Wooley's budget. In a rational world, they would have been cutting back.

Rogerson said, "It wouldn't look right, two of us ganging up on Sylvia."

"But I would *agree* with her on lots of things."

"Well, in that case . . ."

"But not all!"

Rogerson offered to intercede with Gilbert and Fallor came along. Fortunately Gilbert was not in his office. He seldom was. He had

17

acquired an aerie in the library, a carrel meant for students, a little room off the stacks, about the size of a phone booth, but it had a window on the world and another in the door through which Gilbert could peer longingly at unaware undergraduates perusing the books. Several times he had been reported to the librarian by winsome youths who did not know he was a member of the faculty. Gilbert seemed almost to relish the indignity of rebuff. Rogerson assured Fallor he would speak to Plummet-Finch.

"I'll be in my office."

"He can phone you there?"

"I'll keep the line clear."

It seemed a day when he was destined to be the bearer of bad news. Now to Plummet-Finch and, as a result, to Fallor—he had no expectation that Gilbert would invite the ardent chairman—and to Marge. Poor Olson. Again the old phrase formed in his mind. May he rest in peace. There was an unlikely image, Olson before the throne of God. Would the Particular Judgment have to be repeated to his defective ears?

"You're impossible, Matt, you really are," Sylvia said.

The voice-over faded, the camera lights went out, the discussion, such as it was, was on tape.

"I don't know how your wife stands you."

"How can a spinster understand a wife?"

But of course it was impossible to think of the twenty-seven-year-old Sylvia as a spinster or, as the term suggested, devoid of sexual experience. Not for the first time, Rogerson found himself speculating about her. Times had changed, really changed. He had come to believe this despite himself. By temperament he was a *nihil sub sole novum* type, but what had happened to the view that virginity is precious, marriage an honorable estate and pre- or extramarital hanky-panky perforce prohibited? The fixed star of the conjugal bed no longer served to chart the course of girls like Sylvia. The pill, decades of pornography, propaganda and drugs had brought about what Rogerson, in his hot-blooded youth, would have viewed as an earthly paradise. Girls as horny as boys, restraints gone, coupling random. Rogerson saw this in its intensified form on campus, he saw it with a father's eye and he was alarmed. But the eye with which he met Sylvia's steady amused gaze was not paternal. She was undoing the microphone from about her neck and the deed seemed provocative: a woman unpinning, unbuttoning, unfastening, undoing, is the essence of the seductive. Man is born nude and everywhere he is in clothes. Plummet-Finch returned from his exchange with the director.

"He can take care of your more outrageous remarks, Matthew. Must you always overdo?"

"It is the most effective way to undo."

Sylvia snorted. " 'Supine,' " she said, which had been Rogerson's answer to Gilbert's question as to what in his view is the proper position of women. When the subject of women in sports came up, he had suggested "Girls' Athletic Supporter" as a bumper-sticker legend. " 'A woman isn't all she's cracked up to be,' " Sylvia quoted.

"That had a trace of wit," Gilbert said.

All three on their feet now, Rogerson lit a cigarette and got the conversation away from his indiscretions. It was true that he felt an impulse to shock whenever he appeared on *FOF.* He suspected that explained his rather frequent appearance on the program. But Sylvia had been a good sport.

"I asked Gilbert to have Fallor on to lend you moral support," he told her.

"Never," Plummet-Finch said. "The suggestion did put me in mind of Keane, but I was unable to reach him. He would have been of genuine help."

"Are you telling me I did badly?" Sylvia asked.

"My dear, you were wonderful."

"You were indeed," Rogerson agreed. To Gilbert he said, teasing, "Fallor seemed to think you had promised him."

"I did no such thing."

Rogerson hummed. "Better straighten it out with him, Gilbert. Mustn't have a departmental chairman down on you."

The hairy brows went up and would have waggled if Gilbert had ever mastered the Groucho art. Rogerson's watch read after five.

"Let me buy you both a drink," Gilbert said.

"It will have to be quick," Sylvia said.

"Very quick." Rogerson thought of Marge at home, in tears, the printed telegram in her lap. Perhaps he would be of more help to her after a drink.

"Better make it the faculty club then," Gilbert said. "See you there."

"Do you have a car, Matt?"

"No. I do have a bicycle."

Sylvia offered to walk with him. When they came around to the back of the faculty office building, Tommy's bike was not there. The two remaining bikes were both chained and locked.

"My bike has been stolen. My son's bike."

"Was it locked?"

"Do you think I'd leave an unlocked bike on this campus?"

"What are you going to do?"

"Walk. I'll report it to campus security tomorrow."

Sylvia laughed, as well she might have. On campus the unsolved crime was the rule. Retired cops and pensioned watchmen found ready employment on the security force, their main function writing parking tickets and screwing up traffic. Reporting the theft would have the efficacy of prayer. He did not mean that. Why was it his character always to be out of character? Tommy would be heartbroken. The bike was not a year old. Tommy did not take it to school for fear that it would be stolen. Rogerson had proved his son's fears founded. Well, the bike would have to be replaced.

It was twilight when they arrived at the faculty club, a low brick-and-steel edifice which had replaced a homier predecessor. Rogerson disliked the place. Too few of the people he liked went there. They preferred any dingy saloon to this hearty, prosperous setting. Gilbert awaited them at the bar. Rogerson decided on a soft drink. He would face the task of consoling Marge without the boost of booze.

When he left the club, Sylvia was joining a glassy-eyed table of junior faculty. Her passage among the tables was a thing of beauty, the sway of her hips a metronome which set the music of desire going in the heart of the beholder. Rogerson, pausing to watch the watchers and the watched, felt the memory of illicit desire stir in his pagan depths, the unmarried marrow in every man. The dilemma of horniness. From impalement thereon, *libera nos, domine.* Bastable.

The bastard. Rogerson left the club and went in a jogging trot to the bus stop. It was good that he had eschewed alcohol. Virtue is the function of a clear head, routine and the absence of opportunity. Was Sylvia an opportunity? That seemed a question best left unpursued. Adultery is first committed in the heart. No doubt Bastable had hungered and hankered for months, for years, in imagination revising the significance of his past until, reduced by fuming enthymemes to fancied bachelorhood, he was more than ready for epithalamion again when the mating Dolores occurred in the crook of his wakeful arm. Rogerson again felt the need to condemn Bastable vocally, to subject his treachery to extended analysis, he and Marge sipping drinks before the fire, domesticating the dread such antinomian antics stirred in the soul. That would have to wait now. The death of Marge's father had taken the lead in the sweepstakes of dissolution.

Home was a houseful of querulous teen-age kids wondering where Mom was and when dinner would be ready. The car was not in the garage. Marge had not returned. Rogerson asked Barbara why she hadn't started fixing dinner.

"Fixing what? I don't know what we're having."

"Let's see what there is."

"Where's Mom?"

"I don't know."

Barbara stared. "Is she lost?"

"Don't be dramatic. She had class today. Something must have detained her."

"Till nearly six?"

"They went on a field trip. How about spaghetti? Easy, fast and good. Even I know how to make spaghetti. Put on water."

He assigned her the salad as well. Best to make their festive best of Marge's unaccountable absence. Best in busyness to down his own emergent doubts. Bastable again. Falling apart in the forties was, after all, the rule. Both he and Marge had flirted with it, Marge more than flirting, but during the past three years the saving cement of things had set again. Cement. Olson. Riding home in the crowded bus, jostled, pressed, his insides aching, Rogerson had looked forward to his organized household, kids scrubbed, food on the table, welcome home, Daddy. Where the hell was Marge? Barbara's anxiety had wakened his. Suddenly the whole day seemed a sequence of disasters, already in sharp declension when he received the call from Bastable. The pain that had been bothering him intermittently seemed to have settled in his rear and become a dull ache. The old fear of going as his father had returned. Cancer of the prostate. My God.

"Dad, the water's boiling."

He had been staring sightlessly out the kitchen window. Now he broke thin, brittle sticks of dough in half and dropped them into the boiling pot. Jars of Marge's homemade spaghetti sauce were on the shelf. Garlic bread? Forget it. Spices, like alcohol, threatened to churn up his ache to pain again. Barbara had set the table. She had Marge's profile, had become a person without his noticing. Lovely, but still all in all a blank slate on which life had yet to write. How could Bastable imagine living with a girl not so very much older than Barbara, wedding the weight of his already to her yet-to-be? Rogerson hollered for his sons and served the children. He would wait for Marge. Leaning against the stove, he watched his progeny eat, half happy performing this primordial duty of the parent. Like arrows in his quiver, the psalmist sang. Like young olive plants about his board. They had lost their last grandfather and did not know it. Would they lose a father too? If they did, it would be to cancer, by God, and not to a coed.

The sound of a car in the driveway, the slam of a door and Rogerson's heart swelled with relief and then with apprehension. Marge burst into the house as he came from the kitchen. Haste made her beauty glow, lips parted, open raincoat billowing, her hair alive with out-of-doors. She sniffed approvingly, dropping her books on the telephone table.

"Oh, good, you didn't wait."

"The kids are eating."

"Aren't you?"

"No." The fear that somehow she had found out about her father, that that explained her lateness, was dissolved by her distracted manner, her vague good humor. She could not know. Her ignorance seemed almost a fault. What right did she have going off to class on the day her father died, staying late, leaving the kids to starve? Irrational, of course. Marge went into the kitchen and met a chorus of accusation. Rogerson heard them complain that the spaghetti was like paste and the sauce cold. So much for self-congratulation, the little bastards.

In the living room, he paged through the paper, a day's quota of bad news. Dear God, what a world. There must have been a dozen entries in the divorces-granted column, but the average age in the obituaries was seventy-six. Not bad. Add in Olson and he could up the average. The kids came in to be watched by television some more. Tommy, even in stocking feet, was taller than his father. Rogerson forbore to give the usual humanist homily about the stultifying effect of television. He wanted them occupied. He went into the kitchen. He and Marge were having spaghetti too.

"Where have you been?"

"I went to the library after class."

"That was hours ago."

"I know." She tossed back her head, moved it slowly from side to side, eyes closed. She seemed to be having a vision. Knowing what she did not know, his heart broke for her. She is beautiful, Rogerson thought. She is the kind of woman for whom the forties are the fullness of time. Ripeness is all. What did Theresa Bastable look like now? She had been pretty enough years ago, her pale Irish face freckled and fresh, but he could imagine her faded with the years, flesh puckered and sagging, Hopkins' ruck and wrinkle. Would she have grown thin and juiceless, unquickened by humor or brains? Thank God for Marge. Fidelity to her was the path of least resistance. She opened her eyes.

"Matt, it is so good to be *doing* something again."

"I know what you mean. I hadn't made spaghetti in ages."

"I lost all sense of time."

"How was class?"

She thought. "All right."

"I understand it met outside."

"Yes. You should try that."

"Was the lecture any good?"

She was not enthusiastic, but even her faint praise damned Rogerson to jealousy. Why should Keane's competence pose a threat to him? He had long since decided that the criteria of academic success point the road to hell. Woe to him through whom the scandal comes.

"I made another tape with Plummet-Finch."

"What topic?"

"Women."

"What about women?" Her noodled Medusa-like fork stopped on its way to her mouth.

"Their role, their place, their plight. The usual garbage. Sylvia Wood was on too. She explained to me that your taking Keane's class is symbolic of your dissatisfaction with your life."

"She said that on television!"

"Afterward. You are trying to awake from a domestic nightmare and fly free."

"I just want to use my mind again."

He had seen this coming, he had tried to ward it off. The kids were all in school now. Marge had begun to calculate how old she and Matt and each of the kids would be in ten years' time, in fifteen. Life slipped away unlived before such reckonings. Marge, rendered sterile by her hysterectomy rather than elective barrenness, yearned now to bear a mental fruit. Rogerson had suggested she read, but she had always been a great reader. Perhaps they were both reminded of Dowlet, gone now to greener pastures. What was the point of reading if nobody knew? She became involved in a discussion group for faculty wives. Courses at the college were bound to follow. Courses in what? In history, English, anything. Marge's eyes brimmed with a borrowed discontent. She coulda been a contendah. Marriage had robbed her of a career. The trouble was that this was true.

"Career? You can have mine. I'd like a peaceful house to myself all day."

"I'm not a nun, Matt. I want to be with people."

Aha. André Malraux telling Julian Green that the motive for travel is sexual adventure. Who could deny it? Consider travel brochures and airline commercials. Did Marge want to travel outside the life that had been theirs for over twenty years?

"Have you ever read, Pascal, Matt?"

She pushed away her plate and lit a cigarette. Exhaling smoke, directing it from a corner of her mouth, she looked, with her elbows on the table, like a colleague rather than a wife. He was reminded of years before, the two of them at a table in the rathskellar in Madison, two students with a common task, Marge the star of semi-

24

nars, no matter that professors were stunned into receptivity as much by her perfect face and body as by the tentative groping of her talented mind. But what did a graduate degree have to do with marriage, her ostensible destination? Acquaintance, friendship, love, courtship: the process had eased Marge into a secondary role and neither of them had ever questioned this. If one of them continued, it must be him. Who could blame her if she wondered now about the justice of the arrangement? God knows she would have made a better teacher and scholar than Keane, than most of them, so why must she sit in tutelage to that callow youth, she who had been in graduate school when he was a child?

Perhaps the revival of such thoughts would alone have stopped him from telling her of Jimmy Bastable now with that story's potential for calling into question all previous arrangements. But what truly kept him silent was the expected ring of the doorbell. A rush of footsteps, cries of "I'll get it." Rogerson looked at Marge, at her mild curiosity, seeing her as he would never see her again. He felt like God.

She said, "I wonder who that is."

Any desire Rogerson might have had to be clairvoyant was stifled then. He knew the meaning of the indistinct exchange at the door, he knew what it was that Tommy brought to his mother. Marge opened the envelope without expression. She read the message. She seemed to read it again.

"Dad's dead."

Tommy was thunderstruck. "Grandpa Olson!" He looked at Rogerson as if he had invented death and brought it home. Marge was numbed by the news.

"I'll have to go up."

"Of course."

"Can't we all go?" Tommy's deepened voice shifted to alto.

Marge looked blankly at Rogerson.

"No," he said. "Mom will have to fly."

2

On Saturday morning, awakened by the sound of dribbling in the driveway, Rogerson stood at the bedroom window and looked down at his gangly son working the ball in against imaginary opponents, observed by an equally imaginary audience and one real father strangely affected by the sight of the tall, normally awkward Tommy rendered agile and adroit by a sphere of caught air. Inflated bladder. Stream of consciousness. Rogerson's thoughts turned to his morning ablutions.

Marge had been gone three days. Today was the day of the funeral. Rogerson, razor at his throat, looked at his lathered face. Would his own death someday be someone else's thought while shaving? Of course. Tommy. Tommy's children . . . All over the globe the pullulating species replaced itself without let, more than enough new feet to fill the shoes of those who dropped. Helluva thought with which to start the day. But mornings were odd with Marge not here, her empty, still made bed beside his, the kids already up, feeding themselves, doing what they did. No school today, however. Bobby was watching television. Barbara? He consulted the kitchen calendar, its scribbled squares the chronicle of the house. She was baby-sitting. Marge away and he still slugabed, but the life of the house went on. He felt superfluous.

What had most angered him in Bastable's desertion was the image of a house devoid of father and mate, the little ones wide-eyed and wondering where daddy had gone, Theresa, a handkerchief balled in her hysterical hand, staring vacantly from a window. The truth seemed to be that the spring of habit unwinds much as before. But Marge's absence was scarcely comparable to Bastable's defection. The kids knew she would be back. What had Bastable told his brood? I don't remember my wedding day, this household is not really real, farewell, my parthenogenic progeny. The sonofabitch. May he suffer a hernia proving his manhood to his child bride.

Rogerson's own routine was little altered by Marge's absence. The lecherous male escaped from the watchful eye of his spouse? Ha. The faithless Bastable had forged a chastity belt for those who would condemn him. Like the kids, Rogerson just went on as before. The kids, Bastable's *exemplum horribile,* his forty-seven years, explained that. As for the kids, who knew what they noticed? At Barbara's age, at Tommy's, he himself had seen the world with a grand inquisitorial eye, unforgiving, stern, only two columns in the ledger he kept. Age, experience, corruption perhaps, had led to multiple-entry moral bookkeeping. Why then his hard-nosed lack of compassion for Bastable? Because the rat tried to pass off his failure as a meritorious deed: deserting Theresa and the kids was on the same ethical level as an act of God. Compassion is for acknowledged weakness. Bastable, a true child of the times, chose to redefine the concepts. A brief unpremeditated dalliance would have been entirely different. With whom would Rogerson dally if he did? Sylvia? Her air of receptivity was too diffuse and general, an indiscriminate invitation. Dear Occupant. He pushed away his cereal bowl, decided against making coffee, stared out the window. Olson. Poor Olson.

Several times during the day, moved by a wistful sense of duty, he offered to do something with the kids, but they were never all there at once or all willing, and where after all was there to go in Fort Elbow? He made his first drink at two in the afternoon. TV dinners, the kids watching the eponymous TV; finally he shagged them upstairs. What did it matter that he was smashed? He told himself that he was drinking in Olson's honor. When the time came, he watched *FOF* with the sound off: the world as it had appeared to his deaf father-in-law. On the screen, Gilbert looked the soul of sincerity compared with his facetious self. Sylvia was lovely, though not as attractive as Marge had been at that age.

"Let's go to the Newman Club," Barbara said next morning when they piled into the car.

"No," Rogerson said firmly.

But the boys too wanted to go to the Newman Club.

"The Mass there takes too long," Rogerson objected.

"But it's more fun."

Fun? No wonder Marge had stopped practicing her faith. It required a martyr's fortitude to go to church anymore. Banners, singing, balloons, endless haranguing of the congregation by usurpative laypeople: stand, sit, sing, breathe. It was like camp. Boot camp. Rogerson found it a parody of his Protestant youth. He preferred the Polish parish downtown, where one could count on orthodoxy and speed. Nonetheless, he drove to the campus and the Newman Club and an hour's assault on his faith.

When he and Marge had married in a Milwaukee rectory he had promised to raise their children Catholic. Eventually he had joined the Church himself, signing on with Dante and Cervantes and Aquinas. And Newman. What would the ethereal cardinal make of the rite as it was rendered in this student center named for him? Rogerson's keeping his side of the bargain did not depend on Marge's keeping hers. The idea of the father as chief observer of religious obligations appealed to him. It had a Jewish solidity. Let men pray and the women be spared. Surely God would not go hard on Marge for refusing to take part in the orgy-porgy worship of Him had lately become.

Things were worse than Rogerson had feared: the nadir had a trap door. Women in miniskirts distributed communion, demanding a lot of eye contact when they announced, "The Body of Christ." The lessons were read from a translation of scripture that must have been done by machine; the sermon was a critique of capitalism. Jesus hates Nixon. It was good to escape from the chapel, difficult to get the kids to come along. Bobby stared covetously at the ceiling, to which balloons released at the kiss of peace still clung. Were they left there to rot like the red hats of cardinals hung high above the sanctuary of their cathedral church? Outside, Rogerson heard a familiar voice and turned to see Plummet-Finch.

"Gilbert! Don't tell me you were at Mass?"

"You mean the eucharistic assembly." Plummet-Finch made a fastidious *moue* with his fleshy lips. "Young Merlin invited me. He suggested that I would be reminded of my Anglican youth now that the R.C.'s are using the vernacular." Gilbert passed a hand over his face.

"You don't find it lively?"

"I'm sure children do." With a long-fingered hand he ruffled Bobby's hair. Barbara and Tommy had headed for the car.

"Suffer little children."

"Indeed. Did you happen to watch the program last night?"

"Only the picture. Sylvia is very persuasive with the sound off."

"As what woman is not? Do you know Larry?"

"Larry?"

"Larry Merlin. The priest here."

"No. I gather you do."

"Matthew, he makes Candide seem a man of the world. It is impossible to insult him. Everything, absolutely everything, strikes him as synonymous with the nonsense he believes. You are an atheist? So, in a way, is he. You loath collective manifestations of emotion, i.e., worship? He understands perfectly. Matthew, it is a new phenomenon—a zealot without convictions."

"A topic for *FOF.*"

"Perhaps. I could ask Larry to participate."

They parted, Gilbert going with a malicious glint in his eye to where the Newman Club chaplain stood in his doorway, looking out at the world and finding it good.

Rogerson drove to the faculty office building. The kids enjoyed visiting his office, as if its standardized neatness made up for the basement lair at home. As they were approaching the back door of the building, Tommy stopped.

"Hey, that's my bike."

There was a single bicycle in the stand, but it was chained in place. Tommy's thumb was already twirling the combination. In a moment, surprisingly, he rolled the bike free.

"How the heck did it get here?"

"I rode it the other day."

"And just left it here!"

"It was locked, wasn't it?"

"But outside!"

Rogerson was more mystified than his son. Had some Samaritan noticed the unlocked bike and repaired his omission? Somewhat uneasily, Rogerson recalled his exchange with Ketchum, the chief of campus security.

"I suppose it was a good one," Ketchum had sighed.

"A ten-speed."

"It always is." Ketchum was of middle size, thin, his bald head narrow and knobby as a spinal column. "Well, we'll go through the motions. Fill out this form."

"Don't you expect to find it?"

Ketchum did not expect to find it. Bicycle thefts were one of the most common complaints received by his office. He speculated that there was a clearing house in the area and that, dismantled, parts mixed and reassembled, serial numbers altered, the bikes were trucked out of the city a day or two after they were stolen.

"The joke is that the thieves sell them for peanuts."

"Addicts?"

"What else?" That easily Ketchum accepted the decline of the West. Perhaps that had been the perspective of the cop for centuries.

"But there are all kinds of thefts on campus," Rogerson protested. "The bookstore, offices, resident rooms. Not all that stuff can be sold."

"Bikes can be sold." Ketchum had no interest in a general theory of larceny. He had offered Rogerson an explanation of bicycle thefts.

Tommy was now riding around the parking lot. Clearly he had lost interest in visiting his father's campus office. So had Rogerson. He would have to let Ketchum know that the bike had been found. He almost looked forward to it. Even if the bike had not been stolen, it counted against Ketchum. The chief's men should have discovered it if the bike had been here all along.

Another bike appeared in the parking lot, its rider making easy circles around Tommy. It was Sylvia. She waved, Rogerson waved, the kids stared. Sylvia's shorts had flaps fore and aft to simulate a skirt. She left the parking lot and wheeled up to Rogerson.

"Are these your kids?"

He introduced them. Tommy was impressed by Sylvia's bike and she explained that she had bought it in England and shipped it home.

"Isn't Marge back yet?" she asked Rogerson.

"No."

"And you've been baby-sitting?"

Barbara did not like this interpretation, but Sylvia did not notice. Her bike was a male model, the crossbar bisecting her as she stood straddling it. Sylvia brought the back of her wrist across her forehead. "I must have ridden for miles."

The kids asked where she had been and she said to the airport and back. They were suitably impressed.

"It's the only exercise I get. Apart from swimming."

Her body seemed in tune with the cosmos: ruddy cheeks, clear eyes, the sinews of her limbs taut, there seemed no excess anywhere, at least none that Rogerson was inclined to lament. Clearly she regarded it as a moral obligation to take care of her body. Why? Did there have to be a reason beyond health and longevity? It seemed a mark of their difference. His fitful concern was for his flabby soul. Sylvia swung her leg over the crossbar and pushed her bike toward Barbara.

"Want to try it?"

"She can't ride a racer," Bobby said.

Barbara ignored him, walking the bike to the parking lot, where Tommy was once more riding around the asphalt surface.

"Going to check your mail, Matt?"

He nodded. So was she. The kids were occupied. On the stairs, he was conscious of Sylvia's healthy sweat, the spring of her steps, her youth. "Did you watch us last night?" she asked.

"I watched."

"Gilbert keeps interrupting."

"Does he? I guess I've stopped noticing."

On the third floor they went to their respective offices. Rogerson stood at his window and watched Barbara wobble around the lot on Sylvia's bike. He had the obscure wish that the children had not met her. He sat at his desk. Was he waiting for Sylvia in order to go back down with her? It seemed important not to. He rolled a sheet of paper into his typewriter and began to peck out what he could remember of the Gettysburg Address. The machine came with the office. He seldom used it, preferring a less complicated middleman between thought and expression. Marge professed to envy him this machine, huge and electric, one more assault on the taxpayer's pocket.

A tap on the door. Sylvia peeked in. "I'm leaving."

"Tell the kids I won't be long."

"Okay," she said after a moment. She pulled the door shut. Rogerson continued his sporadic typing until he was sure she had started downstairs. Men will not long remember what we typed here, but faithful Rogerson, loyal of loins, single-minded upholder of the sanctity of marriage, shall not perish of lustful longing on this earth.

From the window he watched Sylvia reclaim her bike. His children clustered about her. Was she the future? They stood looking after her when she mounted and rode away. Rogerson was outside before he realized that he had forgotten to check his mail.

"How's everything going?" Marge asked when she phoned that night.

"Fine. How is your mother?"

"Good."

He hesitated. "Did everything go all right?"

"Matt, I think I should stay a little longer."

"Sure."

"Another week?"

"That's all right." His tone was brave.

"What did you have for dinner?"

He told her, in absurd detail. How odd that the daily doings of the house should be news for Marge. He wanted to hear of the final obsequies for Olson. In the afternoon his pain had begun again and there was no doubt of its location. His prostate was flaring up. Lying down had not helped. He sat in a tub of very hot water, sweating, in pain, frightened. The precedent of his father could not be ignored. His life, like his features, was a reprise of the paternal model. He had come increasingly to resemble his father; he grumbled and complained in the same ways, was no longer surprised to find himself echoing him. Rise and shine. Soup's on. Sleep tight, don't let the bedbugs bite. Such nonsense phrases, he now knew, encoded an embarrassed affection. We are the time capsules of previous generations. What wonder then that his insides too should resemble his father's. Cancer of the prostate. Sitting in the tub, unable to relieve the pain, sure that his end would be his end, Rogerson had cried, the tears mingling with his sweat. If he told Marge of his intention to make an appointment with a doctor, would she express more grief for her father's death? Why the hell was she being so stoic? But he knew the reason must be Mrs. Olson somewhere within earshot.

"I don't like missing class," Marge said.

"You won't miss anything."

"Will you tell Gerry why I'm not there?"

Gerry? Why was she so sure he would notice her absence? Students had no idea of a teacher's indifference. Rogerson could not imagine himself explaining to Keane why his wife was not in his goddam class. Was he meant to apologize for Olson's death?

"Will you talk to him, Matt?"

He lied and said that he would. Why couldn't he tell her how he missed her and that he loved her, that he would be true to her till death? Which might not be so imminent as he had feared. During the phone conversation his pain disappeared. How good it would be to go to bed and fall asleep before it could resume.

"Say hello to your mother."

"Tell the kids I miss them."

"Okay."

"And don't forget to talk to Gerry Keane."

Heep the urologist had his offices in a building from which the medical sharpies who had built it as a tax shelter had long since fled to safer quarters. There were loose tiles in the corridors and the doors, hung unevenly, stuck, then surprisingly gave way. Thus it was that Rogerson hurtled into Heep's office, shoulder lowered, a determined look on his face. He arrested himself at the reception counter, where he was booked by a woman whose pale eyes seemed to search him for symptoms. Rogerson felt that he was signing on for a cruise with Charon. How many on the verge of checking out had this woman seen? No doubt this was how it began, the final chapter, handed from doctor to doctor while one wasted away. Rogerson produced the Blue Cross card of the college plan.

The waiting room was small, its occupants elderly, their expressions the doleful ones of those whose genitals are exacting an ultimate revenge. There being no empty chair, Rogerson stood and paged through a vintage issue of *Newsweek*. None of its dated predictions had come true, thank God. The issue read like the Apocalypse. Yesterday's hysteria was almost restful. The appeal of history. Perhaps the daily newspaper would be palatable if allowed to mature for a week or so.

How patient these patients were. They sat inert, staring straight ahead. They might have been examining their consciences. There was an electric clock behind the receptionist and its red second hand seemed to be forcing its way through water. Finally movement. From offstage, a voice. An old man was helped to his feet by a younger woman, perhaps his daughter, and led to a door next to the receptionist's counter. While claiming a chair, Rogerson got his first glimpse of Heep, who had appeared in the now opened door to greet his new patient, having laughed the previous one on his way. Heep reminded Rogerson of a janitor at the college who had been fired for exposing himself in the window of a third-floor washroom, flashing his dilly at the jaded indifferent coeds below. It had been a departmental secretary who had intercepted his anonymous message.

Rogerson felt caught up in some parable whose moral he did not know as he advanced slowly yet inexorably to the chair nearest the inner door. When his turn finally came, he stood up, feeling that he had just passed some obscure test. Heep greeted him and led him down a hallway to an office. Inside was an old desk of yellowing wood into a chair behind which Heep sank with a sigh as if he was inviting Rogerson's sympathy for his harried life. Heep was in his fifties, leathery of face, his steel-gray hair *en brosse,* shirt sleeves rolled up, a loosened tie at his open collar. He lit a cigarette, for all the world like a doctor in the magazine ads of yore, picked up a fountain pen with which to inscribe Rogerson's vital data on a form. A diploma on the wall behind him announced Heep's graduation from a dental college. As if he had willed Rogerson's upward glance, Heep's amber teeth appeared beneath his clipped mustache. He was smiling.

"Mine is an unusual story, Professor Rogerson. I was an Army dentist. I used the GI Bill to go to medical school. Five years as a GP and then back for urology."

"You must like school."

"I hated it."

"I know what you mean."

"How long have you been at the Fort Elbow campus?"

"Twenty years." Rogerson said this as if he expected to be contradicted. He could scarcely believe it himself. It was like serving a life sentence on a volunteer basis. Heep put down his fountain pen and rocked back in his chair. He had the look of one about to reminisce. "I haven't been feeling well," Rogerson said quickly.

As if chided, Heep sat forward. "Who referred you to me?"

"Cashman." This medico, in whose Jamaican tan Rogerson felt himself to be a partial accomplice, had said that appointments with urologists were hard to arrange, but then, having hummed a few bars of "Yellow Bird," he suggested that Heep might be the man.

"Good for him. Most GPs would have fed you pills for months before surrendering you. What seems to be the trouble?"

Rogerson inhaled and recited his woes. He urinated around the clock, his bladder never felt empty.

"Is it painful when you pee?"

"And when I don't. I have a persistent pain in my rear."

Heep grinned knowingly. "What do you know of the prostate?"

"My father died of cancer of the prostate."

Heep ignored this. He had begun a little lecture. Rogerson was to imagine a doughnut. When swollen, the organ caused the discomfort Rogerson described. "How old are you?"

"Forty-seven."

"Some men have this trouble in their thirties."

"I was always a late bloomer. What do you do for it?"

"Massage will probably do the trick."

He took Rogerson into another room, an examining room. On a table in the corner rubber gloves lay in a row, covered with dusty powder, ghostly.

"Drop your pants."

The humiliating memory of the physicals of Army days returned. Heep talked incessantly over Rogerson's shoulder. The prostate was definitely enlarged. Heep proposed a series of massages, more or less what he was doing now. Direct contact was the only effective remedy.

Feeling violated, Rogerson pulled up his shorts and then his trousers. He fastened his buckle as if he were girding his loins. He could not meet Heep's eyes. He had the ridiculous feeling that they had just shared some intimacy.

"Make an appointment with Mrs. Every."

Heep came down the hall with him, to speak to the receptionist, to fetch his next patient. With the door of the waiting room open, he said to Rogerson, "You're not circumcised."

"No." An absurd blush suffused Rogerson's cheeks. His bottom too burned in embarrassment and in the aftermath of Heep's rubbery probe. Was he to have no secrets here? Mrs. Every seemed to be jotting something down. Malice aforeskin? Bidding the urologist farewell, preparing to dash through the waiting room, Rogerson wished that he had more confidence in Heep, wished that Heep did not seem such a confidence man. He put the prescription Heep dashed off for him into his pocket. The pills it would get him would cause him, Heep said, to pee green.

"That's about all they'll do too." Heep smiled as if they were sharing a joke.

The image of the large-bosomed Mrs. Every pursued Rogerson to his car. Seated behind the wheel, he was filled with sudden longing for Marge. It was as though health would return with the familiar contours of her body. Comfort me with apples. A nibble a day keeps the doctor away.

Fallor popped out of the inner office when Rogerson stopped to check his mail.

"Have you given any more thought to summer school, Matt?"

"No."

Fallor's surprise was a futile attempt to put Rogerson on the defensive. Actually, it was a lie to say that he had not thought further of summer school. His health had added another variable to the formula he could not formulate. The summer school salary could make them a two-car family, liberate Marge, put her on wheels. On the other hand, the summer could be used to give Marge and the kids a genuine vacation. Thirdly, and why not, there was the resurgent desire to do some writing; not, God forbid, in response to academic demands and pressures, but rather to the primordial hope of leaving something behind when he himself was gone. Absurd? Of course.

36

But what is not? Breathing, walking, lying to one's chairman. *Sub specie aeternitatis,* anything temporal has a tinseled tacky nuthouse look.

"You said you needed time for creative work." Armed now against the magic adjective, Fallor allowed his voice to grow skeptical.

"Yes. I shall be devoting myself full time to my poetry. I have long dreamt of such an opportunity."

"Your poetry? I didn't know you wrote poetry."

"Shame on you. You should know. Brenda knows." Rogerson beamed at the wizened secretary who clawed at the keyboard of her typewriter. She gave him a quick darting smile, then glowered at the notes she was trying to decode. "Copies of my published poetry should be in my dossier."

"I wish I had time to read them. I'm lucky to find time to prepare for class."

"Are *you* teaching summer school?"

Rogerson knew that Fallor planned to drive his camper up the Alcan Highway in pursuit of the haunts of his literary idol, Jack London. The chairman mumbled about previous commitments and went into his office. When the door shut, Brenda stopped typing.

"I hate working for that man."

"Get a transfer."

"And start all over in another office? Don't be silly." Brenda eased an extra-long filter-tipped cigarette from a pack on her desk. Rogerson lit it for her. Settling into clouds of smoke, Brenda said, "I've been meaning to say how sorry I am about your wife's father."

"Thank you." Rogerson felt that they were exchanging lines from an outmoded book of etiquette.

"Sad. How old was he?"

Rogerson told her. Brenda seemed aggrieved. "George was only forty-five."

George was Brenda's late husband, dead now these ten years.

"My age, more or less."

"Oh, much younger. I mean in appearance. I was in purchasing. So was George. That's where we met. I had to get out of there. Afterward."

"The memories," Rogerson said helpfully.

"You wouldn't believe the way they ran that office after George was gone."

"It was a heart attack, wasn't it?" Rogerson did not remember George, if he had ever known him.

More clouds of smoke. "If only it had been. A heart attack is swift."

"Well . . ."

"You have children, Professor Rogerson. There's something I'd like to talk to you about." Brenda flicked the switch that turned off her typewriter, pushed back from her desk and put her cigarette in the corner of her mouth. Smoke curled toward her closed eye. Brenda's winking expression bothered Rogerson. He did not know what to say. This was no place for confidences and Brenda had the look of someone about to unbosom herself.

"I have class at ten."

"Not on Monday." Brenda, alas, would know. She stood. "Could we talk in your office?"

There Brenda settled across the desk from him, put out her cigarette and lit another.

"Have I ever told you of Eric?"

Eric was her son. He must be thirty now, still at home, a ne'er-do-well. Brenda's term.

"Mr. Rogerson, I think he's on something."

"Drugs?"

"Marijuana for sure. He smokes it in the house. My God, we could be raided."

"Oh, I doubt that."

"Mr. Rogerson, I think he steals too." She gripped the edge of the desk and stared wide-eyed at Rogerson.

"What makes you think so?"

"The garage is full of bicycles."

"Perhaps he repairs them."

Brenda sat back. "Do you think so?"

"Is he mechanical?" In his imagination, Rogerson picked up the phone and dialed campus security. Chief Ketchum. Rogerson here. I've cracked the case. The bike ring is broken.

"Some of them seem taken apart. He gets very angry when I look."

"In your own garage?"

"I never use it."

"Have you asked about the bikes?"

"I'm afraid to. Mr. Rogerson, would you talk to Eric?"

"Me? Brenda, what could I say?"

"He would listen to you. I know he would. I'm so confused."

Her dissolving into tears seemed more than a tactic; Rogerson thought it genuine grief, encompassing more than a garageful of bicycles. He got up and went around his desk. How bony her shoulder felt beneath his hand. She pressed her cheek against him. His own pain put in an appearance. Brenda might have been weeping for him as well.

"You're like George, you know. When he was young. When he was alive."

She sobbed. Rogerson felt his throat constrict. George Mapes cut down at forty-five; Rogerson dreading cancer of the prostate at forty-seven. He had outlived George already. It was a thought difficult to milk for sadness. He had grown used to outliving far more public points of reference than George. Once he had made a list. Crane, Pascal, Fitzgerald, Fallor's Jack London too. And he had outlived Kierkegaard. The game was poignant only if he was meant to do something of note. But his fate was to be Matthew Rogerson, nobody special on an afterthought campus, his professorship a job in civil service. Sobeit. Sobeit. George had been head of purchasing.

"Okay, Brenda. Okay. I'll talk to Eric."

He let his hand slip across her back and she pressed closer to him. Poor old doll, pushing sixty, missing George all these years.

"I blame myself, Mr. Rogerson. I shouldn't have gone to work. I should have quit when I married George. What did I ever do for Eric? I should have been his mother."

The tears were more theatric now. Another sob. The door opened and Sylvia Wood looked in. Her eyes widened with surprise. She stared at Rogerson and he stared at her. Brenda had not heard the door open. Sylvia closed it again slowly on the tableau of Rogerson embracing the weeping secretary whose face was pressed to his side. Sylvia's overheated imagination was bound to mislead her. Rogerson stepped free and Brenda went to work on her face with a Kleenex.

"Have Eric come see me."

"Oh, he doesn't like to leave the house during the day." She rubbed her eyes. Rogerson wished she wouldn't do that. They were already fiery red. "He says he can't stand to look at all the hypocrites."

"He's home all day? When would be a good time to see him?"

Brenda thought midafternoon might be best. Rogerson almost looked forward to the visit. The lad apparently had some notions on what was wrong with the world. Who could resist the avuncular *obiter dicta* of a bicycle collector?

"Does he have a girl?"

Brenda's eyes crossed expressively. "I'd rather not go into that."

He helped her to her feet, assured her she looked just fine, lots of people have red eyes; nobody really looked at Brenda anyway. He stepped into the hallway with her, looked at Sylvia's door, but returned to his own office. Let Sylvia imagine what she would. But seated at his desk, he was annoyed that Sylvia would suspect that if he were disposed to cheat while Marge was out of town, the departmental secretary, accosted at nine in the morning, would be the extent of his ambition.

His class over, at home, still before noon, Rogerson went down into the basement workroom he had fashioned when his upstairs study became impossible because of the sonic boom of the television. Marge's Singer now stood where Rogerson's desk had been.

There was a workbench in the basement, L-shaped, belly high, okay as a desk once Rogerson found a stool high enough. He felt a bit like Bob Cratchit, heels hooked on a rung of the chair, stooped forward. A fluorescent lamp over the bench and Rogerson's Underwood on the short leg of the L. Marge had put down an indoor/outdoor carpet, but above, the studs were visible and pipes and air vents. It was still a cellar. An overstuffed chair in which to read, serenaded by the furnace blower, hot-water heater, water softener, washer and dryer, a veritable symphony of indebtedness. Rogerson complained, but he loved it. There was something ghoulish about spending so much time below ground level, six feet under, as a matter of fact, but a fact he did not choose to dwell on now with his prostate giving him hell.

He had an appointment with Heep tomorrow. What difference

could a day make? It might already be too late, thanks to Cashman and Heep. He would not be the first victim of medical incompetence. His doctors would learn from the autopsy. It was like leaving his body to science. He had read somewhere of a moribund physician who kept careful notes on his illness, his reaction to various treatments, the whole record. The man had turned his own death into a spectator sport. And he had received the unstinting praise the mad deserve.

Rogerson was convinced that he in similar circumstances would become a desert father of asceticism, preparing to meet his God with much prayer and fasting. Meanwhile he lit a cigarette and wondered what it would be like to devote a summer to the writing of poetry. Once he had hoped, as what classroom critic has not, to become himself a fashioner of the wares undone and talked to death to indifferent students. The artifact treated as a natural object, classified, analyzed, mastered, understood. But from what mysterious unknown did they emerge? Rogerson, like others of his ilk, had mimicked the poems he taught. Art imitates art. The ventriloquism of the amateur. But once or twice he had written something that seemed genuinely his own and not wholly bad. Of the handful that had appeared in print, he liked "For Sale" best; it had been written when they had left their previous house for this one.

> Under the eaves sparrows have left nests
> And bees the gray geometry of theirs, guests
> Gone with the lost season. Trees rattle
> Goldenly, leaves thoughtless in their leaving mottle
> The withered grass or go a gamboling
> Coin on the currency of wind. The humbling
> Nakedness of fall comes over limbs whose
> Decency lies misspent on lawn and street.
> The garden being cast out, we treat
> The coordinates it crowded with green news
> Of a primal country as if a box of space
> And a few spectral mementos could efface
> The essential loss. Our abodes abide
> Our leaving, left habitats survive
> Inhabitants who ride the southern slide
> Of blood. Here where we'll no longer live

I watch autumn answer autumn
Either side of glass, the savor gone
From the season while outside like drawn
Swords leaves flank the sign on the lawn.

Could he spend a summer writing things like that? More likely they
would take a trip.

There was a standing invitation from Felix Freeman, who wrote
plangent epistles from his retirement home in Arizona. Felix had
arrived to find his lot located in a wasteland south of the Grand
Canyon, the developer working out of a mobile home by the side of
the highway, perhaps three homes completed on the square miles
that made up Southwestern Estates. But if the homes were only in the
visionary eye of the developer, the streets and intersections were
already there. For miles and miles a grid of asphalt avenues baked
in the merciless sun and where they crossed, street signs stood like
crucifixes of the Penitentes. Grove Avenue met Rosebush Lane,
Wisteria crossed Catalpa, each ghostly street name plucked from the
banality of the developer's imagination. The more or less main thor-
oughfare through this imaginary city was the Avenida de los Conquistadores and it was on this imposing road that Felix found his modest
adobe house. At night, listening to the coyotes, knowing that if he
lived to be a hundred he might have neighbors, Felix wrote to those
of the Old Bastards who still plied their trade on the Fort Elbow
campus. Rogerson was sent the developer's brochure (the opus-
culum that had won Felix's Midwestern heart) and snapshots of the
place so that he could savor the contrast. Rogerson was torn between sadness that Felix had been jobbed out of his savings by a
charlatan's scheme and the thought that Felix really rejoiced in his
desert isolation, deriving as only an Old Bastard could satisfaction
from the fact that he would exit life as he had lived it, one of the
lowly, a loser, but with thumb to nose and fingers waggling defiantly.
The sunset years indeed.

Would Marge agree to a trip to Arizona? Would the kids find the
thought attractive? Even to ask such questions was to invite doubt.
Could he go alone? He imagined sitting with Felix in the desert,
watching the sun go down, reminiscing about Wooley and Laplace.

Come get your ass roasted in the Arizona sun, Felix had written, and Rogerson was inflamed by the thought that solar therapy might after all be the answer: did not the ailing of the nation repair to the desert for repairs? The unrelieved sunlight of Freeman's adopted state might do what neither Cashman nor Heep was able to do. He must bring the matter up as soon as Marge got home. He could even suggest that the idea was the doctor's. It would take Marge's mind off her father's death.

When his knock on the front door received no answer, Rogerson went around to the back. The sight of the garage prompted the thought that he might creep out there and surprise Eric among his bicycles, at work on sub rosa transplants, scraping off serial numbers, repainting. If he wasn't in the house. The back door flew open before Rogerson could lay a knuckle on it.

"Professor Rogerson! I thought that was you at the front door."

"You heard my knock?"

"Mother isn't here."

"I've come to see you."

The idea that he was here to give fatherly advice to Eric invited hysteria. Wild-haired and bearded, Eric's head looked like a trick picture whose upside-down is merely another right-side-up. Bare feet emerged from the bottoms of his Levi's, toes irregular, knuckled and hammered, the prehensile feet of a carnival performer, one who plays an accordion with his knees and toes while plying a violin with his upper limbs.

"Come in, come in."

The kitchen table bore evidence of breakfast. "I was eating," Eric explained. "Just when I decided you wouldn't stop knocking, you did."

Eric lounged at the table. Rogerson leaned against the drainboard. Eric said, "It's been nearly ten years, hasn't it?"

"Since when?"

"You don't remember, do you?"

"Help me."

"I took a course from you."

Eric Mapes? But he could not summon the roster of his current classes, let alone those of a decade ago.

"What have you been doing since?"

"Nothing."

"Sounds hard."

The large, too-bright eyes dimmed with thought. "Leave it to you to understand. It is damned hard. My mother thinks I'm a freak." Eric lifted a bare foot to the chair he sat on, rumpled his hair with his hand. The dish before him held scrambled eggs liberally splashed with catsup. A visit to the zoo.

"She doesn't understand you."

The bare foot returned to the floor, where it seemed to grope about. "Has she talked to you about me?"

Rogerson sat opposite Eric. "What kind of nothing do you do?"

"The absolute kind. I sleep, eat, watch the tube . . ."

"And grow hair. But this welfare state is financed by your mother's labor."

"I chip in."

"Where do you get the money?"

"What has she told you, anyway?"

"She thinks you're on drugs."

Eric laughed. "Everyone is on drugs."

"Your mother isn't. I'm not." He thought of Bastable, and of others, a veritable litany of fallen friends. There are other ways than drugs of going to hell.

"Aspirin, codeine, nicotine, alcohol. As I remember, you're quite a drinker."

"Your news is ten years old."

"Oh, I get over to campus from time to time."

"To steal bicycles?"

"Anything that isn't nailed down."

Rogerson had not expected a confession. "So you are a thief?"

"Let it be our secret. Property is theft."

The sound of television was audible from another room. A game show. It would make anyone a nihilist.

"Would you like a beer, Professor Rogerson?"

Why not? Eric managed to get a can from the refrigerator without leaving his seat. Rogerson lit a cigarette.

"I could offer you a more interesting smoke."

"No doubt. Eric, this isn't fair to your mother. If you want to be a bum, why don't you leave?"

"She'd like that."

"You know what she'd really like. You're throwing your life away."

Eric's squeal of disbelief might have come from Rogerson himself. What the hell was he doing, giving advice to this slovenly dropout? What did Matthew Rogerson care if one more young man decided to turn himself into a sentient vegetable? They could sit here for hours, lecturing one another, wallowing in rival righteousness. On the one side, Eric, rebel and scourge of the bourgeoisie, a cross on his mother's shoulders; on the other, Rogerson. And what was he? Whose representative was he? He got to his feet. The moral code did not need Matthew Rogerson as its champion. He was one supporter it might not be able to survive. Eric had known him when they were both ten years dumber. He looked at Eric's plate.

"Bon appétit."

"What?"

"It's a Parisian curse, guaranteed to bring on the German disease. Watch it, Eric. We're on to you now. You're never out of our sight. Would you like to show me the garage?"

"Cut it out."

"I can't force you, of course. Next time I shall bring a warrant."

"Come on, Rogerson. What is this?"

"Don't whine."

"I'm not whining. What's this crazy monologue?"

"Don't bother to get up. I'll show myself out. Thank you for the offer of tea, but I never drink when I am on a case."

Arms akimbo, Rogerson backed toward the door. He felt for and found the knob behind him, turned it, opened the door. Slipping outside, he cast a maledictory look at Eric.

"Beware."

Rounding the house, heading for his car, he broke into a trot, chin up, arms close to his sides, knees pumping. His lungs protested; so did his legs. Undercover agent Rogerson, the scofflaw's nemesis. He could have kicked himself out to his car. Only a mother could weep for Eric.

Back on campus, he took the far stairs to the third floor to diminish the risk of running into Brenda Mapes. Let her talk to her son first.

His phone was ringing when he came into his office.

"Professor Rogerson? This is Dean Laplace's office calling."

"Hello, Norah."

"Dean Laplace wonders if it would be convenient for you to come see him."

"Now?"

There was the sound of turning pages. "The dean is free tomorrow at three."

"Good for him."

"Is that convenient for you?"

"The dean's freedom is invariably an inconvenience for me. How is the officious bastard?"

"I'll put you down for three tomorrow then."

"Miss Vlach?"

"Is that all right?"

"Norah?"

A long pause. "What is it?"

"Goodbye."

"Goodbye."

"Norah, wait. I can't come at three tomorrow. Make it four."

Again the riffling of pages. "Four o'clock will be fine."

"I have an *important* appointment at three."

"The dean will see you at four."

Replacing his phone, Rogerson made a face at the world. He saw Norah Vlach less and less and this glacial formality was the rule. They had known embarrassment together several years ago. First in her living room, where Norah had filled him with martinis; they were engaged in an all but priapic embrace on the couch when the aged Mrs. Vlach surprised them. Again they had sought refuge in the room of Harry the bartender of the old faculty club, cowering on the second floor while beneath them a meeting of the club committee droned on. After her mother's death, Norah, a probable matricide, left Fort Elbow for a time, but in a few months she was back, once more Laplace's secretary. Poor Norah. Ever since, her life had been a series of what pass for triumphs in the academic world.

As Laplace added more assistant deans to his fiefdom, Norah's job grew in importance. She was not only bossed, she bossed in turn. She had a deserved reputation for efficiency and a concomitant one as a bitch. He and Norah had not quite sinned together. Circumstance had conspired to act as contraceptive, consummation was only wished for and ultimately despaired of; they had drifted apart. Rogerson sometimes wondered if his difficulties with Laplace were due in any degree to Norah's lingering animosity. She had not been a woman scorned, but frustration too infuriates. The one advantage of the pullulating bureaucracy was that it put added buffers and barriers between Rogerson and such satraps as deans, assistant deans, administrative assistants, and the secretaries of the above. He did not relish coming from Heep's office to Laplace's tomorrow. Perhaps he could have Mrs. Every telephone Norah and announce in a sultry equivocal voice that Professor Rogerson was indisposed. His phone rang again.

"Matt?" It was Laplace. Oz himself.

"Nobody else's butt."

"Come on over here, you nitwit."

"What time is it? What day is it?" Rogerson flapped a memo pad at the mouthpiece of the phone.

"You don't have a class. I checked."

"I see I have an appointment with you tomorrow at four."

"Matthew," Laplace said sweetly. "Would you like me to come over there?"

"At your age? Nonsense. Remain where you are."

With the transfer of many offices from the main building to new structures, Laplace had been able to lay claim to more and more space, until now what Rogerson referred to as the deanery occupied half of the first floor. Classroom after classroom had been converted into office space, old walls knocked down, new ones installed, carpeting laid with Armenian abandon, counters erected to keep the rabble at bay. To get to Laplace it was necessary to negotiate three progressively larger anterooms, and the inner sanctum was seldom attained. It was Laplace's boast that he could get through an entire semester without seeing a student in the line of duty. It was the tough case indeed that could not be handled before it threatened his solitude.

Norah Vlach was in the last room before the dean's. By the time he got there—the faculty was not exempted from the ritual it was necessary to observe to achieve access to the dean, not even such old campaigners as Rogerson—he felt that he had solved the mystery of the Great Pyramid. Norah attempted to acknowledge his presence without looking directly at him. She was a reminder that he might have gone the way of Bastable, and sooner. Is accident the hinge of character? Lead us not into temptation. Meaning, Don't test us, Lord.

"You may go right in. The dean is expecting you."

Oh, the hell with it. Norah was probably right. Let the past be past. Norah seemed well preserved, well groomed, handsome if not beautiful. Still single. Ah, sweet mystery of life. Her vacations were alleged to be flying trips to unlikely places: Hong Kong, Tahiti, Helsinki, Bagdad. Did her heart flutter at the possibility of flying out of range of the moral law, bedding down with dusky natives, drinking exotic brews? Not likely. From what he heard, she was more probably out there at the airlines' farthest reach distributing tracts and Bibles.

Herb Laplace, hair shot through with white but allowed to grow over his ears, covering those protuberances like a mansard roof, sat close to his desk, elbows and forearms flat upon it, right hand atop his left, hunched forward, watching Rogerson approach.

"How is Fallor doing?" he asked before Rogerson sat.

"He is everything we expected him to be."

"Pretty bad?"

"Is that what you expected?"

"Of course, the first year as chairman is the toughest."

"This is his second. What's so tough?"

"Dealing with bastards like you."

"Has he been complaining about me?"

"Still smoking?" Laplace watched hungrily while Rogerson lit a cigarette. "Pall Malls, huh? Why the gold pack? Do they give you that when you've smoked a million?"

Rogerson blew smoke at the dean. "Have you quit?"

"I couldn't breathe."

"Try a pipe."

"I don't like them." Laplace tried to talk without moving his upper lip. Dentures. No doubt that made smoking a pipe difficult. "God, that smells good." Laplace pushed back from his desk, went to the window and punched a button on his air conditioner. The outside world seemed to fascinate him. Still looking out the window, he said, "Remember how this place used to be?"

"How do you mean?"

"The Old Bastards." Laplace turned. "Remember Schmidt?"

"Vividly."

"I hear he's doing well at Harvard."

"I'm not surprised."

"Wooley misses him. He sends Bismarck copies of everything he publishes." Bismarck was Laplace's name for the chancellor. "And he sends them on to me." Laplace pulled a book from a shelf and threw it onto the desk. Rogerson picked it up and glanced at the title. *The Phenomenology of Hockey.* In the foreword, Reinhardt thanked the Olympic Committee for the grant on which he had written the book. Rogerson pushed it away.

Laplace said, "Fallor wants to bring in outside people to teach summer school."

"Does he?"

"He says none of his staff is available, at least not enough are. What are you doing this summer?"

"A little monograph on the phenomenology of jai alai."

"Bullshit. What are you going to do?"

"Felix Freeman has asked me to visit him at his desert home."

"You heard from Felix?" Laplace looked hurt. Didn't he know that Felix hated him?

"He suggests that we collaborate on a general indictment of higher education."

"Ha. What would you two know of higher education?"

"Then there is my verse play on Ivan the Terrible."

"You could teach two classes. That would pay."

"No, thanks."

"Damn it, Matt, I don't want to be hiring outside people. There are too damned many people in your department as it is. There should be competition for summer teaching. In the old days we would have sold our mother for a summer job."

"Speak for yourself."

"You know what I mean."

"Times have changed." Rogerson looked significantly around Laplace's office, but the dean was not to be distracted. Rogerson felt like strangling Fallor. Why had the chairman mentioned him when the question of reluctant summer school instructors arose? Of course, Laplace was perfectly capable of remembering old enemies unaided. It was even possible that Laplace meant to do him a favor.

"Naturally I can't make you teach summer school."

"That's right."

"Would there be any point in appealing to your loyalty?"

"To what?"

"To the school." Herb blushed. "To me."

"Is this what you called me over here to talk about?"

"I realize it doesn't strike you as important. You don't have to explain to Wooley the need to cut back in your department while at the same time outside people are asked in to meet our summer school commitments."

"What do you mean, cut back?"

"How many classes do you teach, Matt?"

"I'm a senior man," Rogerson said.

"I know. If you weren't you wouldn't be carrying so heavy a load. Fallor teaches only one class."

"He's chairman."

"I could do that job standing on my head." Laplace snorted.

"Well, after all, with your experience."

"Matt, what is your candid estimate of the humanities department?"

"Uh uh. Not me, Herb. If you want an estimate of the department, ask the chairman. He owes you a report. I don't."

"Maybe you think he's a friend of yours."

Laplace's smile was demonic. It's only a tactic, Rogerson assured himself. But he could not help wondering what Fallor's written reports were like. Professor Rogerson does not publish, which would be less serious a matter if only he were a good teacher. He refuses to pass out the teacher evaluation form to students, but word-of-mouth assessment of his classroom performance is not good. He marks below the departmental average (A—), but it is impossible to say that he makes greater demands on his students. He has a reputation for being whimsical, ill-prepared, unserious. On and on, the somber truths that summed up his life. He did not care. At least he wanted not to care. Dear God, why should he want to receive a good report from someone like Fallor? Twenty years in the classroom had sapped his faith that the effort was worthwhile, but he was incapable of doing anything else. To dig I am not able, to beg I am ashamed. Rogerson got to his feet.

"I won't take up any more of your time, Herb."

"Think about summer school."

"Maybe Reinhardt Schmidt could be persuaded to come back for the summer."

Herb uttered a filthy word which left the room with Rogerson and lifted Norah's brows as he passed her.

Keane sat on the steps in front of the faculty office building.

"I understand your wife is still out of town, Matthew."

"Yes."

"Her father?"

"Yes."

"Has she said what she thinks of my class?"

Rogerson looked thoughtful. "She has long wanted an introduction to modern poetry."

Keane laughed apologetically. "Actually I've been going rather far afield."

"Teaching under the trees? She mentioned that. She'll want to take your summer course too, I think."

"My summer course? But I'm not giving one."

Rogerson feigned surprise. "Does Dean Laplace know?"

"Fallor must have told him I'm going to Europe."

"It's a shame they won't give you a summer course. I'll tell Marge."

"Where did she get the idea I was teaching this summer?"

"I've no idea. What will you be doing in Europe?"

"Research. Some writing, I hope." Keane lied with a sly smile.

"A grant?"

"It didn't come through."

"Too bad. Maybe that is what confused Laplace."

Upstairs, he got past Brenda Mapes without being stopped and into Fallor's office. The chairman was in a corner of the room, brooding over the opened drawer of a file cabinet. His fingers traveled like a musician's over the protruding tabs of the folders. He was made uneasy by the unannounced entrance of Rogerson.

"I've just been talking to the dean."

"Grovel?" Grovel was the assistant dean in charge of academic affairs. Laplace called him Gunga Dean. Grovel came from Trinidad and held black activists in more contempt than did Laplace himself. Ms. Script, a hulking sociologist, was the college's deferential nod to the fairer sex. Phobes was in charge of budgets, a cold, implacable robot who, like the latter-day coin of the realm, seemed to have some baser metal in him which diluted his face value further.

"Laplace."

Fallor actually blushed. The young man was relatively new to the deviousness of administration and a vestigial conscience sometimes blunted the efficient execution of his duties.

"I suggested Keane for summer school," Rogerson said with the air of one who has hit upon a perfect solution. "Herb is reluctant to bring in a visiting professor for the summer."

"But Keane intends to do research abroad."

"His grant didn't come through."

"I hadn't heard that."

"It's not something he's likely to shout about. From what I've heard—don't repeat this—he could use more experience in the classroom."

"Oh."

"Of course, there are rumors about everyone's teaching."

"Isn't your wife in Keane's class?"

"Laplace agreed that summer school is not the place for me."

"He seemed sure he could persuade you to teach when I talked with him."

"Keane himself is anxious to teach."

"Are you sure?"

"So Sylvia Wood tells me. They're thick as thieves."

"She is already teaching summer school."

"I suppose she agreed on the assumption that Keane would be here too."

Fallor groped for a chair and sat down. This conversation had lost its thread. Rogerson chuckled.

"She might even be the reason Keane changed his mind."

"You definitely do not want to teach summer school."

"Definitely not."

"Professor Rogerson?" Brenda's voice was like a hand on his arm. Miss Ortmund too was in the outer office, ostensibly checking her own mailbox, actually taking inventory of everyone else's. There were rumors that she stole examination copies of books sent to her colleagues and crammed everything but first-class mail, regardless of addressee, into the huge leather pouch whose strap somehow clung to her sloping shoulder. "Did you see Eric?"

"Yes."

"Well?"

Rogerson glanced at Miss Ortmund, who, with a shoplifter's dexterity, had just put something in her bag. "Lots of mail today, Celette?"

Miss Ortmund wheeled, squinting through round steel-rimmed spectacles over the tops of which, irregular and spiky, her bangs fell. "The usual." She got a thumb under the strap of her bag and hitched it higher on her shoulder. "So much junk." She turned away, but Rogerson had need of her.

"I think half the mail is lost on its way to this office."

"Really?"

"I've seen the student helpers dump armloads into trash cans."

Miss Ortmund was horrified. "Did you report them?"

"For what good it did."

"But that is a federal offense." Peering at Rogerson, Miss Ortmund might have been a photograph on the post office wall.

"The kids claim it's stolen after it gets here."

Again Miss Ortmund hitched her bag higher. A twitching at the corners of her mouth was the closest she came to a smile. "A likely story."

"You know Keane's theory?"

"No."

"Of course, he has an extremely suspicious mind."

Brenda said, "I am here whenever the office is open. I see everyone who goes near that mailbox."

"That's just Keane's point," Rogerson cried. "He wants you to keep a log, make a note of everyone's mail, note who comes in and out."

Miss Ortmund moved uneasily toward the door, murmuring about a student who awaited her.

"I wouldn't get another thing done," Brenda objected.

"Exactly. His alternative is a small television camera, mounted there." Rogerson pointed. Behind him, Miss Ortmund made her excuses and fled.

"Is Professor Keane serious?" Brenda asked.

"So far as I know." He looked at his watch. "Good Lord."

"What about Eric?" Brenda cried as Rogerson went loping down the hall.

"Later. Later."

Later he was lucky. Brenda had stepped out of the office. Rogerson went to the mailbox and scooped the contents of Keane's slot into Miss Ortmund's. While he was at it, he put Sylvia's mail in Keane's box. Busy as a bee, the zip code of a fly. Let raunchy Sylvia turn her attention to salivating Keane. No marriage admitted impediments to their false minds. If Keane was as avid as she claimed, he would find surer solace with her than mooning over Marge.

"I am serious," Sylvia insisted, warming to the subject. "It is a classic case."

"Marge as Lady Chatterley?"

"You are so goddam sure of yourself."

"Sylvia, your mind has been addled by higher learning. In the real world, evil is largely in the mind. Action requires opportunity, the breaking of routine, risk."

"Read the newspapers."

"God forbid."

"They are full of it."

"Indeed. Indeed."

"Sometimes I go out with a city detective. You should hear the stories he tells. Half his shift is spent keeping husbands and wives from one another's throats. She says he is whoring around and he is sure someone is with her while he's at work. I rode patrol with him one night, posing as a reporter. Don't tell me about the real world."

"That sounds like fun."

"What?"

"Riding around in a patrol car. I'd like to do that."

"I'll talk to Gunther. You're a romantic, Matthew. That's your problem. You think in terms of courtship, being put off, writing sonnets. It all comes down to a piece of ass, which can be a very beautiful thing, of course. Men have always known that. Now women know it too. It's a lot healthier. Maybe your wife is more modern than you are."

"Maybe."

"You think Keane is a clown, don't you?"

"Don't you?"

"In some ways, yes."

"What are the other ways?"

His question caught her in midsip. Over the white horizon of her coffee cup her great gray eyes looked steadily at Rogerson. ESP, something, dirty thoughts traversed the distance between them. Rogerson felt Samson to her Potiphar's wife. Was she serious? In again, out again, show me yours, I'll show you mine. Chock-full of estrogen, she was in a ruttish mood. Not with a whimper but a bang, gang and otherwise, the whole world humping itself to death. Sylvia, he was sure, would be clinically knowledgeable, proud of her seraglio skills. Would she even blink if he locked the door and suggested a sweet, thoughtless session on the floor behind his desk? Her eyes sparked with a small triumph. She had finally hit old Matthew Rogerson below the belt.

"And what was Brenda Mapes weeping about this morning?"

"You noticed that, did you?"

"I should have knocked. You should lock your door first."

"Just what I told myself."

"What was it all about?"

"She couldn't stand it any longer."

"After all these years she had to confess a consuming passion for you?"

"You're not that far off."

"Tell me." Sylvia slid to the edge of her chair. What an appetite for venereal trivia she had.

"Has Keane ever indicated to you this penchant he has for older women?"

"What have I been telling you?"

"Marge? Don't be silly. I mean much older."

"You can't mean Brenda."

"I know, I know. I found it ridiculous too. But just try to convince Brenda it is."

"What has he done?"

"She was reluctant to give details. Like me, she is an old-fashioned romantic."

"Tell me you're putting me on."

"Ask Brenda. Better still, ask Keane."

Sylvia, having confessed herself credulous about the general horniness of the real world, Krafft-Ebing her Baedeker of the tides of love, could scarcely dismiss out of hand this preposterous suggestion. "I can't just ask him outright."

"You'll find a way."

"You better believe it."

Heep said, "Forget about your prostate. Massage will take care of that. If you want to worry about something, worry about that foreskin."

Rogerson grunted.

"If you get cancer there, you'll know you have it."

"Cancer?"

"This one old fellow, it swelled and swelled." Heep's hands widened as if to receive a basketball. Rogerson cried out inwardly.

"What did you do?"

"Cut it off."

"Cut it off!"

Heep grinned. "Did one last week. Whack!"

"My God."

"It really hurts. Mentally, I mean."

"Is that kind of cancer common?"

"I'll tell you one thing. I've never seen a circumcised man with cancer there. Old men are the most common victims. They get careless, and then . . ." Heep snapped his fingers.

"Is that connected with my trouble?"

"I'm only making a suggestion."

"Circumcision must be very painful at my age."

"You won't feel a thing. I do several a week. Many men your age. Oh, I admit it. It's a crusade with me. I see the risk you'll run when you get older. Take a man seventy-five, eighty years old: you cut that off and it's as if his life is over. It doesn't matter that he only uses it to pee with. He feels he's no longer a man."

"How does he pee afterward?"

"I'll spare you the gruesome details. I'd think about it if I were you."

"When I get well," Rogerson said meaningfully.

Marge's plane descended through the rain to the runway of the Fort Elbow airport. Through a steamy window Rogerson watched his wife cross the ramp to the terminal. She clutched her coat and her head was ducked into the rain.

"Here I am," Rogerson said, getting to her through the crowd.

Marge looked at him woefully. The copy of the airlines magazine she had held over her hair on the run from the plane dripped in her hand.

"Have a good flight?"

"Why don't they provide umbrellas, for pete's sake?"

"I should have brought one."

"Look at my coat!" The coat was yellow, boxy cut; Rogerson liked her in it. It looked soggy. Marge slipped it off. Her dress seemed new.

"Mom bought it for me."

"Nice."

Marge brightened. "The stores in Milwaukee, Matt. You don't realize how disadvantaged you are until you get out of this town."

Disadvantaged? The word had an echo he did not like. "How is your mother holding up?"

"Wonderfully."

"I don't suppose the loneliness has really hit her yet."

"She'll do all right."

The luggage was a long time coming and there was little point in trying to talk while they waited, jostled by other impatient passengers. Finally bags began to appear, transferred by hand from carts to pickup shelves. The crowd surged forward, Marge and Rogerson borne along with the rest.

"There it is," Marge cried. Rogerson lowered a shoulder and went over tackle for the score. Another hand met his on the suitcase handle. A squat, mahogany-haired woman glared at him.

"That is my bag."

"I believe it's my wife's."

"It is mine!" An air pocket formed; the woman's voice was shrilly accusative.

"Marge," Rogerson bawled. "Come here."

"What is it?"

"Is this your bag?"

"I guess not. It looks like it, though."

Trying to smile, Rogerson ceded the bag to the crone. "Do you see your own bag?" he asked Marge.

She did not. Others reached around, over and under them to claim bags, those taken away were replaced by others, but still Marge did not see hers. It was among the last to be delivered. They should have waited in dignity at a distance.

"Let's have a cup of coffee," Rogerson suggested.

"I've been drinking coffee steadily for hours."

"A Coke then."

"I have to go to the ladies' first. Watch my bag."

When Rogerson entered the restaurant alone, the mahogany-haired lady was seated at the counter. She looked suspiciously at the bag Rogerson carried. He dropped it on a seat of a booth and sat opposite it. He ordered two Cokes.

Marge was wearing the yellow coat when she joined him. Her hair showed no signs of rain, her mood had brightened.

"You didn't have to hurry back," he said, glad she was home.

"I really think Mom wanted to be alone. People think it's a crime to let a widow be by herself. As if she might commit suicide or something. And nobody knows what to say. It's awful."

"Will she be able to handle things?"

"Money? Don't worry about that. She got down to the bank and cleaned out the safety-deposit box before the obituary notice appeared."

"What for?"

"Once the death is official the bank has to seal it. They can tie up things forever in probate."

"I didn't know that."

Marge lit a cigarette, looking wise. "And it doesn't matter that she owned everything as much as Dad did."

58

"She's pretty well set then?"

"Very well," Marge emphasized. She seemed about to say something, then did not. "Let's get home."

"I explained to Keane," he said, picking up her bag.

She looked puzzled.

"Your absence from his class."

She seemed to have difficulty dredging up the memory. A vacant half-amused look came over her face.

"What did he say?"

"He was sorry to hear about your father."

"He's such a funny little guy."

"Sylvia Wood is sure he's after your body."

"She said that?"

"Words to that effect."

Marge laughed. "Can't she do better than that if she wants to dream up a lover for me? Where's the car?"

He pointed to it. Marge's manner seemed brisk, assured, different. He had noticed it first when she told him of her mother and the safe-deposit box. Rogerson could imagine the old bitch swooping down on the bank before Olson's body was cold. Marge's remark about what people say to widows sounded like a quote from her mother. And the importance she had once attached to Keane's class now struck her as amusing. He should have welcomed this, but he did not like the new self Marge seemed to be trying out in the wake of her father's death. Rogerson had always resented the influence Mrs. Olson had on Marge, even from what should have been the saving distance of Milwaukee. A visit home had often brought her back acting like a junior version of her bitchy mother. No doubt Fort Elbow would, as it had before, work its dimming effect and in a few days Marge would be talking up Keane and his course.

"When did you talk to Sylvia?"

"When? I don't know. I see her every day."

"When she made the remark about Keane."

"Oh, she's said that several times. I thought you'd find it funny."

"Not coming from her."

"So forget it."

"I don't like her speculating about me and talking to you about it."

"Neither do I."

"Tell her that."

"I have."

"Tell her again."

"I'm sorry I mentioned it."

They drove in silence. Rain battered the roof, ran down the windows, turned the windshield wavy.

"How are the kids?"

"They won't be home from school yet."

He stopped in the driveway and Marge dashed for the house. When he came in with the bag, she was already upstairs. He left her bag in the hallway. In the kitchen he put on coffee. It had been stupid to mention what Sylvia had said. He wanted to talk with Marge, tell her of his visits to Heep, of the suggestion that he be circumcised. What a ridiculous thing to have done at his age.

"Oh, good. I feel like coffee now."

Marge had changed into slacks and a baggy sweat shirt. She looked around the kitchen as a stranger might. Before leaving for the airport Rogerson had made sure the house was shipshape. He could see her relief. She sat down.

"I've got news."

She was smiling, a Christmas Eve, let's-open-the-presents smile.

"You know the cabin on Lake Walleye?"

Rogerson nodded.

"It's mine! Ours. Daddy left it to me."

"You're kidding."

"No. It's not in my name yet, but that's being taken care of. Mother never liked the place and Dad wanted me to have it, so it's ours. Isn't that wonderful?"

Olson had built the lake cabin fifty miles northwest of Milwaukee on land he had bought for a song way back when. Over the years he had modernized it, added to it, made it suitable for year-round use. It had been his hope to live there when he retired, but as Marge said, Mrs. Olson did not like the place. She found it too isolated. She did not like to fish or swim, the radio and television reception was erratic, she had nothing to do. For Olson those things were the attraction of the place. In the past, Marge had taken her cue from her mother and professed to find the place boring. They could have had the use of the place for months every summer. Now, in the

60

exultation of ownership, Marge's attitude toward the cabin had changed.

Rogerson sat down. This was undeniably good news, great news, wonderful news. The chair against his bottom reminded him of his affliction. Old mortality. But that did not explain his inability to share Marge's elation. He resented this acquisition, the cabin she had called "mine" before she called it "ours."

"So guess where we are going to spend the summer!"

Marge leaned toward him, offering her lips.

3

There was no wait for a table in the bar of the faculty club, but this advantage was outweighed by the fact that there they would be easy prey to the garrulous types who preferred a liquid lunch. Nonetheless they accepted the steward's offer. Following Marge to the table, Rogerson noticed Plummet-Finch at the bar, seated sideways on his stool, one hand curled around his whiskey sour, the other holding his pipe. Gilbert was staring at Marge with some of the surprise he might have shown if this were a men's room. He saw Rogerson then and before recognition introduced a saving hypocrisy, Gilbert was a study in accusation. Rogerson waved at him, got seated across from Marge, ordered martinis, studied the menu and, in peripheral vision, saw Plummet-Finch get down from his stool, steady the floor beneath him, hesitate, then start toward them.

"Damn it," Rogerson muttered.

"What is it?"

"Plummet-Finch."

"Oh. Where?" She turned her look of amused curiosity directly at the approaching Plummet-Finch, who, drink in hand, gave a creditable performance of one surprised to be noticed just passing by.

"As I live and breathe, Mrs. Rogerson."

"Hello, Gilbert," Marge trilled.

Gilbert kissed her hand, having somehow anchored his pipe in the hand that bore his drink.

"You look so youthful I was certain Matthew had taken a student to lunch."

"But I am a student."

"Say it isn't true."

"Sit down," Marge said. "Are you having lunch?"

Gilbert was careful not to look at Rogerson. "It is lunchtime, isn't it?" He put his drink and pipe on the table, drew out a chair and sat.

"I hope I'm not interrupting a conjugal tête-à-tête."

"We were just engaged in a little foreplay," Rogerson said sweetly.

"I honestly did not recognize you when you came in," Gilbert said to Marge. "You didn't get that dress in Fort Elbow."

"Milwaukee."

"I've never been there."

"I've just returned."

Gilbert's face wrinkled with expressive recognition. "Your father. So sorry." Gilbert sought solace in his drink. "Then you missed the *FOF* Matthew was on."

"I'm afraid so."

Gilbert leaned toward her. "It was not up to standard. No fault of Matthew's, of course. Perhaps it was the topic."

"Wasn't it the role of women, something like that?"

"Something like that. What is this about your being a student?"

"Isn't it awful?"

"I thought you enjoyed Keane's class," Rogerson said.

"Matt, I had forgotten how futile it all is. Trading little bits of information, knowing a few books most people wouldn't care to read, discussing them with an air of superiority. Nine people out of ten could play the game if they wanted to."

Their drinks arrived and while the girl put them down Gilbert drained his glass, put it on the tray and asked for another.

"Will you be eating too, sir?"

"Of course I shall be eating." Gilbert was offended by the implication that he would spend the lunch hour at the faculty club and not have lunch.

"I'll bring another menu."

"Do that. When you bring the drink." The girl gone, Gilbert rolled his eyes heavenward. "This place."

"It's convenient," Rogerson said. He would have liked to order while the girl was there.

"What is your favorite restaurant?" Marge asked Gilbert.

"In Fort Elbow?" As who should say, In the desert?

"What on earth keeps you here?"

"God only knows." Her directness had startled Gilbert.

"Do you know that we have been here twenty years?"

Gilbert clutched at his heart. "Not even time off for good behavior?"

"Twenty solid years," Marge said with dismal eloquence.

"You both will go straight to heaven when you die. Purgatory, Fort Elbow, what's the difference? You have suffered sufficiently."

"I like Fort Elbow," Rogerson said. "It is itself and not another place."

He was ignored by them both. "Surely you escape in summer?" Gilbert said.

"We will this summer."

"Ah."

"My father left me a lake cottage in Wisconsin."

"What luck! On a lake, you say?"

Marge told Gilbert all about Lake Walleye, all about the cottage too. The girl brought Gilbert's drink, they ordered the chef's special ("I believe it is a hamburger festooned with cole slaw," Gilbert said) and Marge resumed her narrative. Rogerson told the girl to bring him another martini.

It had occurred to him, on the walk across campus to the club, that this lunch would be as good an occasion as any to tell Marge of Heep's insistence that he be circumcised. He continued to withhold consent to the operation and hoped Marge would veto it.

"Felix Freeman has invited us to visit him this summer," he said loudly.

"Who?"

"Felix Freeman."

"I don't believe I know him," Gilbert said.

"You don't. He taught here but is now retired."

"He lives in the Arizona desert." There was horror in Marge's voice.

"And he's lonely."

"I don't wonder. Why did he bury himself away like that, far from his friends, in a strange place? It's insane."

How could he explain the enthusiasm that had been kindled in poor Felix by the developer's brochure? The desert would flower, the very air was curative, there was water within a hundred yards of every site (straight down, Felix mordantly explained in a letter), a planned community far from the rancor and risk of the typical urban environment. Felix's twilight years were to be spent in peace and contentment among cacti and coyotes.

"We needn't stay long."

"I am not going to Arizona. I am going to my cottage."

"Is it far?" Gilbert's tone was plummy. Did there dance on the horizon of his mind the possibility of an invitation to a Wisconsin lake, a week in the wilds? Marge, bless her, did not catch the significance of the inquiry.

"Less than a day's drive," she said.

Three chef's specials arrived and Gilbert, with hand signals and nods, adroitly ordered another drink. Marge, picking at her food, full of her subject, went on and on about the cottage. For Rogerson the lunch had taken on the aspect of a meal for the condemned.

For it was as a threat that he now viewed the acquisition of the cottage. It had been the single subject of Marge's conversation since her return. In the evening, with the children gathered about her, she pored over photographs taken at the cottage. Some went back to her childhood, most to the time before they had met. The cottage might have been the promise of a return to her girlhood, to the carefree freedom that had been hers before she married. To the children, on the phone to friends, he heard her refer to the cottage as "mine," sometimes as "Daddy's," less frequently as "ours." It was hers. He wanted no part of it. His resentment was childish, he knew it and it became the fiercer for that knowledge. He did not try to pretend that he was bothered by the fact that the bonanza had come their way as a result of Olson's death. Poor Olson, but it was Olson who had wanted Marge to have his lake place.

That he had actually dreamed of the cottage proved how deeply he was disturbed by its intrusion into their lives. He had seen himself lying on the boat dock, his body white and flabby, Marge hovering over him, a huge scaling knife in her hand. The fishlike body on the dock tosses, flips, out of its element, drowning in air. Knife in hand, Marge kneels beside him. Rogerson was wakened by the sound of his own cry to find that he had cupped his privates in his hand, protecting them from the jagged scaling knife.

Absurd. Freud's influence has come to shape our very dreams. Analysis kills the child in the womb, breaks short the young man's courting, analysis brings age into youth, it lies between the bride and bridegroom, analysis is against nature's increase. Nothing is itself alone, thing for thing, word for word. Rogerson remembered a long-ago nightclub in Sparta, Wisconsin, two blond entertainers singing saucily, He's got the cutest little dinghy in the Navy. Smut is a fallen love of language. Sigmund, cigar in mouth, cancer, you bastard, and will my gentile foreskin breed the deadly cells, the organ swell, a sick erectile? Lying awake, prostrate with prostatitis, his manhood threatened by the knife, an heirloom looming as a threat, Rogerson told himself that he did not want to spend the goddam summer in a cottage bequeathed them by his father-in-law. My cottage, my cottage. It curdled his soul, Wisconsin cheese.

"Are you circumcised, Gilbert?" Rogerson asked during a lull in Marge's eulogy.

"I beg your pardon." Gilbert's eyes popped. A drop of catsup clung to his upper lip.

"Are you circumcised?"

Marge concentrated on her food. Gilbert was actually blushing.

"The reason I ask . . ."

"Yes," Marge said. "Why would you ask such a thing?"

"My doctor suggests that I be circumcised."

"When?"

"Soon."

"Why?"

"He fears I will get cancer in my old age."

"There?" Gilbert was horrified.

"He claims it is rather common. Once you've got it, the only solution is to lop it off."

66

Gilbert went pale, which answered Rogerson's question.

"Who is your doctor?"

"Heep. He is a urologist."

"I never heard of cancer *there.*"

"Neither had I."

"My God!"

If his intention had been to silence Marge, he had succeeded. But what a price to pay. How could she ever treat the topic as serious after this?

"The thought of any operation, let alone that one, paralyzes me."

"Matt too," Marge said. "He would never agree to it."

Such is the nature of perversity that Rogerson decided then and there, if only *in petto,* to have the operation. On his next visit to Heep he would set a date. Heep had said there was no danger, there were no adverse side effects. It would even enhance his sex life. His sex life. Rogerson thought of the meager menu that phrase picked out.

"What a dumb thing to talk about at the table," Marge said later in front of the club. Gilbert had made his excuses and regained his stool at the bar, no doubt intent on washing away memories of chef's specials and penisectomies.

"You're right."

"You always take advantage of the fact that Gilbert has no sense of humor."

"There are times when I fool even myself."

"If you bring my books, I'll take the bus."

Meaning that she would leave the car for him. Her books were in his office. A goodbye kiss, husbands love your wives, wives be subject to your husbands, a brush of lips against her cheek, playing to a cosmic audience, behold how these Rogersons love one another.

His attempt to peek unobtrusively into the outer office to see if Miss Ortmund had left any mail in his box was not unobtrusive enough for Brenda Mapes, who wheeled back from her typewriter and said in an urgent whisper, "Professor Rogerson, I must talk to you."

Rogerson stepped into the office. Brenda came to him and put her hand on his upper arm.

"Thank you for talking to Eric."

"I'm afraid I didn't do much good."

"Oh, but you did. A world of good." She came closer and, on tiptoe, whispered, "The garage is empty."

"Good."

Rogerson already knew this. An irate Ketchum had called to inform Rogerson that he and his security force had made goddam asses of themselves by believing Rogerson and persuading the city police to stage a joint raid on the Mapes garage. It was pretty clear that Ketchum had oversold the importance of the operation the better to conquer the reluctance of the municipal constabulary to have anything to do with the Keystone irregulars who made up Ketchum's force. There had not been so much as a tire track inside the garage and Ketchum, who had been taken to the scene in a city police car, emerged from the empty garage to find that he had been left to return to campus on foot. His own men had skedaddled at the first hooting of the cops. Rogerson tried unsuccessfully to persuade Ketchum that he had not been playing a practical joke on him.

"Did you ever find that bike you lost?"

"The bike that was stolen? Yes, I did."

"You did!"

"Someone returned it to the rack behind the faculty office building."

"Isn't that where you left it?"

"Maybe one of your men found it."

Ketchum made an indecisive noise.

"Or the thief had an attack of conscience. Or both."

Ketchum had slammed down the phone. Rogerson could hardly blame him. Had Eric observed the big raid from an upstairs window of the house, doubled over with merriment?

Brenda said, "Eric wanted you to know that he was grateful for the warning."

"That's something, anyway."

"Do you think he's a bad person, Professor Rogerson? It is so difficult for a mother to be objective about her own son."

"He seems a little lethargic."

"It's his diet. I tell him that. He won't eat sensibly."

"He should exercise too. Tell him I suggest bike riding."

Fallor was drawn by this conversation from the inner office. He too wished to have words with Rogerson. They went into Fallor's office, leaving Brenda to her typing. She seemed only slightly puzzled by the suggestion that her son become a cyclist.

"Thanks for telling me Keane wanted to teach summer school."

"He brought it up?"

"The very day you did. Honest to God, I'm sure he said he had absolutely no desire to teach this summer. Of course, that was when he thought he'd get a grant to do research abroad. I had thought he was going grant or no grant. Anyway, we got it straightened out."

"Your troubles are over?"

"They've just begun. Laplace is madder than hell at me."

"Whatever for?"

"He had already written to the man I suggested as a summer-session appointment."

"Well, he can always write him another letter."

"You should have heard him when I said that."

"How many courses will Keane teach?"

"Two."

"Lucky him."

"How I long to get out of this office."

Meaning, out of this job, out of this department. Like most of the others, Fallor saw this hybrid department as a sure road to obscurity, an academic cul-de-sac. Far better to specialize, departmentalize, and leave the putting together of the various offerings to the students. It was a respectable point of view. Rogerson did not mock it. Whatever hope the humanities department was meant to embody (and of course theory had followed fact; originally it had been a mere expedient to make a single department of professorial odds and ends), it certainly did not convey to students any vision of the whole. Who could blame teachers for wanting to do a small thing well rather than court almost certain failure on a wider scale?

"I can imagine."

"Laplace says you'll be taking over."

Rogerson laughed. "That's an old dream of his. To corrupt me with advancement. I won't be taking over."

"It's not so bad."

"There are others who would want the job."

"Who?"

Rogerson thought. "Miss Ortmund?"

"Say, have you noticed anything strange about her lately?"

"Like what?"

"The other day a guy came in here, flashed some sort of badge and asked about our procedures for distributing mail. He said he had had a complaint from Miss Ortmund."

"What did you tell him?"

"That Farthing in philosophy was the man to see."

"And?"

"Farthing has scheduled a lecture on the secret police."

"Good for him."

"Someone *has* been screwing around with the mail. I was expecting a very important letter from Alaska. It had lain for a week in Sylvia's box."

"A week!"

"She thought it was junk mail." Fallor frowned.

"How about Keane for chairman?"

"Haven't you heard? He's switching to English."

"I hadn't heard." Keane to English. Fallor to philosophy. They would soon be down to a mere handful of faculty. That is how it had been when Rogerson arrived. Once he had been the youngest man in the department. Now he was the oldest.

Keane, sweaty, earnest, holding a very hot cup of coffee gingerly in the claw of his hand, pulled a chair up next to Rogerson's in the faculty lounge.

"Preparing for class?"

Rogerson put down the copy of *The Philosophical Review.* An article which asked whether "maybe" implies "however" had been lulling him toward a learned sleep. "I'm through for the day."

"The semester will soon be over," Keane observed.

"Hosannah, *Deo gratias,* amen."

"I shall be teaching summer school after all."

"So I hear."

"Yes, I mentioned it to Mrs. Rogerson."

"Yes."

"You might take one of these." Keane pressed a dittoed sheet into

Rogerson's hand, thereby empurpling his fingers. The page contained write-ups of two courses Keane would teach that summer.

"Thank you."

"I hope those are clear enough." A wistful look. "I wish I could make them sound more appealing."

Rogerson glanced at the first write-up. *"Paradise Lost;* the Miltonic Line: caesura and irony."

"How can you lose with Milton?"

"The Baudelaire may be more of a draw."

"Perhaps."

"I'll have the class read the *Fleurs du Mal* in French. It won't matter if they don't understand. Baudelaire's poetry is quite independent of conceptual content."

"That's an interesting theory."

"Well . . ." Keane stood, splashed scalding coffee on his knee, danced across the room in pain. He dumped his cup, coffee and all, into a wastebasket. Farthing looked up from his reading as Keane limped from the room.

"What's wrong with him?"

"Coffee on the knee."

Farthing shrugged and returned to *Playboy.*

The following week Rogerson dropped in unannounced on Herb Laplace. The dean was talking to Norah Vlach and started to flee toward his sanctum when he saw that it was only Rogerson who had managed to get to him unmediated by secretaries.

"I've been meaning to call you, Matt. Come inside."

Norah's look was civil if not affable.

"That goddam Fallor," Herb said when Rogerson was seated.

"He's always been a favorite of yours, hasn't he?"

"It's really your fault."

"What is?"

"We are running the risk of a lawsuit, that's what. Over this damned summer school appointment. Fallor begged me to make an offer to some clown he knew in graduate school, great guy, they always are when they're out of a job, so I wrote the letter and now we have no opening and I had to write again and rescind the offer. He'll sue."

"You're sure of that?"

"Of course I'm sure. The AAUP and those goddam unions have poisoned the atmosphere of higher education. He'll take us to court. Why not? What else does he have to do? He's out of a job."

"Buy him off."

"Too simple."

"Why?"

"I mean for him. He can amuse himself for a year or two by suing us, then sock us with his legal bills. What has he got to lose?"

"It turned out that Keane wanted to teach summer school."

"The sonofabitch. He's also switching to English."

"And Fallor to philosophy."

"I need a chairman, Matt."

"I know you do."

Laplace perked up. He sensed a deal in the offing. "You'll like the job, Matt."

"Bullshit."

"There's nothing to it. You can teach one course less and there is a salary boost of a thou that goes with the job."

"I don't want it."

Laplace glowered. "You're not going into another department, Matt. That's flat. I'll block it."

"Acting chairman."

"Acting! Why?" But Laplace was delighted. "Take it permanently."

"No. Another thing. I want to teach summer school."

"Not this summer."

"It would be hard to teach summer school in the fall."

"But you don't want to teach summer school. Nobody wanted to teach summer school. I have to go in search of temporary faculty and now everybody wants to teach summer school. What the hell is going on?"

"I suppose the money is attractive."

"For the younger guys, maybe. No, Matt. I am not going to rock the boat again. No summer school."

"All right." Rogerson got up and stubbed out his cigarette in Herb's ashtray. "And no acting chairman."

"Sit down."

72

"I have to write some letters. There must be someplace that can use a man with my experience in their summer program."

"Sit down! What course do you want to teach?"

"Paradise Lost."

"You? Milton? You're kidding."

"Did Milton write *Paradise Lost?*"

Herb was flipping through papers. "That course is already being offered." He looked up. "But then you know that. It's one of the courses Keane is teaching."

"No kidding."

"You want to teach *Paradise Lost?*"

"In the worst way."

"No doubt. Is that your deal—one summer school course and you will be acting chairman of the humanities department?"

"For one year."

"Fair enough." Herb put out his hand, then took it back. "What's the point of shaking hands? This is no gentlemen's agreement. Those days are gone forever. I'll have Norah type it up. Everything in black and white." Laplace heaved a sigh. "God, what a life. I feel like a guardhouse lawyer."

"Retire early, Herb. Join Felix."

"I wrote that bastard and do you know what he sent? A brochure."

"That's what won his own heart."

"But this is for a new retirement community in Arkansas. I had asked Felix to tell me about Arizona."

"Felix always had a sense of humor."

"Well, I never appreciated it."

"Will you tell Fallor I'm teaching that course?"

"The hell with Fallor. He was dealing with Horst to get into the philosophy department before he even warmed his chair in the humanities office. And Keane was sucking up to Herrick in English. Matt, these young guys have no sense of the tradition the humanities have enjoyed on this campus. You do. You represent continuity. You remember the men who began the humanities program."

"The Old Bastards. A department is a better place to change schools from, if it comes to that."

"It's going to come to that for a lot of them," Herb said grimly. "And they know it."

"It's leveled off, Matt. The boom has run out of gas. Some of these young freaks who came here demanding big salaries, expecting tenure as a matter of course, are going to find out what it's like in the real world. The way it was for us at the beginning. How many of them will be willing to face that?"

"The salary scale has changed."

"It's too high."

"Maybe we'll all be fired."

"Tenure," Herb snorted. "That's the ace in the hole." His mind veered. "Say, why aren't you and Marge playing Wednesday-night bridge at the faculty club?"

"I don't like bridge."

"There's going to be a summer program."

"I'll mention it to Marge."

Like hell. What would she care about bridge at the faculty club now that her sights were set on a summer in Wisconsin?

That night Rogerson descended into the basement and his workroom there. He gathered together the poems he had written over the years, from manila folders, notebooks, envelopes. He was a saver. Whether or not he was a poet was another matter. Wasn't it ridiculous to dream at forty-seven of blossoming into a bard? As an ambition it was both lofty and humble: a few lines arranged on the page, a meager result of days of work, but the hope was that those lines would express in an unforgettable way some moment, mood, thought, scene. And live. That was the motive really—to cheat time and obscurity, to last. Rogerson as survivor, claiming a niche in future surveys of twentieth-century American literature. Why not? Emily Dickinson, Hopkins, others, had been unknown to their contemporaries yet were now considered representative of their time and place. Think of Catullus. In a way. He imagined a paragraph.

Matthew Rogerson, though he lived all his life in the Midwest, cannot (*pace* Winkelmann) be considered a merely regional poet, unless, that is, his predecessors Frost and Horvath too are to be called regional poets. Technical innovation is no more the salient feature of Rogerson's work than it was of Shakespeare's. He is that kind of major poet who takes the forms which are to hand and employs them in a superficially conventional way, though the discerning reader is struck by the liveliness of line caused by what Froward, Rogerson's biographer and the acknowledged authority on his work (it was Froward who established the definitive edition of the poems from manuscripts whose condition had been the despair of earlier laborers in the Rogerson Archives), has called "a scarcely conscious counterpoint." It is as if the two ends of the line rush toward each other, meet, purl, form the caesura and foam sweetly back to their starting points. That lines of such autonomy should also sustain a stanzaic progression is a minor miracle dubbed "the fateful declension" by Hazlitt in his well-known monograph "Stylometric Interpretation of the Rogersonian Stanza." As for the themes of the poetry . . .

"Matt?"

It was Marge, halfway down the stairs, her body half visible.

"What is it?"

"Are you busy?"

"Come on down."

A hesitation and then she descended. Rogerson was seated in his easy chair, Hughes's edition of Milton on his lap.

"What are you reading?"

He told her. She looked around the basement and he did too, seeing it with her eyes. The desk was a jumble of papers and books —closed books, open books, books piled high. More books on the floor. His typewriter, a sheet in its carriage, papers on either side of the machine. Rogerson's chair surrounded by magazines, journals, the paraphernalia of the academic life.

"Why can't you keep this place neat?"

"I like it this way."

"It's a sty. How can you find anything?"

"Nothing is lost. Don't." Marge had put a tentative hand on a pile of books at the end of the workbench.

"Why do these have to be here?"

"They don't have to be there, but they have to be somewhere. That's as good a place as any."

"I'm coming down here tomorrow and giving this place a thorough cleaning."

"Don't."

"No one can work in this kind of squalor. Why are you reading Milton?"

"It's been a while." A chicken answer.

"Three more weeks."

She meant until they would leave for the cottage. She perched on the stool near the workbench and lit a cigarette. She looked around for a place to put the match. "You're going to have a fire down here, Matt. That will clean it out."

"There's an ashtray on the desk."

"I'm sure there are all kinds of things hidden on that desk."

"I'm going to give a course in Milton."

"Good."

"This summer."

It didn't register. She was still looking with distaste at the desk. Removing a pile of letters to unearth the ashtray had not improved matters. Then she turned to him, surprised. "This summer!"

"I had a talk with Laplace. There was a kind of crisis. No one wants to teach summer school."

"Well, neither do you."

"That's what I told him."

"You can't. We are going to Wisconsin. I am not going to spend a summer in Fort Elbow when I have a cottage in Wisconsin, and that is all there is to it."

"You can go to the cottage."

"*I* can go to the cottage?"

"You and the kids. My not being there won't spoil it. I told Herb I'd teach this Milton course."

"To hell with Milton. Don't you want to go to the cottage?"

"Who would take Fort Elbow to a summer at the lake? Don't be silly. That isn't the point."

"You expect me to go up there alone with the kids?"

"It won't be so bad."

"Do you want to teach summer school? Is that it? Are you dying to spend six weeks of summer in a classroom? You couldn't wait until we could afford for you not to teach summer school anymore. What brought about the big change?"

"Herb wants me to be chairman of the department."

"Chairman."

"Yes."

"Did you accept?"

"That's why summer school. It was a sort of deal."

He watched her react. There had been a time when Marge would have been ecstatic over such an appointment. Promotion, as she would have thought. She was happy now, even proud, but at the same time a little sad that so little should be occasion for joy. To be chairman of a moribund department on the Fort Elbow campus was hardly the apotheosis of Matthew Rogerson.

"I'll get a raise."

"They should have made you chairman years ago."

Did she think he had been anxious for such advancement, eager to escape the classroom for the more stultifying atmosphere of academic administration? After so many years did she know him too little or too well? But this was a skit of his own composing. He had invited her pleasure at this turn of events, he himself pretending that he had engineered a coup.

His announcement had the desired diverting effect. Almost without further demur, Marge began to see the summer at the lake as something she and the kids would enjoy while Rogerson labored on in the heat of Fort Elbow. The emphasis on the Ohio heat was Marge's. Actually Rogerson's day would be spent in air-conditioned boredom. A yawn, a perfunctory kiss, and Marge went up to bed. There had been the soupçon of an overture, but he let the hint lie hidden in her yawn. His inflamed prostate made conjugal duty, or opportunity, unwelcome. He had told Heep to make an appointment at the hospital. A few days after the end of school Rogerson would go under the knife, offering a pound of flesh in propitiation of cancer of the penis. Heep the merchant of Venus. It would enhance his sex life. Ha. All he asked was a crab-free crotch.

And now, O lovely prospect, he would suffer alone and unbeknownst to Marge and the kids, to everyone, Rogerson the victim, suffering in awful solitude. To that end he had volunteered for summer school, accepted however temporarily a loathsome administrative post. Acting chairman indeed. It would be a theatrical turn, a mask put on for the nonce, Rogerson on the other side of the line that divides the honest yeomanry from the charlatans of the aca-

77

demic world. For a year he would be a shuffler of paper, an ex officio member of all the futile committees, orchestrator of meetings, father confessor and object of resentment to his colleagues.

"Be careful," Norah had said when he went to sign the agreement. Rogerson looked blank.

"Know your friends." A small oracular smile.

Know your friends. Know thyself. Norah as sibyl was a new incarnation. Did she mean Laplace? He needed no reminder to be wary of so experienced a dean as Laplace. Herb's ethics were the elastic code of the academic careerist.

Rogerson now shifted in his easy chair, conscious of his genitals, apprehensive of his date in surgery under the knife of the uninspiring Heep.

"You'll be a new man," Heep had promised.

"One slip of the knife and I won't be a man at all."

"You'll be your old self again."

"Make up your mind. Will I be conscious?"

"Oh, no. I'll have you put under."

An unhappy choice of words. His sense of foreboding was the twin of self-pity.

4

All night Rogerson had slept with the consciousness that the bed was unnaturally elevated, fully four feet from mattress to floor, and narrow. He woke with his hands clutching the sides of the bed, flat on his back. The room was dark. At the windows a suggestion of dawn. There was a night light at the base of the floor lamp beside his bed. In the hallway some stirring and from far off the muffled sound of voices. Female voices. Nurses.

"Mr. Rogerson?"

Rogerson all but levitated. A woman stood beside the bed, the shadows on her face weird, cast upward from the dim glow of the night light.

"Time for a pill."

"Oh."

"What are you in for?"

"Don't you know?"

"I'm a nurse's aide." Her tone told him that in the curative caste system she was an untouchable. Middle-aged, almost as old as Rogerson, she was short, full-faced, her hair gray and wild. Her smile was toothy and confidential.

"I'm Melanie Jenkins."

Rogerson said hello. His watch was in the bedside table. He asked Miss Jenkins to get it for him.

"*Miss* Jenkins! I've got nine kids. You should never put valuables in a drawer like that, not here. You shouldn't even have your watch." She slipped the watch over his wrist and let the band snap tight. It was like a little ceremony. She gave him a paper cup the size of a shot glass, in which a capsule rattled about.

"What's that?"

"A sedative. It will make you woozy." She took the cup, emptied it into his palm, whisked it away. A maroon capsule. He felt that he had guessed the right shell. It tasted waxy, brittle, indissoluble. It slid down his throat on a swallow of water. He had sat up to take his medicine.

"You're at the university," Mrs. Jenkins informed him. "My kids have mentioned you. I've been taking classes myself for years. Summer school, night school. If I live long enough I'll get a degree."

"What's the point?"

"You sound like my kids."

Across the room was an old man, the foot of his bed aimed at the foot of Rogerson's. His name was Werner Abend. Last night his bed had been surrounded by visitors, among them a minister who had led them all in prayer.

"Nurse," Abend whispered.

"Shh. There's no need to get up yet."

"When's breakfast?"

"Do you get breakfast? I'll have to check your chart."

Abend looked forlornly out the gray window.

"Who's your doctor?" Mrs. Jenkins asked Rogerson. He told her. Did she frown? "Feel anything yet?"

She meant the pill. "No."

"I think it's what they give you in labor. Those are great."

"Will it knock me out?"

"Not quite. Norah Vlach is a friend of mine."

"What are they going to do to you?" Abend asked. He no longer whispered. The doubt cast on breakfast had stirred him.

Shushing, Mrs. Jenkins went to Abend's bed and persuaded him to lie down. Rogerson heard her mention circumcision. He also heard Abend's chuckle.

The pill was taking effect. Rogerson closed his eyes. Mrs. Jenkins came back and talked confidingly of her kids and the mister, of her thwarted academic ambitions. She had married young, too young, you don't know at twenty that those are the years that settle your whole life. The maternal voice, the fact that she seemed to be keeping vigil beside his bed, was soothing. He had not had the sense the night before that he was delivering himself into the hands of a dedicated staff.

A week before, Marge and the kids had gone off in the car to Wisconsin. The station wagon had been packed to the gills when they backed out the driveway and the rear bumper banged on the asphalt when she reached the street. She hesitated, then gunned the motor. Rogerson watched in dread. An oncoming motorist blasted his horn at the sudden appearance of the station wagon. A squeal of brakes as he swerved around Marge, his face contorted with terror and rage. The kids waved to Rogerson and Marge sounded the horn and then they were gone.

Rogerson had spent the intervening time in desultory reading. Drinking beer on a lawn chair in the back yard, putting off the mowing of the grass, he had become aware as seldom before of birds, though birds had always fascinated him, their number, their variety. Trees were alive with them and so was the ivy which clung to the garage. A dove perched on the crossarm of the TV antenna and cooed sadly, the sound one he realized invaded his morning and evening ear but had not been filtered from the sounds of the house, nature and art mingling to the detriment of nature. Aslosh with beer, he resolved to move beyond knowledge of robins, sparrows, jays, cardinals and others. Our friends the birds. Matthew Rogerson, poring over a manual, plane spotter in peacetime, identifies 168 species of birds in Fort Elbow back yard. Urges others to take up this pacific hobby, a stout Cortez staring benignly from the newspaper photograph. Binoculars perhaps, though they might stir pangs of apprehension, or hope, in the neighbor women. He could feel their disapproving eyes upon him while he lounged in the yard, beer can in hand. Doors slammed, mops were shaken, and rugs, some untypical puttering in the garden beds, furtive accusing glances. Why was he lolling away a weekday afternoon in the sun?

Rogerson felt on retreat, prepping spiritually for his operation, shaving away the quotidian confidence that life is a right, illness an alien plague, considering that the body which ingested beer, the bladder that filled with it and sent him periodically inside, all the organs on which he relied, would give out, revolt, break down. If not soon, then sometime. No future could be distant enough that marked the end of Matthew Rogerson. A marker loomed before his mind. Matthew Rogerson, 1923–. To what date was the dash directed? He consoled and saddened himself with the knowledge that Marge and the kids would not even know he was in the hospital. Heep had been uninformative about recovery time.

"You'll be up and out of there before you know it."

"How many days?"

"That varies. If all goes well . . ." He was distracted by the phone.

Rogerson tried to form the question now, addressing Mrs. Jenkins, but his lips felt rubbery and the sounds he made seemed remote, unrelated to his will to speak.

"Just relax, Mr. Rogerson."

What sounded like the voice of Werner Abend was audible. Mrs. Jenkins was no longer beside his bed. He tried to worry about that, but along with drowsiness came euphoria. The impending operation now seemed the merest nothing. Even death was a thought easy to accommodate. A slip of the knife, whoops, unable to stop the blood, who cares? Let me drift, drift.

He had come to the hospital the night before by bus, carrying a small suitcase, feeling like an immigrant or worse. He wished he had used a briefcase instead. A suitcase drew attention, raised questions: Going? Coming? Why by bus? He got off two blocks short of the hospital and walked the rest of the way. No need to announce his destination and assuage the curiosity of his fellow passengers.

The homes around the hospital were huge and old, older than his own house. The streets were paved with brick, uneven, rippling, quaint. Each one laid by human hands. A thought there. The houses were painted oddly and seemed to exude the determination of their owners not to be like the rest of men. Rogerson, made aware of his attachment to his own house, felt momentarily uneasy. But the genial disrepair of his house, its unobtrusiveness behind evergreen and oak, prevented it from making assertions to passers-by. A dog sailed out at him, running low, a growl deep in its throat, aiming for the suit-case. Rogerson, Clyde Beatty at a moment's notice, fought off the beast. From a screened porch a voice called languidly, "Boris. Here, Boris." Boris did not retreat and Rogerson, his body tingling, his hair numbering itself on his head, proceeded up the street. Goddam dog, he ought to be tied up, strung up. Pity the poor postman. But they now armed themselves with Mace. Pft. Pft. The mail must go through.

"Who is your doctor?" the woman in reception asked.

"Heep."

"The elevator is down the hall. Stop at admissions."

It was like booking a room. He carried his suitcase toward the elevator. It was very hot in the hospital. A huge woman in admissions ran a form into a typewriter and tapped out the answers Rogerson gave to her questions. Insurance? Yes. Thou shalt not crucify this country on a cross of blue. Next of kin? Marge. He gave the tele-phone number of the house and thought of the instrument ringing unanswered when he was wheeled lifeless from the operating room by a cheery Heep, saying, Win some, lose some.

"Room 603. Take the elevator."

"Just go up?"

"Report to the nurse on the floor."

He might even help her to her feet. Easier said than done, in any case. The nurses' station was abandoned. Rogerson stood at the counter holding the slip of paper he had been given in admissions. This was not at all what he had imagined going to the hospital for an operation would be like.

A nurse appeared, her glasses hung on a kind of necklace and bouncing on the starched shelf of her bosom. She took the slip of paper. "Robinson?"

"Rogerson."

"Dr. Heep?"

"Right."

"What's he going to do?"

Rogerson looked over her head. "A circumcision."

"I thought so."

"The way I walk?"

"He does a lot of them." She stopped, restrained perhaps by an ethical code, honor among thieves. "We'll get you settled. I hope you've eaten."

He had not. It was not yet six. He wasn't hungry. He lied.

"Good thing. Come on."

When she took his suitcase he felt transformed into an invalid. He did not try to keep pace with her bouncy progress down the hall. He stole glances into the rooms they passed. The occupants looked back pathetically, curious, hopeful, pale.

There were four beds in the room, but the two nearest the door were empty. The nurse drew a curtain around Rogerson's bed. A nightgown appeared.

"I brought pajamas."

"Better wear the gown. It will make things easy in the morning."

He waited for her to leave.

"Ring if you need anything," she said.

"I've been ringing since supper," the old man across from Rogerson complained.

"Just rest, Mr. Abend."

"Where are my visitors? My wife should be here."

"Visiting hours don't start for half an hour."

"She must be waiting downstairs."

"Just lie still and relax, Mr. Abend."

"I'm only in for tests. I'm not sick." The old man spoke defiantly. "What's wrong with you?" he asked Rogerson.

"An old war wound." He had taken off his shirt and slipped out of his shoes. The nurse seemed to escape while Abend's attention was diverted.

"Why aren't you in the vets hospital?"

"I fought on the wrong side."

Abend stared at him, then revealed his denture in an appreciative smile. "Who's your doctor?"

"Who's yours?"

"Upfeldt. I don't trust him. He's a relative of my wife. By her first marriage. i'm in for tests."

Rogerson, down to jockey shorts, put on the nightgown.

"The strings go in back. It's like a goddam bib. They'll make you take your shorts off."

84

Rogerson left them on, turned the nightgown around, sat on the edge of the bed. The curtains were drawn around his bed in such a way that he had nowhere to look except out the window or at Mr. Abend.

"What's your name?" Abend asked.

Rogerson told him and admitted that he lived in Fort Elbow.

"I don't," Abend said. "Gatton. Know where that is?"

"No."

"It's north of Tyler. You take State Road 6 out of Tyler and go north to County Road B. Seven miles east and you're in Gatton. You ever hear of The Homestead?"

"No."

"Best restaurant for miles around. Plain country cooking. No liquor. Emily and I try to eat there once a week."

Emily was the second Mrs. Abend. She and Werner had been married thirty-one years. Werner told her that he had been telling Mr. Rogerson about The Homestead.

"Don't you just love that place?" she asked Rogerson.

"I've never been there."

It was only the first of many places he had to deny knowledge of before Abend's other visitors arrived and commanded his full attention. The son was almost Rogerson's age and looked both older and younger: he was a weathered man, bandy of leg, his torso a huge crate he seemed to be supporting with his pocketed hands. His eye was youthful and naïve. He was a farmer. The daughter's obesity was of the attractive kind; there was the look of the kitchen about her. The minister was treated with great respect. It was a professional call and there was much reference to the Word of the Lord, and passages were quoted to approving nods from the Abends. Rogerson tried to read Trollope's *Ralph the Heir*. The Lord was invoked to look after his servant Werner and to keep him in mind special on the morrow, when tests would be made to check the soundness of his body. Skinny little Werner Abend lay at the center of this impetratory assault, a serene and contented patriarchal figure.

Abend's voice now, then Mrs. Jenkins', versicle and response, an unintelligible liturgy tuned in from the land of the living. His bed was surrounded. He was being addressed. Someone removed his jockey shorts and from seemingly rooms away from the event a Rogerson without inhibitions told himself to take a farewell look at his prick. Laughter. He heard himself babbling joyously as he was lifted from the bed and onto something else. It moved. He was being rolled from the room. He closed one eye and got some sort of focus on the ceiling of the corridor he was pushed along. Mrs. Jenkins was not there. Male voices. An elevator, upward movement, he was and was not present. Off again and through a series of doors and under bright lights from among which Heep looked down at him.

"And how are we this morning?"

"I've changed my mind." But only babble emerged.

"You'll be given the anesthetic now." Heep's face was no improvement upside down. Again Rogerson tried to say that he had decided against the operation. He had had a vision in which he was assured that he would never get cancer. His arm was strapped to something, he felt a cool wetness, a stab and then a great rushing flood. Socrates in his death cell, the effects of the hemlock coursing through him, a great dark tide which almost but not quite reached and extinguished the small bright light behind his eyes.

A moment later, Heep's face again, much talking, when would they begin? He had to stop them before the anesthetic wiped him out entirely. A new face, a nurse.

"I don't want to do it," Rogerson said, almost clearly.

"How are you feeling?"

"Where is Dr. Heep?"

"You'll be going back to your room soon."

Rogerson began to cry with relief. Heep had heard him and understood. Thank God.

"I am forty-seven years old," he told the nurse, unashamed of his tears.

"You're coming out of it now."

"That was close. Is this surgery?"

"You're in the recovery room now."

"What happened?"

"Everything went nicely. When you get back to your room you can sleep."

The return trip was smooth. Rogerson was confused. He had never fully lost consciousness, he was certain of that. But when he was lifted onto his bed and the gown no longer covered him, he saw that his loins were bandaged. Anger almost broke through the lingering euphoria before he fell asleep.

"I never was myself," Werner Abend said. "No need for it."

"My doctor says there is danger of cancer there."

"I did it myself."

"Did what?"

"Circumcised myself."

Rogerson thought about it. "I don't believe you."

It was late morning when Heep showed up. "Well, you talked a blue streak this morning, Professor. How do you feel?"

"What did I say?"

"I'll never tell. It's part of the oath."

"I didn't know I was talking."

"That's what makes it so funny."

Rogerson said nothing.

"It's not just you," Heep said. "Everyone does it. Jabber, jabber, jabber. How do you feel?"

"Numb."

"There'll be a little pain later on. The nurse will give you something for that. Your wife been in?"

"Not yet."

Heep pulled a sheet over him. "You won't be doing much for a few weeks. A month at most. Then watch out."

Rogerson decided not to ask Heep if Abend's claim could possibly be true.

"Does Mrs. Rogerson work?" the nurse asked.

"Why?"

"Has she been in yet?"

"She's out of town."

"Oh."

After that the nurses paid more attention to him, much to Abend's discontent. He had come back from his tests bright and chipper. They hadn't knocked him out, he said. No more fuss than a visit to the doctor's office. He saw no reason why he should be in the hospital at all. He said as much to Upfeldt when the doctor came in.

"I've still got plowing to do."

"We'll have the results tomorrow."

"If I don't get at those soybeans soon I might just as well forget it."

"Don't worry about your soybeans. Fred is taking care of the farm."

"Fred has his own farm to take care of."

"When is Aunt Emily coming in?"

"Not till this afternoon."

"Did they drive back to Gatton last night?"

"Yes."

Upfeldt nodded. To Rogerson he looked bright and urbane. The doctor treated Abend firmly but with respect. He shook the old man's hand before leaving.

"He seems a good man," Rogerson said.

"He lost his faith."

"Did he?"

"He used to attend our church with his parents. Since he became a doctor he doesn't. Maybe he's too smart for God now."

"What denomination are you?"

"No denomination. We just built a church and hired ourselves a preacher."

"Where do you find a preacher?"

"They find us. When old Empson died—he was our first pastor—we had a dozen applications before we had the man in the ground. Jensen—you saw him yesterday—offered to conduct the burial service. He did a good job. He hadn't known Empson, so he couldn't say much about the man, personal, but what he said touched our hearts, so we offered him the job."

"You're a farmer?"

"I am now."

"Weren't you always?"

"I was with the railroad. Until twenty years ago. I did a little truck farming, but until I retired nothing serious."

"A railroad man," Rogerson mused.

"That used to be a better job than it is anymore. Still is better than most. I was after the pension. I figured, put in your time, get that pension, then live the way you want. That's how it worked out too.

When my first missis died, why, the fact I had that pension ahead made me a pretty attractive target. Inside of a year or two I courted eight different women and let me tell you not all of them sent me back to my place when the sun went down. I like to lose my soul during that time. Of course, I told myself I was enjoying life as I never had before." There was a twinkle in Abend's eye. Visibly he reined in his memory. "Emily brought me back to my senses. She drove into my place one day—she and I had gone here and there a couple times. Anyway, Emily came to the house and said, 'Werner Abend, are you going to marry me or lose your immortal soul?' "

"What did you say?"

"I married her. It was like I had made up my mind before she came through the door."

"How long ago was that?"

"Thirty-one years."

To his vast surprise, Norah Vlach came to see him, standing in the doorway until he noticed her, then crossing to his bed.

"What brings you here?" he asked.

"I might ask the same."

"Better not. Are you visiting someone?"

"Melanie Jenkins called to tell me you were here. Is it anything serious?"

Rogerson had a sudden certainty that Norah had already learned the nature of his operation from Mrs. Jenkins.

"Not according to the doctor."

Werner Abend cleared his throat and looked receptively at the wall above Rogerson's head.

"This is Mr. Abend, Norah."

"Pleased to meet you, Mrs. Rogerson."

"Oh, but I'm not Mrs. Rogerson."

Abend was flustered. For that matter, so was Norah. Rogerson let them straighten it out. Norah here. Incredible. When she had placated Abend with a lengthy description of her job in the dean's office, Norah asked about Marge.

"She's in Wisconsin with the kids. We—she—has a cabin up there. How come you know Mrs. Jenkins?"

Norah sighed. "She is a special student. In every sense of the term.

If credits were given for pestering deans, she would have a doctorate by now. Does she really work here?"

"The graveyard shift. Not that they call it that. Hers is the first face one sees in the morning."

"Well, you seem in good spirits."

But even as he spoke to Norah the pain Heep had promised him arrived. Norah was speaking of summer school.

"Laplace says you begged for a course."

"White dean speak with forked tongue."

But Matthew Rogerson, poor forked animal, lay now in acute discomfort.

"Didn't you ask for a course?"

"It's a long story."

"With you it always is." She was at the window now, looking down at the street. "How long will Marge and the kids be in Wisconsin?"

"All summer."

"And you'll join them after summer school?"

"No doubt. Despite my new duties. Don't tell Laplace I'm here, by the way."

"But I already did."

"Damn."

And Laplace came, early in the afternoon, wearing a solemn expression.

"Come on, Matt, cut it out," Laplace protested when Rogerson told him what he was in for.

"Not quite. Just a little nip and tuck. The fact that I have been known affectionately as the hooded cobra by generations of girls poses a problem. What have I metamorphosed into? The bald eagle, perhaps."

"Why would someone your age get circumcised?" Laplace sat, crossing his legs protectively.

"Cancer."

"Oh, my God."

"It's not uncommon, Herb."

"Did they get it all?"

"Just the foreskin."

90

Laplace passed a pacifying hand over his eyes. "I meant the malignancy."

"It's too early to say."

"They don't know?"

"Herb, what my doctor doesn't know . . ." Rogerson sighed. "He used to be a dentist."

Laplace shook his head.

"It's true. An Army dentist. Remember those? He went to medical school on the GI Bill. Then into urology. From orifice to orifice. Now he's in private medicine."

"When will they let you know, Matt?"

"I expect to be out of here in a day or two."

Laplace's smile said, Humor the poor bastard. Any skepticism Laplace might have had disappeared during the conference that now occurred between Werner Abend and his doctor. Upfeldt came in, looking somber, and sat on Abend's bed. He began to talk. After a minute he tugged the curtain around the bed, cutting Abend from view. The results of the tests. Bad news seemed an odor in the room. Poor Abend. The voices behind the curtain were low, grave in tone. Laplace got fidgety, as if misfortune were contagious. He stood.

"Matt, don't worry about summer school."

"Don't you worry. I'll teach the course."

"Of course you will." Herb looked at his watch. "I'll come back tomorrow. How is Marge taking this?"

"She's at the lake with the kids."

Herb sat down again. "Doesn't she know?"

"No."

"That's not right, Matt. She has a right to know."

"Of course she does. I'll tell her. I can't very well just call up and say a thing like this, can I? Marge, I've just been circumcised? Will you love me in soprano as you did in bass?"

"Would you like me to contact her?"

"Absolutely not."

Herb did not understand.

"Promise me you won't call her, Herb."

"Matt, I don't even know where she is."

But Rogerson had little doubt that Laplace could dig up the location of the cottage if he really wanted to. The bed across the room was still concealed by its curtain. Rogerson imagined Herb contacting Marge. The game he had been playing with the dean was childish in the light of Abend's authentic trouble.

"Herb, I'm all right. All I'm in for is a circumcision. That is all. Understand?"

"Of course I understand."

"The operation was only a precaution. Ask my dentist."

Herb smiled tolerantly. "I've got to get back to my office."

He was left alone with Werner Abend. Upfeldt pulled the curtain back when he left and the old man stared vacantly at the window. The news had clearly been bad. Werner had flunked his last test. What did he have? Did he even know? If the results had brought such gloom, precision as to the cause was unimportant.

"Yesterday at this time I was worried about soybeans." Abend spoke wonderingly. Sounds from the corridor; from outside, the sounds of traffic. The world went on.

"Your doctor had news?"

Abend hesitated. "No," he lied. "Nothing definite."

Sylvia and Plummet-Finch came together, alerted by Laplace, both trying to conceal that they had heard the worst of news about him. Their solemn faces cheered Rogerson to flights of revelry. Sylvia had brought him candy, Gilbert the latest issue of *Mind*.

"There's a rather good piece there about mirror images. If a mirror reflects images backward, why doesn't it show them upside down?"

"What's the answer?"

"You must read it yourself."

"I applaud this return to the larger questions, those cosmic conundrums which interested us in philosophy in the first place."

"Without a sound theory of perception," Gilbert said primly, "the rest is only hot air."

Sylvia was certain that Gilbert had invented the article. Rogerson handed her the journal. She read the titles on its cover incredulously. "Is this what philosophy is?"

"For centuries it was only groping," Rogerson said. "At last the way has been found."

"How do you feel?" Plummet-Finch sailed the question over the bed in the direction of the window, where a predicted rain fell.

"Very little. I am still numb from the anesthetic."

"What exactly did they do?" Sylvia asked.

"Removed a wart."

Plummet-Finch, standing at the foot of the bed, exchanged a look with Rogerson. Good show, Reggie. The squadron will miss you frightfully. "A masculine dysfunction," he said to Sylvia, seeking dignity in mystification.

"Oh, for heaven's sake."

"I am told that I shall survive to contribute my upper register to the church choir."

Sylvia stopped giggling before she had started, remembering La-place's message, perhaps.

"Let's open the candy," she said. "It's cheap stuff, chocolate-covered cherries. I love 'em."

Rogerson opened the box and passed it around. Plummet-Finch carried it to Abend, whose Emily had arrived. She must have spoken with Upfeldt already. Little conversation was going on between the Abends. They both refused candy. It was so sweet it made Roger-son's cheeks tingle.

"Good?" Sylvia sucked the tips of her fingers. Rogerson passed the candy and she took another. Plummet-Finch, patting his pouch, refused.

"Look, Matthew. Is it true that Marge is out of town and knows nothing of this?"

"It's true that she's out of town."

"I think you ought to get word to her."

"Doesn't she know you had an operation?" Sylvia asked.

"There is no need for her to know. It was a very simple thing. My doctor does half a dozen of them a week. I'll be out of here tomorrow."

"Are you sure?"

"I have to get ready for summer school."

The suggestion that he might, under any circumstances, devote a lengthy period to the preparation of a course silenced them both. They knew him to be the champion of the extemporaneous. Not even Keane could hope to be as irrelevant as he. Find where the students are and start from there: that was the opposing theory, the educational orthodoxy. Poppycock, as impassioned controversialists say. Rogerson had no intention of retracing his steps into the intellectual chaos inhabited by students. Let them struggle on their own to get within hailing distance of where a quarter century of uncharted study had landed him. Nothing of lasting or at least of a predictable nature happens in the classroom. This was the awful truth experience had taught him. He had no skills to pass on, no content they could not pick up alone if they were interested, which was unlikely. It is wrong to think that what we call education has been going on from the beginning. Mucking around in the twilight of a culture, our efforts are pathetically peculiar.

"You'll have over a week," Sylvia said. "But then you've probably given the course before."

"Never. *Paradise Lost.*"

"I thought Keane was teaching that."

"Apparently he changed his mind."

"Or his mind was changed. No wonder everyone wants to get out of the humanities department."

"Better come in with us, Matthew," Plummet-Finch said. "We need another wise old head."

"Another?"

"Now, Matthew. Be kind. You really should get off that sinking ship, you know. You've heard the rumors?"

"Tell me."

"That they will dissolve the humanities department entirely."

"Nonsense."

"It makes sense," Sylvia said. "What's the point of a department that isn't a department? People are trained for specific things."

"Not I," Rogerson said.

"She meant since the Renaissance," Plummet-Finch said, some of his normal hauteur returned. "Sylvia, Matthew must rest."

"I'll follow in a jiff, Gilbert. Okay?"

Dismissed, not liking it, Gilbert took Rogerson's hand limply. "Do get well, Matthew."

"Just for you, Gilbert."

Tears actually glistened in Gilbert's eyes as he looked down at his dying but so brave colleague. He tiptoed from the room in his gray suede crepe-soled ankle-high Hush Puppies.

"That's not just rumor, Matt," Sylvia said. "I have it straight from the horse's ass. Script told me." Her hand on his bare arm, she kneaded the flesh.

"Laplace asked me to take over from Fallor as chairman."

Sylvia laughed, tossing back her head. Her eyes squinted nicely, a bubble of saliva formed and burst when her mouth opened. Pores, small blemishes, eye liner in the fold of her lids. Her other hand slid behind him.

"And I accepted."

"You didn't. What a silly little gown."

"Just something I wear around the hospital."

"Are you in pain?" Concern, genuine. Why?

"Not really."

"Let me see."

"See what?"

"What they did."

"Sylvia," he growled reprovingly, finding the suggestion exciting. What an odd girl she was. Across the room, Abend and his wife sat silently, in another world. Perhaps they are praying, Rogerson thought. Sylvia herself blocked the view from the hall.

"Please."

"Sylvia, it's a bloody mess."

Her hand slid from his arm and under the sheet. For a moment, it rested on his stomach, its outline etching itself into his flesh. Since he was lying on his back, his stomach would not seem flabby to her. Her hand moved. Rogerson closed his eyes, then quickly opened them. Sylvia's hand now rested on his thigh. He could feel the heel of her palm pressing against him. And then he realized that her fingertips must be on his bandaged self.

"Poor Matthew."

"I can't feel a thing."

"Thanks a lot." Her hand made a sweeping arc up his side and she dug him in the ribs. He lurched and the Abends glanced at him. Sylvia, brisk and aloof, was on her feet.

"I mustn't keep Gilbert waiting."

"No."

"Next time I want to look too."

She turned and strode from the room. Abend stared impassively at Rogerson. Had he noticed anything? What did it matter? Poor Werner seemed already on the other side of the Styx, looking back at where he had been, finding it strange, unreal, elsewhere.

"You really sounded the alarm," Rogerson chided Mrs. Jenkins.

"Oh, you're awake."

He had wakened to the sound of her banging things about on his bedside table.

"Look at this ashtray. You smoke too much."

"I had a stream of visitors yesterday."

"That's nice." She put down the ashtray, put all her weight on one foot, looked at him. "You've read *Moby Dick?*"

"Not for years."

"Melville fascinates me."

"Why?"

While she struggled to overcome incoherence, Rogerson thought that Melville fascinated him too. Early success, dropping out into the civil service, the late poetry. It was the poetry that interested Rogerson now. Herman, sure he had failed as a novelist, devoted years to the production of second-rate verse. Mrs. Jenkins had been talking.

"Does any of that make sense?"

Rogerson looked Delphic. "Why *Moby Dick?*"

"I'm always reading something."

"You should write."

"I do!" Mrs. Jenkins squealed. She rested her hip against the bed and spoke confidentially. "This job? The money is welcome, of course, we can always use money, but I'm here for the experience."

"Don't write about me."

"I already have. Yesterday afternoon."

"Before or after you telephoned Norah Vlach?"

"I needed more background on you."

"Is it fiction, nonfiction, what?"

"I'm really not hung up on genres. Call it a story. And it really isn't you. I'm using certain traits, of course."

"What's the plot?"

"I'm not sure yet."

"You must get a lot of ideas here."

Her eyes lifted. "Hundreds. Literally hundreds."

He went back to sleep when she left. He was wakened again for breakfast and fell asleep again. The next time he awoke, Heep was there.

"Been out of bed yet?"

"Should I have been?"

"I don't see why not."

"You didn't mention it."

"I didn't mention going weewee either, but I'll bet you did."

He had. In the middle of the night. He discarded the thought of using a bedpan. His clothes were in the closet. He put them on. Barefoot, he searched the hall for a men's room. He could not find it. He did find a door marked STAIRWAY. He went through it and started down. How weird to be moving about like this. The place seemed deserted. Perhaps it was, the patients abandoned. He went down two flights, gripping the railing with one hand, cupping himself with the other. His bandage had the feel of diapers. He remembered Sylvia and stopped to think about that. From far below came the sound of humming, a generator perhaps, the soul of the building, sending its warm breath through hallways and into rooms, up stairwells too. The floor he emerged on seemed the one he had left above. He had his land legs now. He found an elevator and took it to the first floor, where he had noticed a men's room. How easy it would have been to leave.

When Sylvia came that afternoon, he realized that he had been awaiting her return. She was everything he did not like in the young. In general. But Sylvia herself, one person singular, with her peering puzzled eyes, her smile which seemed to apologize for her amusement, the swagger that did not convince, was simply Sylvia, a fascinating pagan of a girl. Today she was very prim. It was difficult to believe she was the same girl who had touched his dilly the day before. Perhaps for luck.

"Fallor said he was coming down, but I told him you had probably gone home."

"Thanks."

"It wasn't penis envy."

"What?"

"Yesterday."

"I may develop that myself."

Campus gossip, and then: "Why have you stayed here, Matt?"
She meant the Fort Elbow campus. "I'm lucky to be here."

"I hate it."

"What if it is really typical?"

She shuddered. "Matt, if you remain in the humanities department
and it is dissolved, where does that leave you?"

Upfeldt was with Abend, behind the drawn curtain. Rogerson put
his hand on Sylvia's shoulder, felt bound in her bone and flesh, flesh
fashioned by the God who did not approve of the married Matthew
Rogerson longing for an answering touch from her. She looked at
him, sad, happy, younger. He took his hand away.

"Why isn't your wife here?"

"She finds it hard to bilocate."

"This is where she should be."

He smiled. The young have such severe codes for the married. Did
they imagine a union so intimate that not even one's thoughts remained one's own? He had known the same hope, of course; he
supposed Marge had too. Another disappointment. Our hearts are
restless. A minute later the priest came in.

"Professor Rogerson?"

"Yes."

"Bill Freundlich. Ms. Rogerson." He nodded at Sylvia.

Freundlich wore gray slacks, loafers, a short-sleeved black shirt
with a Roman collar. His thinning hair was brushed forward; spears
of it lay on his forehead, not quite reaching his brows.

"If you want to receive communion, tell the nurse. How about this
weather?" He glared at the gray day, as if to ease the pressure of his
first remark. Sylvia and Rogerson looked obediently at the weather.
The sound of voices behind Abend's curtain distracted the priest.

"One of ours?"

"No."

Freundlich seemed relieved. "You're at the university."

"That's right."

"I suppose you know Larry Merlin."

"I know who he is."

"We were classmates. Well . . ."

A waggle of his raised hand, a lopsided smile for Sylvia, and

Freundlich was gone. Sylvia left shortly thereafter. Today was not the day before. A gusty improvisation refused to recede to unimportance. He could hear her footsteps as she went down the hallway. Who is Sylvia and what is she?

Marge telephoned at seven that evening.

"Matt! What on earth is wrong? Should I come home?"

"Don't be silly. Nothing's wrong."

"Nothing! Herb Laplace sounded as if he were notifying the next of kin when he telephoned."

"I'll be out of here in the morning."

"But what are you doing there?"

"Circumcision." There seemed no way to make the word into a monosyllable.

"What!"

"Dr. Heep thought I should have it done."

Her trilling laughter arrived across the wire from Wisconsin and Rogerson, holding the phone tightly to his ear, looking at Abend in consultation with his wife, accepted Marge's version of his plight.

"Don't tell the kids."

More laughter. Well, why not? It was like announcing, at forty-seven, that his voice was changing.

"Don't worry," Marge said.

5

A glorious afternoon in June, the sun high in the blue Ohio sky, the slightest of breezes to fan the brow and bronzing body of Matthew Rogerson, supine in a lawn chair in his back yard. He wore shorts and sunglasses and a smile under the restorative sun. Who can feel forty-seven years of age while lazing in the warmth of a summer afternoon with only the prospect of inert hours before him, with the smell of early roses, irises and persistent lilac in the air, the twitter of birds and, from a distance, the unmuffled snarl of a mower in someone else's charge, on someone else's lawn? His own grass could stand a trimming, but it, along with the rest of the world, would have to await Rogerson's full recuperation.

He had been home from the hospital two days. His wounds were far from healed and with each passing hour he felt added cause to curse the ineptitude of Heep. Since Marge had the car with her, his transportation was a bicycle. Tommy's ten-speed would have been out of the question. The thought of throwing his leg acrobatically over its crossbar and entrusting his posterior and to some extent his bandaged and still bloody anterior to the untender mercies of the punishing fetish of that elevated seat sent pangs of anticipated pain through Rogerson's. Scarcely healed incisions would reopen were he to churn his legs in such a canted jackknife position as the bike required. It was not for the ten-speed that he had looked in the garage, but in any case it was gone. He could only hope that Tommy had dismantled it and somehow taken it along in the already overloaded station wagon. He had been left Barbara's bike. When he felt better, he would give it a whirl.

For the nonce, however, he was thoroughly content to lie in the sun and permit even his rage at Heep to sink in his sun-drenched lassitude to the status of a theoretical tort and one which, upon his return to more diurnal concerns, might be permitted to engage his will. But mañana, domàni, tomorrow; not now. Now was for dozing under this pleasantly purgatorial sun, feeling the sweat no sooner form upon him than it evaporated and blew away on the breeze. Beside him, half hidden in clover, a can of beer sweated too. On such a day, in such conditions, only the cadences and chattily cosmological lines of Browning seemed appropriate: the mutterings of a rabbi, of a homicidal duke or of Roberto himself: that Art remains the one way possible of speaking Truth, to mouths like mine, at least. So with artful half-truth mused Matthew Rogerson under a sun which six hours earlier had smiled on Italy.

Last night Marge had called again, to make certain that he was indeed safely home from the hospital.

"Why didn't you tell me that you were going to have an operation? I could have put off leaving until afterward."

"There was nothing you could do."

"That isn't the point. What will people think?"

"I didn't tell people either."

"Then how did Herb Laplace find out? Let me tell you there was a very strange tone to his voice when he called."

"Nothing is less strange than a strange tone to Herb's voice."

"That's why you didn't come up here, isn't it? The operation."

"Of course."

"Can't you come up now?"

"I agreed to teach summer school."

"Herb seemed to think you wouldn't be able to."

"He formed an exaggerated notion of the seriousness of the operation."

"He certainly did. To hear him talk, you'd think you were dying."

"Good old Herb."

Herb himself had phoned this morning, shortly before ten, waking

101

Rogerson, who plucked the phone from its cradle at bedside and, eyes still shut, said hello.

"I hope I didn't wake you up." Herb spoke with funereal deference.

"At ten o'clock?" Rogerson had opened his eyes.

"They told me at the hospital you'd gone home. I couldn't believe it."

"As well here as there."

"What?" There was the catch of dread in the dean's voice.

"Sleep till ten."

"Then you were awake?"

"I had to get up to answer the phone."

Herb sighed. "You're really something, Matt. Do you know that?"

"Why did you call Marge?"

"Matt, a wife has a right to know. I suspected that you hadn't told her. When will she be back?"

"Late August or early September."

"Isn't she coming home now?"

"I wouldn't hear of it. There are some things a man can only do alone. Like teach summer school."

"Matt, about that. I'm not going to hold you to your contract. I can find someone else to give that course."

"Lose *Paradise Lost?* I wouldn't hear of it."

"You still want to give the course?"

"More than ever, Herb. In a way, now it somehow seems even more appropriate. . . ." He let his voice trail off.

"Sure," Herb said gruffly. "Sure."

"Sort of a thanksgiving for my health."

"Have you heard something new?"

"Only what I told you at the hospital."

"Oh."

Did Laplace really believe that Rogerson had cancer of the dinky? Herb was the most credulous cynic Rogerson had ever known. Once several years before he had been similarly quick to believe that Rogerson was as good as dead. Some wish fulfillment going on there, perhaps, though why Herb should regard him as anything but a throwback to a worse, or better, time, depending on your point of view, was hard to see. But what was Herb's point of view? A few weeks ago he had professed nostalgia for the *vita ante acta,* had actually written Felix Freeman and received a deserved rebuff for his pains. Surely that was not the real Herb Laplace. The dean had made the transition into the newer academic madness without missing a stroke; he along with Wooley flourished in this moneyed educational egalitarianism. Members of the legislature had been conned into thinking, or at least saying, that there was no hierarchy among the various campuses of the state university system, that, in principle, the regional campuses were on a par with that at Columbus. The principle involved was monetary. Chancellor Wooley outearned the lieutenant governor and Herb himself was alleged to make the better part of forty thousand a year. Where the treasure was, there must their hearts also be.

"Look, Matt, who is taking care of you?"

"I'm not an invalid, Herb. I feel great."

"I want you to come to dinner some night soon."

"That's very nice of you."

"Tonight's out, unfortunately."

"For me too."

It was enough that Herb had made the gesture. Rogerson had no desire to spend an evening with the Laplaces. Mitzi Laplace was a thin, mousy person who seemed to have no mind of her own while in the presence of her husband and what she did on her own was a matter of conjecture. The rumor was that she drank like a fish, but if so, she was never seen in a bombed condition. Rogerson, who had himself started the rumor as a favor to Mitzi years before, wanting to confer some distinction on the woman, had found himself susceptible to its plausibility when the tale returned to him. Perhaps he had made an inspired guess. His efforts to convince his colleagues that Mrs. Wooley had begun life as a male and subjected herself to a Scandinavian operation so that she and Wooley could come out of the shadows fared less well. Felix had derided the suggestion. "They do a much better job than that," he opined. Good old Felix. Odd to think of him sweltering under the same sun down there in his old Arizona home.

Rogerson sought and found his can of beer in the grass beside his lawn chair. Beer dribbled down his chin and onto his chest while he drank. Damned cans. Only the noseless can drink from them with impunity. The trick was to ape the birds: fill the mouth, then tip back the head.

At the sound of a voice helloing him up the driveway, Rogerson sat forward. Another half-yodeled yoohoo and Sylvia sailed through the gate and into the back yard. She braked so that her front wheel came to rest against the sole of Rogerson's right foot. Sylvia dismounted. She wore navy blue shorts and a white halter; a polka dot kerchief was tied round her head as a sweatband. Her lithe brown body bore witness to hours in the sun, her limbs were sleek with perspiration, her mouth remained open as she breathed heavily.

"Good afternoon," she said demurely.

"You have the advantage of me."

"Hmmm."

"Where are you headed?"

"Here." She pushed the bike to the garage and propped it against the ivied wall. She dragged a lawn chair with her when she came back. Rogerson had moved to the edge of his chair, disturbed by this sudden appearance of the scantily clad Miss Wood. In her present apparition she looked youthful and athletic, not at all the importunate young lady whose hand had checked him out on his hospital bed.

"You look your old self," she said.

"I feel my old self."

"You know what I mean. How long have you been out here? You're going to burn to a crisp."

"What time is it?"

"Two."

He had come out after his late breakfast. Perhaps three hours in the sun.

"My God. Why don't we go inside?"

This thought had already occurred to Rogerson, if only to get her out of sight of the neighbors, whose imaginations ran to orgy, at least as far as Rogerson the chaste was concerned. Even the innocent or unlucky were beneficiaries of the current estimate of faculty types. But to remove Sylvia from the view of his hot-eyed neighbors into the house would be to translate an absurd speculation—surely only the depraved could think he meant to spread-eagle Sylvia on the grid of plastic stripping which, with a frame of aluminum tubing, made up her elongated lawn chair—to a far less remote opportunity, repre-

104

sented by the empty house. For if Sylvia had metamorphosed from the forward, faintly feline prober of his hospital room into an outdoors type whose gray-green eyes, now that she had removed her enormous sunglasses, had a horizon-seeking sailor's look, she was nonetheless the same sweet amoral girl who had repelled and fascinated him ever since her arrival on campus. Indecision sent Rogerson to his beer.

"Do you have another of those?"

"I'll get you one." He scrambled to his feet.

"Your grass needs cutting," she said, coming along with him.

In the kitchen, he took a can of beer from the refrigerator, opened it and gave it to her. She wanted a glass and he got that too. His own beer was still in the yard. She poured half a glass and drained it. Her tongue licked her lips in a metaphor of ingenuous sensuality. Rogerson moved toward the door.

"No," she said firmly. "You really can't go out into that sun again."

"My beer is out there."

She offered hers. He took another from the refrigerator. "We could sit on the front porch. That's shaded."

Had he thought she would veto the suggestion and drag him upstairs to his unmade bed? They went through the house and onto the front porch, a vast L-shaped veranda which wrapped around one corner of the house. Sylvia settled on the swing with a clink of chains and Rogerson sank into a wicker rocker. The porch was screened from the street by untrimmed evergreens and from the flanking neighbors by other foliage. Here Rogerson felt as insouciant in Sylvia's presence as he had in the hospital, at least prior to her access of curiosity. Nonetheless, Marge and the children seemed to haunt the house as they had not prior to this afternoon. Rogerson could half believe that at this moment beside her Wisconsin lake Marge felt a twinge of suspicion. Another woman in her home.

"I've got gossip," Sylvia said, putting her feet on the swing and starting to rock in an oblique movement.

"Wooley has decided to run for the senate?"

"You're kidding!"

"I hope so."

"Please don't say things like that." Sylvia settled back, straightening the arc of the swing's motion. "This has to do with the humanities department."

Rogerson groaned.

"Wait. Grundtvig is positive a really diabolical move is afoot."

"Grundtvig." Rogerson lit a cigarette and expelled smoke angrily. Grundtvig was an odious busybody, president of the campus chapter of the AAUP, a short, hairy thirty-year-old who spoke in a rasping whine and whose antennae were forever picking up dark conspiracies in administrative moves. If there was anything to be said in favor of Grundtvig, it was that the new look on campus, the *modus operandi* of Wooley and Laplace, invited the adversary attitude that Grundtvig represented. Of course, Grundtvig would have had his doubts about Eden itself and would be a vocal member of the opposition if the utopia he envisioned should ever be visited upon the academic community. The Grundtvig solution—and this was an old siren song to which Rogerson had cultivated a deaf ear long since—was faculty participation. Student participation too, of course. If only there were three or four watchdogs on every university committee, delegates from the faculty and student body, well, then things would at last go well. The difficulty with this theory was that it was regularly disproved in fact. There were even now faculty and student members on every committee and board on campus. Hours and hours were wasted by purported professors in the discussion of disciplinary problems, parking assignments, building maintenance, the unionization of campus security and dozens of other matters no sane man would wish to clutter his mind with. Grundtvig indeed.

"His sources are unimpeachable."

"A janitor or a trustee? Or both?" A janitor had been voted onto the board of trustees by the students.

"Better. The dean's secretary."

"Norah Vlach?"

"The same."

"So what's the gossip?"

"They are going to dissolve the humanities department."

"You already told me that."

"But that was just guessing. At least it might have been. Now Grundtvig is certain that that is what they plan to do." Sylvia made a face. "And to think I nearly went into that department. Laplace talked it up as if it was the haven for all the brightest kids. He must have known even then that its days were numbered. He could have had it both ways: hire a woman and then not keep her because the department was being dissolved."

"You even sound like Grundtvig."

"I know you don't like him, but he is on our side, Matthew. Others have seen the handwriting on the wall for months. For heaven's sake, look at Fallor. The chairman himself is transferring out of the department."

"Because he wants to be a specialist."

"That is the public reason."

"Well, I don't want to be a specialist. I've always liked the humanities department. It could have been tailored for my special sort of incompetence."

She half closed her eyes and let her mouth droop. "Talking that way is a way of praising yourself, as I guess you know. You really think you're better than most."

Rogerson had never cared for sapient asides from the young, least of all when they pretended to be analyses of his own deeds. Sylvia spoke as if he lay revealed to her inspection, no nooks and crannies out of sight, the wheels and pulleys fully in view. Did she really think people could be summed up in general remarks? Not that there wasn't a bit of truth in what she said. He did not consider himself more brilliant and knowledgeable than his colleagues. Rather, and quite sincerely, the reverse. But he did believe that he had swept out his own Augean stables, got most of the horse ordure out of his life, stopped pretending. Not that he was an apostle of frankness of the assertive kind, nor was he . . . Oh, the hell with it. Her observation had annoyed him and what did that tell him about his bullshit quotient?

"You're absolutely right," he said levelly.

"Oh, stop it."

"You're absolutely wrong," he said in the same tone.

"All right." She tossed her head and looked out toward the street. Some minutes of silence and then she said, "How secluded this house is. You could murder someone on this porch without attracting attention."

"I usually stop at rape."

"Ha. In your condition? Maybe a passionate handshake."

Although her intimacy was this time verbal, it was as surprising and as fascinating as her touch. "Be patient. Time heals all wounds."

She looked at him with speculative eyes, the corners of her mouth first trying, then rejecting a smile. "Uh huh."

"The yard, moreover, is ideal for growing marijuana. Actually, we've grown financially dependent on the resultant addition to my income."

"In that shade you're lucky to grow grass."

"That's what I said."

"People try to grow it in the funniest places. I told you of my detective friend who took me around in his squad car one night?"

"You also said you'd get me an invitation."

"I don't see much of him anymore. Anyway, the county highway department has three crews who do nothing all day but spray marijuana fields. Some of them are wild, I suppose, but most have been planted. It's a waste of time. The sheriff's helicopter is ideal for discovering any sizable crop. For the smaller ones they rely on squealers."

"When I was young, people talked about marijuana, but I don't think anyone actually tried it."

"Haven't you?"

"No."

She stopped the motion of the swing and stared at him. He had finally succeeded in really surprising her. "You mean you have never once in your whole life tried pot?"

"Are you suggesting that you have?"

"Everybody has."

"I haven't."

"The funny thing is, I believe you. But why haven't you?"

"I have also never scaled Mount Everest, visited Ireland or felt any inclination toward speleology."

"Neither have I. And none of them is part of the scene today, not central to it. Pot is. How can you be alive at this point in history and be so out of touch?"

"With drugs? Easy."

"You don't have to become an addict, for pete's sake. Do I look like an addict?"

"Not in this light."

"I don't even smoke cigarettes, and look how hooked on them you are. If you're worried about forming habits, you should quit smoking cigarettes."

"I've tried that. I prefer smoking."

"And why did you start? For the experience. You could have had a couple and let it go at that. I did, with both cigarettes and pot. And I don't regret having tried them. I knew I would regret not having tried them."

"Why?"

She found the question unintelligible. "Why anything, for chrissake? The whys stop somewhere, don't they? It's just something you should know about."

"What a missionary you are."

"I am not!"

"You surely aren't much of a logician. Should I try everything I haven't tried?"

"I don't mean that you should harm yourself."

"Maybe I should give Plummet-Finch a tumble too. I've never experienced that sort of thing either."

"Says you."

Had she? He didn't want to know. Yet he found himself wanting to steer the conversation in raunchy directions.

"I have never even seen marijuana," he said.

"In this town? Come on."

"I know it is supposed to be all over campus, but if I have ever seen it, I don't know it."

"You make me feel corrupt, you really do. But you're right, it is everywhere."

"Where exactly?"

She thought. "Well, it's not easy to find right now, with the students away. And I suppose the summer school students are straight as sin. No, I guess you wouldn't find it on campus at the moment."

"I'll stop looking."

She stood. "Do. Because I am going to get some for you and I want to be there when you try it. After that you can thumb your nose at it all you want—I'll even join you—but at least you'll know what you're talking about."

"Don't bother."

"No bother at all."

He went with her, slowly, while she retrieved her bike from the back yard and wheeled it out to the driveway. She put one leg over it, but did not start off. If only she had. She was posed there, one golden leg over the crossbar of the bike, the other braced on the driveway, her attitude emphasizing the paucity of her attire, when Herb Laplace drove in.

"You've got company," Sylvia said.

The sun glared on the windshield and Rogerson could not see the driver, nor was the car itself familiar to him. Then the car came into shadow and Herb Laplace stared at Sylvia.

"Hi," she trilled as she rode past the car and then picked up speed, whizzing out the driveway and up the street.

Herb got out of his car with a grudging leer on his face. "Was that Dr. Wood?"

"I believe it was."

"Matthew, Matthew. Tell me she has a part-time paper route and was trying to sell you a subscription to the Toledo *Blade.*"

"All right."

"All right, what?"

"I'll tell you that she has a part-time paper route and was . . ."

"Oh, shut up. Come on, give me a drink."

"Beer?"

"I said a drink. Maybe you're on the wagon because of your prick. . . ." At the mention of the sacred organ, Laplace became again the uncharacteristically soft-voiced and concerned old friend he had been mimicking the past few days.

"My doctor says I can drink all I want now. More than I want. It makes no difference."

Herb found this carte blanche depressing. "Maybe I will have a beer. What happened to your face?"

"You don't have to drink beer."

"I want beer. You look cooked."

They sat on the porch, Rogerson claiming the swing and letting Herb have the wicker rocker.

"A wicker chair," Herb marveled. "I haven't seen one of these for

110

years. We had wicker porch furniture when I was a kid. Where did you get it?"

"It came with the house."

"Guard it, Matt. Save it."

"I'll pass it on to my son."

A deepening of Laplace's gloom. But Rogerson had no desire to play for Herb's commiseration, real or feigned. As far as that went, the vision of the half-clothed Sylvia in the drive when he came in had set Herb's skeptical juices flowing, and he was willing if not indeed eager to drop his deathbedside manner.

"Too bad Dr. Wood had to leave," he said, wiping his ruttish mouth with the back of his hand. "It's a shame someone that attractive has to be intelligent too. I'm told she's a feminist."

"I'm afraid so."

"Now I see why you got your family out of town. Rather a nice way to pass the long hours of afternoon."

"With me in stitches? She'd have as much fun with a eunuch."

"Don't be so damned prejudiced."

"Maybe you're right." It was often hard to follow Herb's drift. "She brought me rumors that the humanities department is going to be allowed to sink without a trace."

Laplace frowned. "I suppose it looks that way, with everyone transferring out of it."

"Which came first?"

"The chicken. That goddam Fallor. You remember his candidate for a summer job? Sure as shit he's going to sue because I reneged on the offer. If there was any justice, I could can Fallor and hire the other guy in his place."

"Doesn't Fallor have tenure?"

"Tenure." Herb spat over the porch railing. "All a teacher has to do now is get his foot on your campus and he has you by the balls. I'm serious. Now we have to give reasons for not giving tenure and that means tenure is one of the four freedoms and a God-given right until proven otherwise."

"I hear Grundtvig is against tenure too. There is an ally for you."

"That sonofabitch. Sure he's against tenure. Until he gets it himself, he's against it. Let me tell you about bastards like Grundtvig."

What Herb had to tell was a theory with some validity. It ran along the following lines: A professor who was not particularly eminent in his field turned inevitably to campus politics in a noisy way, he made himself a spokesman for faculty rights, if he was lucky he got elected to office, the faculty senate, some advisory committee, the goddam AAUP. Then he has you. You lay one hand on his balding head and it's reprisal. He may not be able to teach his way out of a paper bag, his own colleagues may regard him as incompetent, but you cannot touch the sonofabitch. No matter what evidence you have about his teaching and scholarship, you are really out for revenge. And Grundtvig was a perfect instance of the type.

"What's his field? Economics. Economics! The bastard is some kind of socialist. His lectures are tirades against capitalism. Who the hell does he think pays his salary? And he's shacking up with a student. Well, she used to be a student. She dropped out after she moved in with Grundtvig. I could have him on a morals charge if they hadn't decided to make eighteen-year-olds adults."

"Statutory adultery, Herb. Your old friends the state legislators."

Herb looked around as if there might be spies in the shrubbery. "Thank God they're as dumb as they are, Matt, or we would still be eating hamburger."

"We still do."

"Aw, you're doing a lot better than you were."

"That was before I was circumcised."

"Tell me something." Herb leaned forward. "Say you got an erection now. What happens?"

"I pop a stitch or two."

"I'm serious. Isn't it painful?"

"The question has not arisen."

"Naw."

"Have you ever had Novocaine, Herb?"

"You're kidding."

"Numb as your thumbnail. Nothing."

"Jeez. When will it wear off?"

A good question, and one Rogerson intended to put to Heep the following day. He had intended to telephone the urologist that afternoon, but first Sylvia and now Herb had made that impossible. He was still swaddled in bandages. He felt maimed and impotent, and he wanted more from Heep than his cheery optimism and allusion to his track record on circumcisions. Rogerson cared naught for the average; he wanted reassurance about his own damaged digit.

The shrill cry of a jay, which swooped through the trees and alighted on the front lawn. The bird had a cruel head, its beak a weapon. Even in this peaceful neighborhood, natural species warred on natural species, gave pause for thought, inspired Rogerson's "Ode to an Insect." He had it right here, scribbled on a slip, marking a page in Milton.

A grasshopper etymologically
comes across the lawn and stops,
his brittle arms embrace a branch
of grass, his armored jaws begin
to munch. He is the color of his lunch,
has threads upon his head to serve
the function of those sightless nodes
which look like eyes not as:
he takes on cheating wings his leave;
names like the named often deceive.

"Is that what you meant to spend the summer doing?" Herb asked. He had found the poem while leafing through Rogerson's book.

"I wouldn't expect to reach that level every time."

"I don't imagine."

Rogerson began—it seemed a way to bring the visit to an end—discoursing on poetry, his theory of, recent. So recent was it that he developed it right there on the porch while Herb squirmed in the wicker chair. Classical syntax, learn from the Latins, word order more faithfully suggesting the structure of thought. For example? How about this? "Wholes not half as please us pieces do. Think about it, Herb." Herb apparently thought better on his feet. He shook his head, saying nay to Horace. "What feathered in the caught one pulses on in two," Rogerson intoned. Herb moved quickly across the porch. "Does in lilting units spiral spun this sound to grimace goad you?"

"You must be better, Matt. You sound crazy."

113

"Your visit has cheered me."

They parted on the front step, Herb to his car, Rogerson inside to answer the phone.

It was Marge. She wondered why he didn't come to the lake and spend what time remained before the start of summer school with his family. The time remaining was less than a week, Marge had the car, he had reading to do.

"This is perfect for reading. Barbara reads all day. There is a hammock slung between trees at the side of the cottage. Cottonwoods," she added, as if that were important.

"Cottonwoods, eh?"

He asked to speak to the kids, but it turned out that she was phoning from town. Besides, the kids were off to a carnival two towns away in the company of a family whose name meant nothing to Rogerson. Marge began to speak in a confidential tone about the opportunities in real estate around Lake Walleye; the place was booming. He could hear other voices in the background. He asked whose they were.

"I'm using Frank Wadley's phone."

"Wadley."

"The lawyer. He's also in real estate. Matt, are you coming up?"

"I'd better not, Marge. I really can't travel yet. You know."

"Oh."

"I have to just sit still for a while."

"You shouldn't be teaching summer school." The voices in the background crescendoed. "I'll get back to you, Matt. I have to go now."

Get back to him? She sounded like a secretary to a dean. Her tone confused him. Real estate? His wife was now a woman of some financial independence; she called him from a lawyer's office and murmured about the opportunities in real estate. Should he have gone up there? He had a vision of himself moving like a pendulum in the hammock, above him the oily leaves of cottonwoods twisting on their stems, a book in his hand, a breeze off the lake.

When he went out onto the porch for his beer, he felt almost inclined to get back to Marge and tell her he would come. He sat on the swing and the tinkle of chains reminded him of Sylvia seated here, broad-hipped Sylvia, gray-eyed Sylvia, Sylvia product of the

114

new amorality, she of the ruttish tongue and fuscous limbs, emboldened perhaps by his years and his incapacity, certainly fascinated by the latter. Penis envy. A curious concept, product of a perverse old cigar chewer who dreaded the young Jung's obsequious overtaking and his own deposition as the wizard of sex. Crotchety devil, testy, the big weenie of Wien, tell me all your bad dreams, my dear. Rogerson now equally full of dirty thoughts, age no respecter of the grizzled loin, the sap also rises in a forty-seven-year-old dried-up professor on a regional campus in Ohio, the instrument of his folly now folded in gauze, soothed with salve, *ave atque vale*, hail to thee, limp coagulated casualty of Heep's scalpel. Even in its current condition, a stirring as if of memory, a dreamlike response to the forwardness of Sylvia. A wiser man would have put a stop to her familiarity at the outset. There, there, my child, I'm father enough to be your oldster. But what man is wise when a quick hand lies uninvited on his thigh? Wisdom needs distance, armor. A medieval moralist would grant him the delight and pleasure and ask only if he had given his consent to it. Kiss you? I shouldn't even be in bed with you. Perhaps he should have spent these last languid days of inactivity with Marge and the kids and the real estate opportunities on Lake Walleye, inhaling the tarry smell of pines, watching the cottonwoods float their seed on the summer air.

"Of course there's some discomfort," Heep said. He seemed not to want to acknowledge Rogerson's complaints. "It's not like having a mole removed."

"You made it sound that simple."

Heep grinned. Was his look meant to be one of cunning? It made him seem an imbecile. "The main thing is it's done. It should have been done years ago. Now you won't have to worry."

Rogerson tried to recapture the worry which had driven him into the haven of surgery. This was difficult to do. Surely he had not allowed Heep to convince him that he was in imminent danger of contracting cancer? Surely he had. But if he was so susceptible to cancer scares, why did he continue to smoke cigarettes?

"Does marijuana cause lung cancer?" he asked Heep.

"This is tobacco." Heep rolled his cigarette between thumb and finger. "The thing to fear from cigarette smoking is heart trouble and emphysema. The lung cancer connection was oversold."

"And nine out of ten doctors smoke Camels?"

"Not a cough in a carload."

"Good for the T zone."

Heep frowned as if these slogans of a bygone day were ineffably sweet to remember. "Most doctors have quit smoking."

"But not all? Just nine out of ten?"

Heep's hand went for his cigarette, then retreated. "Your prostate is okay now, isn't it?"

"My prostate is okay. That's one out of two. As for my penis, the only sensation I have there is pain."

"Let's take a look."

Rogerson, pants at half-mast, in mourning for his manhood, tried to decode Heep's grunts and hums as he surveyed the scene of the crime. Heep tried to undo the gauze strip and Rogerson yelped.

"That's the stitches."

"You sewed the gauze to me?"

"No, no. The scab has formed a kind of cement." Heep stepped back and Rogerson got dressed. "Start taking baths again. That should help."

"When will feeling return?"

"I don't understand."

"I've been trying to tell you. Except for some pain, I can't feel anything there."

"You're imagining that."

"How could I imagine a thing like that?"

Heep lit another cigarette. "Operations are funny things," he began.

"Hilarious."

Heep frowned away this irrelevancy. "Their effects . . . Their psychological effects," he added darkly. "Look, I'll make you a promise. In a week or two you'll be all healed up and raring to go. You'd better warn your wife. You'll be trying to make up for all you've missed, and I don't mean just these past few weeks. Sex will be a totally new experience for you. You will have sensations you never dreamed of."

"You should write a book."

"I've thought of it." Heep's hand went to a drawer of his desk and his smile became shy.

"I'm not surprised."

"I've even dictated a few tapes."

Rogerson groaned inwardly. Doctors were becoming a literary menace: bogus diet books, sex manuals, sexual gymnastics, upbeat popular psychology. *Foreskin and Seven Years Ago: A Retrospect*, by Manfred Heep, D.D.S., M.D.

"What I need," Heep said, sitting forward, "is someone to go over it, for style, for grammar; you know."

"Sounds like a big job."

"Look, would you be interested?"

"I don't think so. I'll be teaching summer school."

"There's no rush." Heep looked sly again. "You can have a mention on the title page."

"No, thanks."

"Well, whatever." Heep opened the drawer, then shut it. "I don't want you to see what I've done so far. Give me some time. Then you can look it over and decide. If it's more work than you care to take on, say so. No hard feelings. Meanwhile, don't pay my bill."

"I haven't received it."

"I won't send it. First you look over the manuscript."

Any way out of paying Heep money for what he had done to Rogerson seemed attractive. He nodded slightly and that was more than enough to seal the bargain.

"I am thinking of gathering testimonials from patients. Real-life stories. The advantages of circumcision for the middle-aged man. You may feel like writing one yourself in a few weeks."

"I hope so."

"I promise you." Heep was beaming again. "With a little luck, I can get a sample of the book to you in a few days."

It felt good to go by the receptionist without making an appointment. In the waiting room the usual collection of patient clients sat flipping through magazines or staring vacantly before them. Not a single familiar face. Heep must be raking in money. When did he have time to write a book? Even a bad book takes time. Rogerson felt almost chastened by Heep's energy. He hoped that it would be a very bad book.

6

Three days later a strange car swept into the driveway with Marge at the wheel. Rogerson, who had been sitting on the porch this cloudy day, got to his feet feeling delight, surprise and apprehension. He had an absurd desire to make a swift circuit of the house to see how messy it might look to her. His breakfast dishes were on the table, his bed unmade, clothes scattered about the bedroom. Cunning conquered unease and he sank back, an abandoned convalescent.

"I'm on the porch," he called out, not too weakly, when the car door slammed.

An authoritative tattoo of heels, a swift ascent of the steps, and a moment later Marge rounded the corner of the porch and stopped. Her summer dress was a soft lemon semitransparent nimbus, her picture hat gave her a modish foreign air, her expression was that of the reassured.

"You look fine," she said.

"So do you. Whose car are you driving?"

She dropped some keys into her open purse, coins in a well, the wish already granted. "I rented it."

"Did you fly?"

She nodded, drawing a chair up to his. "To Chicago. You're tan." She was not. He took her hand and pulled her toward him. A moment of resistance and then she came into his arms to a rustle of dress, a fugitive scent of perfume, almost a stranger. Her lips on his cheek were moistly momentary. She pulled free and sat back in her own chair.

"Aren't you surprised?"

"You flew to Chicago?"

"Yes. With Frank Wadley. It was all on the spur of the moment. But I had to see how you are. What a sneaky thing to do, scheduling an operation without telling me."

"Who is Frank Wadley?"

"I told you on the phone. He's a lawyer."

"You rented the car in Chicago?"

"Frank was flying there and I hitched a ride."

"Does he have his own plane?"

"Matt, it's so small."

How awkward they both were. She brought chatter of Wadley onto their porch and he was bothered by the image of Sylvia seated on that swing only a few days ago. Dear God, if Marge had chosen that afternoon to drive in! Guilt filled him with rancor at the unknown Wadley, the daring young man with his flying machine.

"He's older than you are," Marge countered. "And if he did any stunting he would lose his license."

"His marriage license? He *is* married, I suppose."

"Matt, everyone is married." She stood. "I'm famished."

He remained on the porch after she had gone inside. His delight in her return was spoiled by the unusual way she had accomplished it. Had she ever flown in a private plane before? He had not. And this must be the first time she had rented a car. Such self-reliance was unnerving. Wonder about the kids sent him inside after her. She was in the kitchen.

"Someone's been eating from my bowl," she said, continuing to clean up the table.

"Forget that. You'll get your dress dirty."

"Would you bring in my bag, Matt?" She turned to look at him. "Can you?"

Meaning his wounds. "Of course."

Outside the clouds were darker, threatening rain. The windows of the car were up: it was equipped with air conditioning. He thought

120

of Marge zipping alone across Indiana in cool and rented comfort.

While she changed he finished cleaning up the kitchen. He supposed she was making his bed and tidying up their room. They seemed to be occupying their least common denominator, housekeeping. When she came down, he asked about the kids.

"More luck. They had been invited to the Lairds' and Betty said they could stay on there. They have loads of room and our kids get along famously with theirs."

"Do I know them?"

"They have a place half a mile up the shore."

He didn't know the Lairds. His children were with strangers. Who were not strangers to them. Or to Marge.

"You must have been getting lots of sun."

"In the back yard."

"Sounds relaxing."

She was in shorts and a striped jersey, her hair pulled back. The costume was not appropriate to the day. Great gray puffy clouds moved across the sky, beyond them were yet darker ones, and the temperature was perceptibly dropping. The impending rain seemed a promise of closeness, a way out of the oddly formal way they were acting.

"How's the weather been at the lake?"

"I've hardly noticed."

"Oh?"

"Matt, do you know that land right across the road from the cottage? I want it. There is a boom in the offing and I want to be in on it. That land will quadruple in value at least."

"Who owns it?"

Marge laughed. "Gus Johansen. They call him gloomy Gus. He thinks the land is useless."

"Maybe he's right."

"No." Marge lit a cigarette. "No, he's wrong."

"What would you buy it with?"

"I can afford it."

Even without the assertive pronoun, the claim would have been mystifying. Rogerson could think of nothing to say. Marge smoked meditatively for a moment and then spoke more generically of the economic bonanza land near Lake Walleye would one day soon represent. Others saw this, of course—Frank Wadley seemed to be one of them—but most did not. Hence the opportunities. Clearly Marge had been having a busy and calculating summer thus far.

"Are the kids enjoying it?"

"They love it."

"Where do you go to Mass, in Warwick?"

She sailed a smoke ring across the table. "There's a Catholic church in Warwick, yes."

"Haven't you been going?"

"Matt, we've only been there a couple of weekends."

"The kids have to go."

"Please don't start that."

"It's continuing, not starting. I promised to raise the kids Catholic."

Her frown gave way to a smile. "All right. All right. I'll make sure they go."

The rain had begun to fall. He said, "I didn't make the rules."

"Matt, let me say it once, and for God's sake let's not argue about this. *Priests* have told me it isn't necessary to go to Mass every Sunday. That sort of legalism is a thing of the past. If priests say it, why can't you accept it? You're more Catholic than the Pope. And you're not going to make me feel guilty about it."

He had not told her of Jimmy Bastable, of whom her words reminded him. What would her reaction to Bastable's departure be? He did not want to know. If Sunday Mass was an obligation only when you felt it was, what about other obligations? Were they too at the mercy of whim and feeling? She was right about one thing: they must not argue about this. She had come all this way to see how he was.

It rained all afternoon, rain descending in sheets on the lawn, on the roof, on the eerily bright lawn chairs in the yard, perpendicular rain, the outpouring of a bottomless bucket. The trees wept further water on the roof. Marge changed into slacks and put on a sweater and Rogerson too got into warmer clothing. Marge lay on the couch and fell asleep. Rogerson went upstairs, where he stood at the window of their room and watched rain ping from the roof and hood of the rented car. What was it costing Marge? Marge. Suddenly she had economic autonomy and he felt unmanned. He was conscious of his still unhealed self; he felt weak and wounded. He lay down on the bed and almost immediately was asleep.

That night he made a fire in the fireplace and while Marge pored over a manual that told of requirements for certification as a real estate agent in Wisconsin, he read Milton. The poet seemed to speak to Rogerson from another, saner world, or he did until Rogerson flipped past the poetry to the selected prose in the volume and by God, here was John Milton writing on the doctrine and discipline of divorce. Rogerson, expecting a hell-and-brimstone condemnation, was startled to find Milton carrying on like a columnist in a women's magazine. What the hell was this? That no covenant whatsoever obliges against the main end both of itself and of the parties convenanting. The ignorance and iniquity of canon law providing for the right of the body in marriage, but nothing for the wrongs and grievances of the mind. Without it (divorce), marriage, as it happens oft, is not a remedy of that which it promises, as any rational creature would expect. God regards love and peace in the family more than a compulsive performance of marriage, which is more broke by a grievous continuance than by a needful divorce.

O Milton, thou shouldst be living at this hour. Your logic boggles the Rogersonian mind. Divorce argued for as the preservative of love and peace in the family. Madness. There was more, much more, and Rogerson was reading only the chapter headings. He felt angry and besieged. Did Bastable have guns as big as Milton on his side? Was Matthew Rogerson to be the last man in the West to argue for the importance of rules and promises and hanging in there when the going got rough? To hell with divorce. People should learn to live with their mistakes. Rationalizing like Milton's had undone the fabric of society. He must have had marital difficulties himself. Of course he had. He couldn't get it up, wasn't that it? Beneath every theory there lurks a personal history. What the hell kind of world would it be if we brushed aside as inconvenient the keeping of past promises? Marriage. Sunday Mass. Better to condemn marriage outright than to pretend its dissolution preserves it; better to repudiate the faith than to argue that avoidance of the Mass is an authentic form of worship.

Rogerson slammed the book closed. From time to time, some rain came down the chimney and hissed on the burning logs. Marge went on reading. He had not seen her study so avidly since Madison. Would she give a damn if he went off to bed? She had not asked a direct question about his operation. Was she afraid, alone in the house, without the protective screen of the children's presence, to refer to his manhood?

"The AAUP are convinced Laplace and Wooley are up to something with the humanities department."

"Hmmm?" Marge went on reading.

"Grundtvig thinks they plan to dissolve it entirely."

"What?"

"The rain sounds nice on the roof."

"Doesn't it?" She put a finger in her book for marker and hugged it to her. "It's almost like a night at the cottage. Matt, I just love it up there. I always did. When I was a girl, the happiest months of the year were those we spent there."

"Laplace dropped in the other day."

She seemed to have to think who Laplace was. "Oh?"

"He denied Grundtvig's claim that the humanities department will be dissolved."

"Dissolved!"

"Most people want to be in a regular academic department now. I'll have only half a dozen faculty next year."

"What department would you go into?"

"If Grundtvig is right, I could be out on my ear."

"They can't fire you. You have tenure."

"Tenure is tied to a particular department. It goes if a department is discontinued entirely."

"Do you really think they would do that to you?"

"Anything is possible, Marge."

"But is it likely?"

"I don't know. There has been a steady flow out of the department. Of staff. We keep attracting students, for what that's worth."

"I wish they would dissolve it, Matt." Marge hunched over her knees, still hugging her real estate manual.

"Thanks a lot."

"No, listen. We could move to Lake Walleye, live there the whole year round. If I'm right about the land opportunities, we could make a good deal of money. And it's so healthy for the kids."

"And just what the hell would I do? Fish?"

She had an answer to that too. Had she been thinking of this? "There is a community college in Hayden."

"I've never heard of it."

"I don't suppose they've heard of the Fort Elbow campus either." Touché. "Marge, I've got a job. And we have a house, this house."

She groaned. "This town. I hate this town. And so do you, Matt. We belong in Wisconsin, in our native state."

He hummed a few bars of "On, Wisconsin," but she was serious.

"Matt, you brought up losing your job here; I didn't. If that happens, there is an alternative. That is all I mean." She opened her book.

"Maybe I could go into real estate."

She didn't look up. "You're not cut out for it."

"Why not?"

She read a line or two. "You don't have a head for business."

"That is my boast." He stood up. "Want a beer?"

"No."

He took a bottle onto the back porch, where he sat on a bench and looked out at their cottonwood, huge against a purplish sky, tossing in the wind. Lightning flashed across the sky, but the thunder was delayed and distant. Marge must be going cabin crazy. Move to the lake cottage as their permanent home! He could teach in a community college that would no doubt make even the Fort Elbow campus seem by comparison the very grove of academe. And Marge would make a million in real estate. The very possibility had hardened her, moved her out of his reach. The cottage aided and abetted her fantasies, reminder as it was of a time before their marriage. How much constraint did their marriage present now that she had given up her faith? If there was anything to be said for the Catholic Church, it was that it opposed the modern malaise on divorce. The marriage ceremony was unequivocal; it was a life sentence if there ever was one, and even opponents of capital punishment defended life sentences. Of course, Marge could find some flaky priest to tell her that she wasn't married, really, unless she felt it in her heart. She and Jimmy Bastable could trade theological arguments on the subject, bolstering one another's weakness. Even Milton nods. *Even* Milton?

Rogerson's estimate of the blind bard was in steep decline. Presumptuous heretic. Who did he think he was, Dante? Now there was a man. Rogerson could not remember if Dante had married her, but his fidelity to the girl first seen on the Ponte Vecchio was a model the world needed. An *Amoroso* instead of a muddle-headed *Penseroso.*

"What are you doing?" It was Marge, standing in the kitchen doorway.

"Drinking beer."

"In a typhoon?"

He said nothing. She came outside.

"Look at that rain," she said.

"I wish you'd brought the kids."

"Don't worry about the kids. They're having a wonderful time. Is there more beer?"

"It's warm. I didn't put it in the refrigerator."

"Let me taste."

He handed her the bottle. In a moment she handed it back, making a sound of distaste.

"I kind of like it warm," he said. "I used to drink warm beer all the time. Did I ever tell you of the summer I worked in the bottle house?"

"No."

"At Schlitz."

"But you never drink Schlitz."

"That's the story."

She laughed and moved closer to him on the bench, looking out at the rain. He was almost embarrassed by her proximity. The scene was reminiscent of long-ago intimacy, he talking, she listening. Had that been the trouble? The trouble. My God. What would it have been like if everything had gone all right? Marriage is a task, divorce its defeat. Why did he keep thinking of divorce? Milton. God damn Milton. And Bastable too. But it was already a moral defeat to have a marriage reduced to the parlous state in which his life with Marge now found itself, he in voluntary exile at home, she dreaming of economic coups at the lake. Was she as uncomfortable as he was just to be alone together? For a long time his conjugal gestures had been hidden behind a mask of irony, become comic, a ho-ho progress through life with Marge. No wonder she had been a sucker for harebrained feminist theory, a Stalinist film: find fulfillment as a tractor driver or hod carrier. Or real estate tycoon in central Wisconsin.

"What do you do with the land if you get it?"

"What land?"

He reminded her of her scheme. The idea, she said, was to subdivide, it sell it off in lots, perhaps develop it and put up houses. Rogerson was reminded of the brochure that had lured Felix Freeman to the wastes of Arizona. Better not to have mentioned it.

"This would be nothing at all like that."

"Felix says the brochure never told a literal lie. The illustrations did that. If he tried to take them to court . . ."

"Matt, I don't want to talk about Felix Freeman."

"I'm the one who's talking about him."

Her arms—where had they been?—crossed, she hugged herself, a defensive posture. He did not want to talk of Felix either. Marge and Felix had never gotten along.

"Let's go in," she said. "You'll catch cold."

She was shivering. They went back to the fire, where he threw on another log. He brought her a beer that seemed cooler than the rest. They had been staring at the rain; now they stared at the flames, together, alone. Rain on the roof, rain splattering in the puddles it had previously made, the snap of the fire.

"This is why we fought the war, men," Rogerson droned. "A fire, a beer, a girl at our side."

"Did you really work for Schlitz?"

Well, he had been employed there, in the bottle house, for several weeks after his discharge, before he decided to make use of the 52–20 benefits. His task had been to watch the bottles march past a light on their way to the pasteurizer. Ten minutes off each hour, when they drank warm beer from the pasteurizer. He had worked from six until two in the morning, when he went home half drunk and slept till noon. The best of both worlds, or so it had seemed.

He embellished the memory, as he might have in his prime, brushing it with the warm colors of nostalgia, a better past. He even remembered the names of men he had worked with in those impermanent weeks. But his heart was not in the effort. He had the silly feeling that he was wooing his wife.

127

"Tell me about the operation."

"There's nothing to tell."

He almost resented her remembering to ask. Silence. Into the kitchen for another beer and that was all. He stayed by the fire after she had gone up to bed, already dimly aware that the best moments of her visit had been enjoyed.

It rained for two days. They did not go out. Marge had no interest in seeing anyone; her visit was their secret. She studied the rules of Wisconsin real estate while his dislike for Milton was consolidated by further reading.

At first Marge shook away his question about her father's funeral. Her reluctance to speak of it became intelligible when she finally did. Her father was not buried anywhere. His body had been cremated and its ashes scattered over Lake Michigan. It seemed a somewhat dramatic disposition of Olson's mortal remains, but his fancy had been caught by the radio commercials of a firm calling itself Aerial Burial. Rogerson had no idea what degree of faith had been concealed in his father-in-law's bullet head; his Catholicism, like Rogerson's own, had been contracted with his marriage, but nominal or not, his faith should have been an obstacle to his request.

"What did the priest say?"

"What do you mean?"

"Isn't cremation verboten?"

"Why should it be?"

"Damned if I know, but doesn't the Church forbid it?"

"Father Jawohl didn't go up in the plane or anything."

"Who did?"

"I did."

"You!"

"A member of the family has to go. That was part of the contract Dad signed."

"Tell me about it."

She sensed mockery in his curiosity. "You needn't be so damned lofty about it, Matt. What did you do with your father's ashes?"

For years he had kept an urn filled with Pall Mall ashes on his desk, referring to it as his father's ashes. One night he had dumped them in the wastebasket, a little ceremony of farewell, adieu as he had thought to his farcical self. The occasion had been a solemn one; a believed lie takes on objective weight.

He said, "I donated them to science. Aerial Burial?"

"So it's a silly name. The idea is sensible. We can't keep using land for cemeteries. That day the pilot pointed out how much of Milwaukee is taken up by graveyards. What a waste."

"I should think it's a pretty profitable use of land."

"But it isn't."

The kitchen window behind her streamed with rain. She was due to meet Wadley later that day at Meigs Field in Chicago. He took her bag out to the rented car and came back soaked to where she waited on the porch. Why were they separating like this? Summer school had already served its purpose, granting him solitude for his circumcision. The Milton course held no appeal. At the lake he could recuperate. He did not want Marge to drive away to Frank Wadley's plane in Chicago. These and other velleities failed to achieve the hue of resolution. Marge made him promise that he would come up to the lake soon, take a long weekend. That is all she asked. They kissed and he held her briefly and then she scooted out to the car. A bereft, abandoned Rogerson leaned into the rain, waving after her.

7

Rogerson's class list, three pages spewed from the IBM machine in the administration building, thirty-five names per page, the third not quite full, had to be a mistake. Brenda Mapes doubted it.

"You'll know when you meet the class," she said.

What he knew when he found ninety-odd people jammed into a classroom meant for fifty was that they had indeed signed up for *Paradise Lost.* He did not know why. He managed to squirm into the room, sideways, someone's elbow pressing his Adam's apple, another's plush bosom his ribs. Limbs. Flesh. He was reminded of Plummet-Finch's sighing reminiscences of riding the bus in Naples. Once he got inside the door, a small lane to the desk opened for him. Walking through it, he felt like a professional golfer about to demonstrate an impossible shot.

The desk stood on a platform and from its top the knowledgeable could make a lectern appear. Rogerson did so, placed his folder of notes on the canted surface, his Milton on what remained of the desktop, and surveyed the room. The Last Judgment would be something like this, he supposed, though his would not be so favored a place. Only those near the front of the room had noticed his entry and Rogerson did nothing to attract attention. Predictably, hushing began and traveled sibilantly through the room. The standees leaned against the walls, those who had come early and gotten chairs settled possessively into them. A sort of humming silence established itself.

"This is *Paradise Lost,*" Rogerson said. There was a tentative titter he decided not to encourage. "I am Matthew Rogerson."

He did pause now and the expressions grew more attentive. A hand lifted, that of a small, bald, bearded man in a short-sleeved shirt. He asked in piping voice if this would be the permanent place of class meetings. First Rogerson wished to make certain that everyone here knew where he was. He repeated the title of the course, his own name and the department under whose auspices the course was offered.

"This is not an English department course," he said, and there was a promising undercurrent of grumbling, which did not, however, presage any exodus. There was nothing for it but to launch into the class-winnower he had meant to employ even if the enrollment had required but one IBM sheet.

"Comprising twelve books, *Paradise Lost* runs to a total of 10,565 lines of poetry, certainly a modest amount when compared to Dante or Virgil or, for that matter, *The Ring and the Book.* Milton's poem is not half the length of Browning's. This is a lecture course. You will be expected to write one full-length term paper, a three-thousand-word review of an important work from the secondary literature— I will provide you with a bibliography—as well as weekly exegetical pieces on lines to be assigned. Of course, it is assumed that you already have a more than passing acquaintance with the poem."

With a group this large, it was difficult to gauge the impact of such an announcement. Concentrating on a face or two did not provide a significant enough sample to measure the general reaction. For every satisfyingly glazed look or involuntary falling open of a mouth, there were two or three who listened impassively and with apparent equanimity to the impossible menu of summer labor he had outlined. Even the final fillip failed to bring the expected groan, only one quickly muffled laugh.

"Doubtless most of you have long been teaching *Paradise Lost* to your own students."

There were actually some nods in response to this gloss on his expectation, fraudulent nods, he was sure, but he no longer doubted that he was confronted with something a good deal less than the prospect of a six-week downhill slide into an indolent August. There was something too bright and eager about this crowd of summer scholars, and while much of that could be accounted for by the fact that this was the first class meeting, Rogerson had the sinking feeling that with altogether too many of them the studious fervor would persist. All the more reason to regret that he had been unable to get through *Paradise Lost* himself before the summer session began. He could not recall what circumstances had led him to think of *Paradise Lost* as an unalleviated delight, something to which he could go back at any time to read with pleasure and profit.

"Your own teaching will have acquainted you with the difficulties of a poem whose Latinisms inevitably offend the contemporary ear. Milton's classicism will be a recurrent theme of my lectures." His lectures? He had not the faintest idea how he would get through this first day, let alone the weeks that lay ahead. Visions of a small group of illiterates, of a first meeting whiled away in pruning the group of the random gung ho student who is the bane of any course, followed by an informal get-acquainted session, had emboldened him when he arose that morning. Twenty years of teaching had not wholly destroyed the inviting novelty of beginning a course nor the surprising unsameness of students when his defenses against getting to know them crumbled. Regular students, concealed under the homogeneity of hair and beards and unkempt clothing, were, it was difficult to deny, each unlike the other. Summer school students, on the whole older and squarer-looking, could be literally anything. A lot of high school teachers, of course, but they turned out to be as varied a bunch as a college faculty. And then there were the wild cards. Rogerson had once had a justice of the supreme court of Pennsylvania in a summer class, a Korean ace, a paroled murderer, a nymphomaniac, two actually, a blind woman of sixty who took notes in Braille, clicking away whenever he spoke like an elevator starter of yore or a castanet player fallen on evil days. It was necessary to tread lightly with even a small group in summer school until the lay of the land was clear. How in hell could he know where he was with ninety students? He flipped open his book to the beginning of the poem and read.

"Of man's first disobedience, and the fruit
Of that forbidden tree, whose mortal taste
Brought death into the world and all our woe . . ."

He looked up, smiling knowingly. " 'Arma virumque cano,' of course. No need to emphasize it." Did he only imagine a flicker of remembrance in several pairs of eyes. Reading Virgil in the basement classroom of long ago, Rogerson transported to his youth, to the first surge of the thirst for knowledge, for mastery, for entrance into another, better world. The memory brought with it a twinge of guilt at the con game his own teaching had become, his standards lowered and then abandoned because their application would void the university of students. He launched some further banalities about the *Aeneid* and *Paradise Lost,* returned to the text, fell silent, then closed the book dramatically.

"Clearly there is no point in trying to hold class in these crowded circumstances. I will post on the door of this room the place of the next class meeting well in advance of the appointed hour. You may either check with the departmental secretary or come by this room if you persist in your perversity and wish to attend the next class."

He stepped back from the desk, lowered the lectern into its top, fussed with his manila folder and his book, knowing that it was useless to try to plunge through that crowd to freedom. He prayed that few would come forward to pester him now, but as with so many prayers, the answer was in the negative. He repeated a dozen times the edition he would be using, he should have written that on the board; he said that yes, as he had announced, they would not be meeting in this room again. Where was the departmental secretary located? Again this was information he should have put on the board and, in more normal circumstances, would have. Of course, it was as predictable as nightfall that a third of a new class will come forward after the first meeting to speak to the professor. However truncated a class he might have had, he would have been unable to escape after he closed his book. He was still there in the classroom when the bell rang. The inevitable student who could not be shaken loose by his move to the door, his farewell remarks in the hallway or his brisk walk in the direction of the stairway was female, tall, oddly proportioned and possessed of a smooth blank innocent face that belonged on a twelve-year-old boy. Her hair was cropped close to her well-shaped head, her blue eyes had a confiding twinkle as she leaned toward Rogerson, her milk-white teeth protruded slightly. She had the body of an earth mother. Her hips in the corduroy slacks were high, fulsome, and yet her long legs gave her a coltish look. Her T-shirt ballooned with the burden of her breasts. She spoke in a whisper, so that he had to strain to hear her in the echoing hallway. This slowed his pace. She said that she was chiefly interested in Milton's attitude toward women.

"Ah. You mean his approval of divorce?"

"I didn't know about that."

"What did you have in mind?" He was hoping for some biographical reason for her interest, some deed or saying of Milton's. The girl to his consternation quoted some lines.

> "Meanwhile the heinous and despiteful act
> Of Satan done in paradise, and how
> Hee in the serpent had perverted Eve,
> Her husband shee . . ."

Rogerson cocked his head while she quoted, smiling noncommittally. The mention of Satan, the drift of the lines, suggested that they were indeed from *Paradise Lost,* but he did not intend to take any chances. A student who had lines by heart spelled real trouble and much depended on what foot they got off on.

She said, "Male chauvinism."

"It's all biblical, of course."

"That's what I mean."

"Anyway, it's more satanic chauvinism than anything, isn't it?"

"It would be if anyone took the devil myth seriously. What comes through is the woman dragging down the man."

Oh, my God. They had stopped walking—to continue would have been too overtly impolite—and now she faced him, her weight on one foot, her book held lightly in her hand, her toothy smile inviting him to endorse her ideological reaction to Milton. She was disturbingly hermaphroditic, with that body by Rubens, face by Disney, and husky whispering way she had. He took the coward's way out and asked her name.

"Elpidia Hopper." She said it as if sharing a joke. "My father is a scripture scholar. I have siblings named Pistis and Agape."

"You're kidding."

"Only partly. They're middle names."

"What is your first name?"

"Julia."

"I suppose you have another class."

"No. Are you busy?"

"I'm going to have to do something about that room. I can't imagine why I have such a huge enrollment."

"It's no mystery. You have the reputation of being an easy grader."

"Everybody gives high grades now."

"And not much work."

"You heard what I said just now."

She nodded, smiling, part of the conspiracy. "We were told about that too. A week from now you take it all back."

"Not this time. Pass the word, will you?"

She shook her head. "Not me. Are you free now?"

"First days are pretty hectic."

She accepted this without fuss. Rogerson hustled up the stairs. Julia Elpis Hopper cast a pall over his summer. Her father was a scripture scholar, but what was she? A teacher? A desultory student? A spy? His pace slowed as he savored the possibilities of a conspiracy. His enemies had planted Elpidia in his class to gather information. To what end? Nonsense. She was only a bright young lady with an ax to grind. Milton as male chauvinist. Well, he was not male chauvinist enough for Rogerson, not with his wavering on divorce. In a chivalrous mood Rogerson was apt to speak of equality of the sexes as an acceptable declension of the female, but it was the concept of equality he questioned. Equal to what? To one another or to some *tertium quid*? Surely not to one another. A man is not a woman, a woman is not a man. Whoever thought so was beneath contempt and beyond the range of rational argument. Biology was not the last word, but it could not be wished away as it was by Simone de Beauvoir, an author Rogerson was certain Julia could quote, and in French, no doubt. Gender as existential choice. Bullshit. From penis envy to the dinky as wish fulfillment. Only a philosopher could imagine such nonsense. Did equality mean Marge's right to become a real estate

135

developer in Wisconsin? Economics was the *tertium quid,* man and woman made equal in remunerative labor. Well, anyone who wished to adopt that angle of vision on the world was welcome to it. Equal pay for equal work? But the point of civilization is to dethrone the preeminence of work. Did he dare to lace his lectures with such sound doctrine, subtly to undermine the ideology that had corrupted Miss Julia Elpis Hopper? Obliquity was the only effective attack. Rogerson had never met a woman he didn't like.

The woman he met next was Norah Vlach, emerging from the departmental office wearing the look of sour severity that seemed to be the outward sign of her decision for Christ. She lifted her hand to stay the hurrying Rogerson.

"A word with you, Matthew."

"I have a student who thinks the Bible is sexist."

Norah's brows rose in warning, responding to the word's root rather than its suffix.

"Eve is inferior to Adam," Rogerson explained. "Beneath him, as it were."

"Wives be subject to your husbands," Norah intoned, and there was a wistful twist to the words as she spoke them. Norah had exchanged her glasses for contact lenses and these lent a receptivity to her look which suggested that there still lurked in her some of that fire to which marriage is the Pauline remedy. Milton again, the bastard. Norah, the putative matricide, once hot for the body of Rogerson, this arguing an all but indiscriminate carnal itch, had, since her return from a brief exile after the death of her mother, gone through a somewhat manic period which had been finally superseded by her conversion. An itinerant evangelist, guest of the redoubtable Taggart of radio fame, had prompted her from her pew and down the aisle to make the decision that had changed her life. Norah was now serenely among the saved. Rogerson's own notion of religion involved less a plateau of salvation than the hills and dales of sin and mercy. Still, like a good American, he would defend to the death Norah's right to be a heretic.

"Brenda tells me that you have spoken with her son."

"Yes, I visited him."

"Did you pray together?"

"Actually, he ate scrambled eggs while I told him to stop stealing bicycles from campus."

Norah winced. "He is a thief?"

"That is probably not the worst of it."

"Remember the good thief."

"Oh, Eric was pretty good at it. Apparently he stopped."

"Brenda is still quite worried." Norah came closer and whispered, "Drugs."

"I wouldn't be surprised."

"She says he has filled the house with strange plants. And he is growing mushrooms in the cellar."

"I see."

"I have offered to speak to him. I shall ask him to pray with me. Christ is the only answer, Matthew."

"What is the question?"

"Don't make light of it. In your own way, you know what I mean. Have you any suggestions on how I might approach Eric?"

"Ask him what he has in his pots."

Students attempted to grow marijuana in window boxes in the dorms, but during the good growing times they were away on vacation, so not much came of it. It was said that the new greenhouses of the botany department permitted a choice cannabis to flourish in the winter months, this felony financed by the taxpayer. Probably a wishful lie bruited about by resentful humanists who objected to the way the sciences claimed the largest slice of the budgetary pie.

The departmental office was crowded with confused students seeking direction. Rogerson recognized some faces from his just disbanded class. Better to keep clear of there for now. He should have asked Norah which dean was in charge of classrooms. To hell with it. Brenda could take care of it.

He was struck by the lack of activity in other departmental offices as he went down the hall. The sound of voices from the faculty lounge drew him.

"We will have to drop the Hegel course," Horst was saying when Rogerson came in. "Laplace won't let us carry a course with only two students."

137

"Two students, and one an auditor." Geist, the Hegel scholar, shook his head in disbelief. "The campus is alive with students. What courses are they taking?"

"You've got to be kidding."

Rogerson at the coffee urn, pressed the handle, which permitted an ounce or two of syrupy liquid to stain his paper cup. The dregs of the urn. Behind him, the conversation had stopped abruptly. He was conscious of embarrassed, angry eyes not quite meeting his when he took his cup across the room.

"Have you met your class yet?" Horst asked Rogerson.

"Just."

"Well?"

"The usual aspirants after wisdom. One or two pretty girls."

"How many?" Geist demanded.

"One or two."

"I mean students. How many are enrolled in your course?"

"Quite a few. I had no idea Milton was so popular."

Keane said meaningfully, "It isn't Milton, Matthew."

"Do I detect a sullen note in your voice?"

"My Baudelaire course has been canceled. You got the Milton course I had hoped to give."

"Would you like it back?"

"Don't be funny."

"I'm serious. Do you want to take it? I've done nothing more than meet them and tell them we need a larger room."

Geist groaned. "How many signed up for it, Rogerson?"

"Ninety-one."

There were yelps of disbelief, but Rogerson ignored them. He took a chair facing Keane. "I am perfectly serious, Keane. Do me a favor. I don't want to teach that course."

"Are there really that many signed up for it?"

"You can imagine my dismay. They deserve a better course than I could possibly give them. A Milton man should give the course. You. What do you say?"

"Take it," Horst suggested.

"I had been counting on the money from at least one course," Keane said shyly.

"Of course you were. It's bad enough that you're not teaching two courses." Rogerson looked around at the earnest group. "My wife took a course from Keane this spring. She couldn't stop talking about it."

"She got a C," Keane said.

"And was happy to get it." Marge, after all, had skipped the final.

"It was the second highest grade." Keane straightened his shoulders. "I flunked four."

There had been scarcely a dozen in the course. The others nodded approval of the severity of Keane's grading. An interrupted conversation seemed to resume. Fallor spoke feelingly of the need for standards, particularly now.

"A B.A. is not a civil right," Fallor said firmly. "Neither is getting an A in every course."

Geist said, "We are a laughingstock to the scientists."

"What do you say?" Rogerson asked Keane. "You would be doing me a great favor."

"I expected your wife to sign up for my Baudelaire course."

"She's at the lake, in Wisconsin. She'll be there all summer."

"And summer school is keeping you here, away from your family?"

"Do me a favor," Rogerson pleaded.

"Very well," Keane said. "I will."

They finished their coffee before going downstairs and over to the dean's office, Rogerson not swallowing his but pretending to sip, while Keane gulped periodically as if nectar and ambrosia had nothing on the dreadful brew dispensed from the faculty lounge urn. He told Keane the edition of Milton he had ordered, not that it mattered; there were not nearly enough copies in the bookstore and any order submitted now could not possibly be filled before summer school was over. Keane would have absolutely free rein.

"There are some ideas I had hoped to develop," Keane said.

"Of course."

"What is your view of Book Eight?"

"Tell me yours."

Keane did, in unintelligible detail. Rogerson nodded, smiling. Julia Hopper was going to love Keane. His ear picked up the conversation behind him, a familiar one, true, but engaged in now with unusual vehemence. Rogerson's younger colleagues were appalled by the lack of academic standards on campus and considered the grade point average in the arts college a scandal. If it were accurate, one would have to conclude that only geniuses were enrolled, yet they all knew the level of test scores that was considered sufficient for admission. O'Brien, who was black, introduced a note of caution. Exceptions must be made for the unjustly disadvantaged applicant. Fallor could not agree more. They had to be wary of elevating the standards of middle-class America into criteria of intelligence and capacity, O'Brien reminded them. Geist wanted it understood that nothing he had said was meant to apply to blacks.

"Or Chicanos?" asked Segura.

"No. Nor to Indians either."

It was a conversation Rogerson fairly lusted to enter. He contented himself with asking over his shoulder, "Yes, but what about women?"

"What about women?" Keane asked.

O'Brien said that he resented having women treated as though they were members of a disadvantaged minority. He would be damned if he felt the least bit sorry for a bunch of frustrated suburban housewives. Women who were part of authentic minorities, that was another question, but women as such, why, hell, man, they're a majority, do you know that?

Fallor knew it. Geist knew it. Even Horst knew it. Keane wondered what the problem was.

"Let's get down to the dean," Rogerson suggested. Standards were in good hands, here in the lounge. Until Laplace approved of the transfer of the course to Keane, Rogerson could not rest.

"You say there are some good-looking girls enrolled?" Keane asked lustfully as they left the lounge.

"There are. Of course, they constitute a minority."

"I suppose you want to beat it up to Wisconsin," Laplace said when Keane had been hustled out of the office, the business of switching the course completed.

"I may do that."

"May? Isn't that why you wanted out of that course?"

"Herb, over ninety people signed up for a course in *Paradise Lost.* Isn't that a sign of the Last Days?"

140

"Ask Norah."

"Has she been proselytizing you again?"

"You make it sound almost interesting. God, what a screwed-up mess this summer session is. Do you know how many courses have been dropped because of insufficient enrollment?"

"What's the problem?"

"These young guys can't teach."

"They think it's because they mark too low."

Herb guffawed. "Who told you that?"

"It's an impression I picked up."

"Don't you believe it. Their grades are as high as yours and you've been Santa Claus for years."

"Surely not Keane?"

"Of course Keane. Why?"

"I heard he flunked a third of his class in the spring."

"That's a bunch of bullshit. There were exactly twenty-seven failures in the college this spring, twenty-four of them due to unauthorized withdrawal from class. Dropouts, in other words. Keane may have had one of those."

"Then why did so many classes draw blanks this summer?"

Herb said, "There was only one blank, but a lot had only one or two people sign up. Mostly English courses. The humanities department is the reason for that."

"Why, if everyone is giving high grades?"

"Who knows why? It's just a fact." Herb lit a cigarette. "A fact we'll be hearing a lot more of. Those young bastards want to wipe out the humanities department, Matt."

"I was told that you do."

"Why would I want to wipe out a department?"

"To keep the people in the English department happy."

Herb glowered. "They can't be unhappy enough for me."

"How about Wooley?"

"What do you mean?"

"Maybe he wouldn't mind getting rid of the humanities department. This is the only campus in the state with such a department. It must stick out like a sore thumb when he gets together with the other chancellors."

"The other chancellors! Isn't that a goddam joke? Remember

when every general was a five-star general?"

"I remember when we only had one dean."

"There is still only one dean," Herb said emphatically. "At least in this college."

After he had left Laplace's office, Rogerson realized that he had no destination. The summer stretched before him again as he had meant it should, three months of inactivity, puttering with his poetry, lying in the sun, perhaps a bit of golf, getting out the seven-club starter set he had picked up for thirty dollars at a discount drugstore ten years ago. Others described the university golf course as stale, flat and unchallenging, but Rogerson, in the days when he had played, had always found it vast and unmanageable.

"That was damned nice of you to give up the Milton course to Keane," Fallor said.

"It was his in the first place."

"Even so."

"I was glad to get rid of it."

Fallor with uncharacteristic bonhomie slapped Rogerson on the arm. The locker room gesture turned Rogerson's thoughts again to golf. While these pale and bearded youngsters wasted the summer lecturing to reluctant students, he would be free as the breeze, plodding the fairways of indolence. The building seemed a place to escape from and he did, walking, half jogging, home. He felt great.

Heep had removed his stitches, Rogerson was no longer sore and swaddled and conscious of his pudendum as of an ailing appendage. He could not agree with Heep that the result of surgery was aesthetically remarkable. He half feared the urologist wanted a Polaroid shot for his files. This was not a far-fetched apprehension. The visit to Heep had ended with the doctor pressing a typewriter-paper box into Rogerson's hands.

"Take that along and look it over. Let me know what you think."

"I really won't have time to work on it. I'm teaching summer school."

"Just give me an opinion. It may not be as much work as you think."

Rogerson recognized the pride of authorship in Heep's voice, the hope, the fear, the insistence that others read what he had done. He took the box along. The barter basis Heep had suggested for the exchange was not unattractive, given the cost of the series of prostate massages. Blue Cross had covered the operation but not the massages. The *quid* of his editorial help could thus cover the *quo* of Heep's ministrations.

That night, when he uncovered the box and flipped through the top pages of the manuscript, Rogerson wanted to cover it right up again and drop it off at Heep's office, just put it on Mrs. Every's counter and get the hell out of there.

The English language became a foreign tongue in the hands of Heep. "Circumcision and Sexual Sensitivity" was a title that had been struck out. Several other possibilities had been penciled in. "The Foreskin as Carcinogenic." "You and Your Penis." "Your Foreskin and You." "I Am Joe's Penis." Rogerson tried to laugh, but was saddened by the vision Heep must have had while dictating this shapeless manuscript. And it was clear that it had been dictated. He could hear the urologist speak as he turned the pages. Had Heep been sustained through the long hours of dictation by the hope that one day his book, like those of so many other medical men who had found the pen more profitable than the scalpel, would be a best seller across the land, himself feted and deferred to, a guest in demand on talk shows from coast to coast, with perhaps—oh, nirvana—a felicific appearance on *The Tonight Show,* Francis X. Heep enters heaven? Only an ambition become obsessive explained how anyone could have filled so many pages with tedious banality. Heep had taken the route staked out for him by his many mentors: case studies. Mr. A and Mr. B and what Mrs. C had said, an alphabet soup of ciphers, less distinguishable than the letters which lent them a saving anonymity. All Heep's patients, after an interlude of sexual inactivity as the result of circumcision at an adult age, returned to the fray unencumbered by the prepuce. "It was like I'd never done it before," averred one happy client, while another contented customer, ringing changes on a barracks adage, said that it was like taking a shower without a raincoat on. Yet another, a Mr. F, testified that he had hitherto thought French ticklers were a fraud, a con man's overpromised delight. Now he knew the titillating truth. These testimonials had something of the uneaseful effect of the reports of religious conversion. The great difficulty, so far as Heep's hopes for a book went, was that there was no point in multiplying them. One was as good, or bad, as all; each said essentially the same thing and the message, Rogerson was sure, was Heep's, not theirs. As with Rogerson himself, Heep had so convinced himself of the benefits of the operation, quite aside from its prophylactic and preventive aspects, that he drummed into the prospective patient the words that would express the desired result. For his own part, Rogerson knew these to be lies. Not that he had put himself to the ultimate test. Infidelity aside, there was no immediate prospect of experimentation, but the promised effects, short of undreamed-of connubial joy, had simply not put in an appearance. Heep's surgical technique was minimal and no amount of healing seemed likely to make his organ look other than it would have if a third had been severed in some awful accident and then clumsily sewn back on. Nor was his case unique.

In the box, along with the manuscript, was a large legal envelope containing snapshots Heep had made of his patients, before and after. Shuffling through them, Rogerson felt that he had come upon a pervert's album, though these pictures were covered by that commodious ideal, the quest for scientific knowledge. The parade of privates, in lurid color, taken with a Polaroid to eliminate the middleman, did not tell the story that Heep would address to the world. The unmaimed members looked healthier and happier to Rogerson. Bah. With a rueful sigh, he returned the pictures to their envelope, the envelope to the box, and covered it. "Foreshortened Perspective: The Scalpel's Edge," a memoir by Severus Heep as told to Matthew Rogerson. He pushed the box away.

If Rogerson had any specific complaint, it was that he had no feeling in his penis. It seemed numb, an arm or leg fallen asleep while the rest of him remained awake. At the urinal he had to have visual verification that he had matters in hand; he might have been wearing one of Heep's rubber gloves.

"That's your imagination," Heep had said.

"No, it's my penis."

Heep flicked the tip of it with his fingernail. Rogerson felt nothing. Heep frowned at him. He tried again. Nothing. Heep began to say something, fell into a professional silence, finally said, "Well, yes, that sometimes happens. A slight trauma."

"Trauma?"

"It's like a virus. Give it a little time."

Rogerson suspected the worst. Heep had severed nerves, no messages received at that outpost would ever again be conveyed to his brain. If he was still erectile, as he was—proof positive of that was available in the usual matutinal manner—he was little better off than if he were impotent. Pain that you cannot feel is no longer pain, and the same holds true of pleasure.

"I'll sue you if it stays the way it is."

"Ha ha."

But Heep's eyes darted about the room and he retreated to a sink to wash his hands. The mention of litigation made him nervous as a cat. Perhaps he had had more than his share of it.

Now, with Heep's manuscript on his desk, Rogerson felt half accomplice of the scalpel-happy urologist. How many others had permitted themselves to be wheeled into surgery, the inflated hope of renewed sexual prowess vying with the fear of cancer of the genitals, only to find that their last state was worse than their first? Were they too embarrassed to complain? Of course, they could always fall back on the fact that they had not caught cancer, Heep getting credit for the calamity that did not befall them. How would he tell Heep his verdict of his book? Gently, of course. God only knew what the fury of a urologist scorned might be; hiking his bill well beyond what he knew Blue Shield would cover?

But enough of prose. Rogerson drew lovingly toward him the notebook into which his verse was put.

> These circles from
> a further heaven
> than the rain
> that makes them
> come, appear
> when drops alight,
> wheel outward from
> the central splash
> to an ordained
> periphery
> till they unlike

their prototype,
and me, are gone.

A mood of melancholy reverie, that from which his verse emerged, descended upon him and he felt abused by Marge. As Herb had said, he was now free to join her and the kids in Wisconsin for the summer, but he could not face the prospect of months at Lake Walleye. What then? If he told her he was not teaching summer school, she would insist that he come to the cottage. He formed an image of Marge insisting that he come at once. This was strangely hard to do and unconvincing when done. Did she really give a damn whether he was with her or not? After all, she had Wadley, with whom to talk about possible real estate deals, and should things become dull, they could go up in his plane and do the loop-the-loop over the lake while below the kids cheered.

Rogerson was drinking gin and tonic, more gin than tonic, and he had left out the slice of lime after the first one. He moved from the desk to the chair in which he read, overstuffed, unsprung, comfortable as old slippers. Ah. The basement was cool; through the open window over the desk, filtered by the arborvitae which sheltered the window, came summer sounds: children at play, the sound of tires on the street, a sustained kissing sound, birds. A cardinal sang with passion somewhere near. Rogerson sipped his drink. The good life was a matter of recognizing moments of perfection when they occurred. He rejected the thought. The good life should be a matter of character rather than accident. Very well. It took character to receive with good grace the perfect moment granted by God. Much more acceptable stated thus. What a lovely drink is gin.

Marge liked gin only in martinis. Marge. During their courtship he had called her Margarine, almost risqué in the dairy state, that term of endearment. Courtship, marriage, a day almost a quarter of a century ago yet imaginatively near for Rogerson. From it stretched so many years that nonetheless seemed not so long a span, reaching to today. Today, when Marge was in Wisconsin, at a cottage with their children, inhabiting an inheritance from her father which connected her too palpably with pre-Rogerson days and he, five hundred miles distant, here, alone, drinking gin. A strange situation, but if it was in any way culpable, he decided that the guilt could not be his. After all, he was home. Home, in the first place, because he had had an operation and applied for summer school to disguise that fact. He had wanted to free Marge for the summer, wasn't that it? His magnanimity, remembered over gin, loomed enormous, brought tears to his eyes. In retrospect, those days in the hospital, more particularly when he had been under the anesthetic and, worse, under the knife, Marge all unknowing, seemed poignant. He saw himself as self-effacing, a sacrificial lamb of sorts, his prepuce offered as propitiation, so that Marge might have the summer at her cottage. Her cottage.

Rogerson's thoughts turned to Sylvia Wood. She was the new woman, amoral as the day is long. The mind is a tireless negotiator. His operation, Heep's manuscript, the urologist's prediction as to the sensitivity of his healed self, the loss of moral fiber as it crept into his home in the form of Marge's discontent, his own sense of being somewhat badly used, Sylvia Wood. No worse for being unclear, this sequence added up in Rogerson's gin-clouded mind to the imperative that he discover, for scientific reasons, whether Sylvia's straightforwardness was bluff or a genuine invitation to a still pretty agile if forty-seven-year-old Rogerson.

He was wakened by the doorbell and sat up quickly. The room was warm, his head ached, he was very hungry. His watch read three o'clock. The doorbell rang again and he swung his legs off the bed.

Plummet-Finch and Grundtvig stood on the porch, staring at the screen door they could not, with the sun upon it, see through. Rogerson let them in.

"Matthew, you look awful," Plummet-Finch said.

Gilbert himself had the deepest tan Rogerson had ever seen on the old Oxonian. Grundtvig said briskly that he had stopped at Rogerson's office and not found him in, whereupon Plummet-Finch had suggested they try to reach him at home.

"Do you have a drink?" Gilbert asked.

"There may be a drop in the house. As you know, I myself do not drink."

"Don't drink?"

"I gave it up."

"I don't believe you."

"Is gin all right?"

"Gin would be lovely."

"Grundtvig?"

"I'd like a beer if you have any."

"No beer. Have some gin."

"No, thanks."

Rogerson made a gin and tonic for Plummet-Finch and another for himself. He opened a beer for Grundtvig.

"I found one," he announced, giving the bottle of beer to the president of the campus chapter of the AAUP.

He had to go back to the kitchen for his own drink. Why had Gilbert brought Grundtvig here? Rogerson disapproved of the bogus proletarian look affected by Grundtvig. Denims, a filthy shirt, beads of some savage tribe dangling from his neck. He wore his long hair in a ponytail. His mustache was flowing, giving him a piratical appearance. His extra-academic specialty was Jane Austen.

Rogerson moved them out onto the porch, where Grundtvig, after standing and brooding over the lawn as if that much untilled land pained his serf's soul, said abruptly, "Did Laplace take away the summer course you were assigned to teach?"

Rogerson sighed. "Bad news travels fast."

"What reason did he give?"

"He'd had a request."

"No doubt. It was completely within Keane's rights to want a course, but for Laplace to wrest yours from you is another matter."

"You mean that Keane's rights can't be respected?"

"It depends, it depends. How were you informed?"

"Does it matter?"

Grundtvig glared at him. "Rogerson, this concerns all of us. Of course it matters. Whenever a dean or a chancellor, or a chairman, treats the faculty like shit, it matters."

"I suppose you're right."

"Of course I'm right."

Rogerson looked at Plummet-Finch and saw only skepticism in his eyes.

"I've never seen Laplace more ruthless," Rogerson said, sitting back in his chair. His headache had settled behind his eyes and he

148

rubbed them. When he opened them again, multicolored circles spun through the air between himself and Grundtvig. "And remember, I've known Laplace a lot longer than the rest of you. I knew him before he became drunk with power. Have I ever told you of the Reinhardt Schmidt case?"

"We have a dossier on Laplace a foot thick," Grundtvig assured him. "Tell me what happened this morning."

Grundtvig was so thirsty for injustice it would have been churlish not to feed him deep draughts of it. But first Rogerson set the scene; no matter the impatience of the president of the local chapter of the AAUP, the thing could not be appreciated if the setting was not given. Upon entering the dean's office, the outer office, actually, he came upon Laplace's secretary, Norah Vlach, crying at her desk. Thinking, with the egocentricity of the oppressed, that she had been moved to tears by his own misfortune, Rogerson stopped to soothe her. Imagine his surprise when she informed him that she wept not for him but for herself. Laplace had just spent fifteen minutes mocking her religious beliefs. Grundtvig's eyes narrowed. He had the agnostic's passion for freedom of worship.

"I tried to console her as best I could and then proceeded, on her instructions, into the inner office. The dean, Herbert Laplace, was standing at the window, his back to me. I announced myself, but the dean did not turn around. 'Sit down,' he barked. Stunned, I nonetheless sat. A full minute passed in silence. When the dean turned I saw that he held a small but powerful pair of opera glasses in his hand. His eyes seemed to bulge from his head as he came toward me. He held out the glasses. 'Come, take a look,' he said in a guttural voice. I took the glasses, not understanding his intent. At the window, he told me to direct the glasses at a given spot on the mall in front of his office. 'The one in the red halter,' he rasped. 'Those are the biggest tits I've seen today.' "

Plummet-Finch snorted. Grundtvig glared at Gilbert. "Go on, Rogerson."

"I said something inappropriate and returned to my chair. The dean sat behind his desk."

"Yes?" Grundtvig sat forward.

" 'I'm taking you out of *Paradise Lost,*' he said."

" 'You can't,' I cried.

149

'O for that warning voice, which he who saw
Th' Apocalypse, heard cry in Heaven aloud . . .'
But you know the lines.''

Plummet-Finch did. " 'Woe to the inhabitants on earth,' " he quoted.

Grundtvig said, ''What reason did he have?''

" 'What reason can you have?' I asked. 'Reason!' he snorted. 'I have no need of reasons. Bismarck proposes and I dispose.' "

''Bismarck?''

''The chancellor.''

''Wooley?'' Grundtvig was excited now. ''Wooley himself was behind this?''

''Of course, Laplace could have been lying.''

''Why would he lie?''

Rogerson shrugged. ''I asked him what reason Chancellor Wooley might have for summarily removing me from a course on the first day of summer school, particularly after I had already met the class.''

''You had actually begun teaching the course?''

''The class met as scheduled at nine that morning.''

''Good.''

''Shouldn't you be taking notes?''

''No need for that.''

''I thought you considered the matter important.''

''Of course I consider it important.''

''He is recording all this, Matthew,'' Plummet-Finch said sweetly. ''Do go on.''

Grundtvig's recorder, a Japanese model comprising the latest in miniaturization, had looked to Rogerson to be a transistor radio. He had found it credible that Grundtvig, like the students he lionized, went about with the cacophonous rock blasting in his ear.

''It's all bullshit,'' Rogerson said to Grundtvig.

''You can say that again.''

''I mean what I've been telling you.''

''I don't understand.''

Plummet-Finch said, ''Dear Grundtvig, he has been pulling your leg.''

Grundtvig still did not understand. ''Why don't you finish?'' he said to Rogerson. Plummet-Finch opened his hands and looked at the ceiling. Rogerson, with his disclaimer recorded, saw no reason not to go on. He went on until Grundtvig was out of tape, sketching a drama of such cavalier mistreatment on Herb's part and such long-suffering innocence on his own that he became quite caught up in the narrative. Plummet-Finch went inside to freshen his drink, unable to act as witness without support.

"I think we have him this time," Grundtvig said, snapping off his machine.

"Do you really think so?"

"Look, you did sign an agreement, didn't you? A contract?"

"I told you I did."

"So it's a legal matter. This time there won't be time wasted over ethics and intention and all that rot. Where is your copy of the contract?"

"I have it somewhere."

"My God, I should think so. Where?"

"Probably in my office on campus."

"Guard it with your life." Grundtvig stood and drained the beer bottle. He placed it carefully on the ledge of the porch. "I would advise you to bring that contract home. We have reason to believe that our offices are systematically searched from time to time. Do you have a safe-deposit box?"

"What makes you think our offices are searched?"

Grundtvig looked shrewd, or tried to. His expression suggested a man examining the tip of his own nose.

"Who goes through the offices, in your opinion?"

"Laplace, for sure. He may bring another dean or two along."

"What would they be looking for?"

Grundtvig shrugged.

"Miss Ortmund's vibrator is missing," Rogerson mused.

"Her vibrator?"

"She has arthritis. Anyway, it's missing."

"Miss Ortmund is missing most of her marbles," Grundtvig said.

"Then you've heard about that?"

Grundtvig was puzzled. "About what?"

"Her marbles. Small Indian sculptures, erotic poses, some in marble, but most in jade. The most valuable was the 'Jaded Embrace,'

151

which dates from the eighth century. The Ding dynasty."

"I hadn't heard."

"Of course, they were insured, but they are irreplaceable."

"I think Laplace is after bigger booty."

"Miss Ortmund has a small foot," Rogerson agreed.

"Correspondence, evidence of scholarly work; particularly, I think, any indication that a person is angling for a job elsewhere."

"You think he might try to steal my contract?"

"You said you know him better than the rest of us. I wouldn't put it past him."

"You may be right."

"I'm going," Grundtvig called into the house.

"Go along," Plummet-Finch trilled. "I shall be staying."

Plummet-Finch waited inside until Grundtvig had gone off up the driveway, then slipped out onto the porch again. His drink looked very fresh.

"Isn't he the most complete ass you've ever seen, Matthew?"

"It's hard to tell when he's seated."

Gilbert made a wet, reproving noise. "Grundtvig as faculty advocate! Ah, well, I suppose we deserve no better. Do you know he had the effrontery to tell me he is an expert on Jane Austen? I forbade him to continue on that subject. There ought to be a law, an international law, preventing people like Grundtvig from reading Jane. He could not possibly understand a word she wrote."

"How was Morocco?"

"Who said I was in Morocco?"

"Sylvia."

"That girl cannot keep a secret."

"What's the secret? After all, Gide spent a lot of time in North Africa."

"Did he?" Gilbert said frostily.

"You got a nice tan."

"Africa does have that effect on one."

"You don't want to talk about it?"

"No."

"Very well."

"Oh, it was pleasant enough. I hate short trips, in and out; they leave one a wreck."

"I should think so."

Gilbert took a long drink from his glass, then sighed. "You do realize that Grundtvig thought you were telling him the gospel truth about your interview with Laplace?"

"He'll figure it out when he listens to the tape."

"Put that in the form of a wager and I would be inclined to oppose you."

"Then someone else will listen to the tape and explain to Grundtvig that he is stupid."

"That too I should bet against."

"Morocco has given you a low opinion of your fellow man. Did you meet a robot in Rabat who didn't know what's what, who wouldn't take the bit between his teeth, a robot who when censured declared that he was insured, and wouldn't be the under of your neath?"

"I'd never heard that before."

"You couldn't have."

"Matthew, what about summer school?"

"I gave up my course to Keane. He was delighted because his other, on Baudelaire, was undersubscribed. Over ninety souls signed up for *Paradise Lost.*"

"Curious."

"They certainly were. There was a young lady named Hopper . . ."

"That sounds like a limerick."

"She could hardly wait to have a dialogue."

"Aha. Then Marge is still away?"

"For the summer. I have been abandoned."

"Poor you. What will you do?"

"Apart from write poetry? I shall await replies to the notice I ran in the *New York Review of Books.*"

Rogerson often consulted this paper in the library, not to read the unconscionably long reviews of books that the reviewers often neglected to mention, but to study the personals in the back pages. What if any was the sinuous connection between the hand-wringing moralism of the articles and reviews and those perverse pleas in the personal columns? "Moody forty-seven-year-old professor, no joiner, member of ACLU, Soren Kierkegaard Society and Home Canners

Association, into haiku, John of the Cross and tatting, cosmopolitan, lifelong resident of Midwest, would like to meet neurotic matron on Tuesdays, 1:05 to 2:31 P.M., her place." "Achtung: my bête noire is bestiality, so you sheepdippers south of northwestern Ohio watch it . . . my back is up. You're not much wisewise if this word does not suffice."

"Poetry?" Gilbert said.

"Mainly limericks. You were right. There was a young lady named Hopper, who put up my giggy a stopper . . ."

Gilbert had put down his drink and clamped his hands over his ears. Rogerson's head still ached. He was hungry. He had not eaten lunch. Gilbert moved his hands away from his ears, tested the silence, picked up his drink. He sighed with boredom.

"I have half a mind to ring up Eric."

"Brenda's boy?"

"Going cold turkey is a difficult thing. Eric never lets one down."

"I'm told he grows his own."

"Nonsense. He imports from Cleveland. Rather good stuff."

"You can't use my phone."

"You are such a prig, Matthew. Would you care to join me?"

"No, thanks."

"You don't care for it?"

"I've never tried it."

"You're not serious."

Was he really the only holdout? He would have thought his gray hairs protected him from such condescension. First Sylvia, now Plummet-Finch. But pot was part of the larger picture: porn, infidelity, women's lib, contraception, divorce. What the hell did Sylvia and Gilbert care about the future of the family? Their anomie put Rogerson on the ramparts, defending a doomed civilization. Was Grundtvig too a hophead? No doubt. The moralizers were always the worst. That was the link between the editorial stance of the *New York Review of Books* and those wretched ads in personals. Morality had ceased to be personal; it had been reduced to other people's public acts, the oppressive nature thereof. But surely a nation of ass hounds deserved all the tyranny they got. His headache apart, Rogerson's head spun with the contradiction. People professed to want a well-ordered society, a just distribution of wealth and goods, while behind every closed door every imaginable kind of perversion was indulged. His head spun too with the thought that Sylvia Wood would doubtless bed with him for the dual purpose of short-circuited conjugation and the lamentation of administrative iniquity.

"What did you do in Morocco, Gilbert?"

"I won't bore you," Plummet-Finch said, draining his glass and getting to his feet. "And I won't use your telephone either, you old fuddy-dud."

"Thanks for bringing Grundtvig over."

"I am sorry about that."

"Ta ta."

The following morning at nine o'clock, Herb Laplace was waiting on the first tee when Rogerson arrived carrying his bag of discount-drugstore clubs. Herb wore checked shorts and an ill-fitting polo shirt. The rain hat pulled down over his eyes gave him the appearance of a soda fountain habitué of long ago.

"Son of an habitué, anyway," Herb said, slashing about with his driver. "Hurry up. We go out after that threesome."

The reference was to three students about to tee off. Their drives snapped off with an authoritative crack, rode a rising line for two hundred yards out onto the fairway, dropped and continued for another fifty yards. Herb watched these performances with nodding approval. Was he capable of as much?

"How about a buck a hole?" he asked Rogerson.

"Are we going to play eighteen?"

"Why not? We can finish in time for lunch."

Rogerson agreed. He agreed too that Herb should hit first. The threesome had arrived at their balls and in minutes three picture approach shots were on the green.

"They're pretty good," Rogerson said.

"I don't think they'll hold us up."

Herb teed up his ball, took a number of practice swings which were reasonable imitations of those the threesome had taken, stepped forward and addressed his ball. Half a minute went by, Herb frozen in concentration, then slowly, slowly his club head moved back until it was well behind his ear, parallel with the ground. This auspicious beginning was shortly negated when Herb brought the club down in a lunging, go-for-broke movement. Club met ball, Herb twisted, nearly losing his balance. The ball rose swiftly, going straight for the middle of the fairway, but then, fifty yards out, veered sharply to the right, described a great lazy arc and disappeared over a bush into another fairway.

"Shit," Herb said, stooping to pick up his tee. He sauntered to his clubs and Rogerson had the impression that the dean was not wholly displeased with the result.

When he had teed up his own ball, Rogerson stood over it and was filled with uncertainty as to the proper position of his feet, his arms, his hands, his distance from the ball and the general drift of the universe. He had no memory whatsoever of having hit a golf ball before.

"Hit the damned thing," Herb urged.

Rogerson remained immobile. Once he started his backswing, he would be committed. Why had he thought of golfing, why had he phoned Herb the night before to suggest that they go out together? As if in a dream, seemingly of its own accord, his club head began to move. Rogerson allowed things to happen. The only rule he remembered was to keep his eye on the ball. He swung. The ball was gone. By the time he looked up, he could see no trace of it.

"Where did it go?"

"You skyed it," Herb said.

"But where did it land?"

"It hasn't yet."

Finally the ball came to earth, about seventy-five yards out from the tee but in the fairway. Herb had already started off the tee, pulling his cart, loping in the direction of his ball. Rogerson walked alone to his. The green was still two hundred yards away and a wood shot was out of the question; Rogerson did not trust them. But which iron? A three. Rogerson took it from his bag and looked at it. It seemed to have no more loft than a putter. He exchanged it for a seven. Again he felt a sense of complete unfamiliarity when he stood over the ball. He chopped at it and it went grudgingly another seventy-five yards. From the other fairway, screened by bushes, Herb's voice was audible, his language obscene. Apparently he had dubbed a shot. Some minutes later, a ball entered the first fairway and dribbled to a stop ten yards ahead of Rogerson's. Herb came up while Rogerson again stood over his ball, a seven iron in his hand.

"What club have you got?" Herb asked.

"A seven."

"You're crazy."

"I like it."

"It's your dollar."

Rogerson meditated for a moment, liking the look of the white ball half buried in the grass. He swung. His divot was taken well behind the ball. The ball itself settled a short way beyond Herb's. Herb laughed tolerantly.

"You bent your elbow."

"I should hope so."

"Your left elbow should remain straight."

"Show me."

Herb did. His ball rose magnificently, as if it had been shot from a cannon. It came to rest in a sand trap next to the green. Herb swore.

"It was well hit," Rogerson said.

Herb glared at him. To placate his partner, Rogerson exchanged his seven for a five iron. He told himself not to bend his elbow. He topped the ball, an error which conferred on it a saving overspin. It trickled onto the green.

"Was that your fifth?" Herb asked.

"No. My fourth."

"We both lie four," Herb said.

Herb was out of the trap in three more strokes, though the third sent the ball clear across the green into some heavy grass. With his putter, Herb knocked the ball onto the green. Rogerson needed three putts to get his ball into the hole. So too did Herb.

On the second tee, Herb got out pencil and card. "What did you have?"

"Seven."

"We halved the hole. I retain the honors."

Herb sliced his drive into the first fairway and went immediately after it. Rogerson, unobserved, hit a seven iron from the tee. He used his seven iron all the way and was on the green in five. Herb seemed to be lost. Rogerson was about to go in search of him when a ball dropped onto the green and Herb burst through the bushes, following the shot. Seeing it drop on the green, he whooped. "On in three," he yelled.

Before the putting began, Laplace asked Rogerson how many strokes he had taken.

"Five."

"Be careful."

The warning had an adverse effect on Rogerson. Again it took him three putts to get down. Herb too needed three putts.

"My hole," Herb crowed. Rogerson bristled at the triumphant tone. Doubts about Herb's arithmetical abilities rose in him. Somewhat defiantly, he drew his seven iron from his bag on the third tee.

"What the hell are you going to do with that?"

"Just hit your ball."

Herb did, a beautiful long ball. Unfortunately it headed straight for the fence and out of bounds. He topped his second try and it dribbled out twenty yards from the tee. Rogerson with his seven iron got an easy hundred yards. Herb took out a four wood and managed to advance his ball fifty yards before the grass slowed, then stopped, its progress. Rogerson got another decent seven-iron shot. Herb hooked his next shot, but it stopped short of the fence. He was stymied behind a tree. Rogerson saw him kick his ball five yards, but said nothing. Herb's next shot went into a trap bordering the green. With another seven iron, Rogerson was on.

"On in three," he cried. Herb said nothing.

Again it took Herb three tries to get out of the sand, but his third put the ball inches from the hole. A tap in. Rogerson needed three putts.

"Six," Rogerson said.

"Me too." Herb shook his head with disgust.

"Six?"

Herb stared at him, but said nothing.

Rogerson said, "You hit one over the fence."

"You want me to count that?"

"What does it matter what *I* want?"

"I thought this was a friendly match."

"Of course it is. But let's use the series of natural numbers, all right?"

"What is that supposed to mean?"

"Forget it."

"Forget it? Are you accusing me of cheating?"

"Herb, I saw you take eight shots, not counting the ball you hit over the fence or the time you kicked your ball out of a bad lie."

"You sonofabitch."

"Did I win the hole or didn't I?"

"Listen, Rogerson. All bets are off. On the golf course, a man's word is his bond. If you're going to doubt me, there isn't much point in playing with you."

"I agree."

"All right."

Rogerson strode toward the next tee. So did Herb. They reached it together, neither acknowledging the presence of the other. Rogerson teed up his ball. So did Herb. Rogerson addressed his ball with his seven iron, keeping his head down; he must not look at Herb. He swung. He all but missed the ball. It trickled perhaps thirty yards into very deep rough. Meanwhile Herb's drive seemed to gain power from his wrath. The meeting of club head and ball produced a resounding crack. Rogerson's eye was drawn toward the fairway. High in the sky, almost invisible, a white speck seemed to accelerate as it went. Herb had driven his ball well over two hundred yards. Despite themselves their eyes met. Herb, made bashful by success, was moved to magnanimity.

"Okay, Matt. You won the last hole."

"So we're even?"

"We're even. Still a buck a hole?"

Rogerson hesitated. After one stroke he was scarcely off the tee, in grass that hid his ball, while Herb was an easy chip shot from the green. "All right."

In two more strokes, Rogerson was on the edge of the fairway. Herb, as if fearful such example might influence his own game, headed for some bushes to take a leak. Rogerson teed up his ball and drew his driver from the bag. He addressed the ball quickly and swung. He missed everything. He stepped back and began to flay with his club, trying to create the impression that he was taking practice swings in case Herb had been watching from his bush. On the next try, Rogerson connected mightily. With his heart in his

159

throat, he watched his ball soar effortlessly and drop beyond Herb's drive. He stamped his tee into the ground and set off down the fairway.

"Sounded good," Herb said, coming out of hiding.

"It was all right."

"What do you lie?"

"Four."

Herb smiled. Rogerson felt hatred for the dean. His inward joy was exquisite when a moment later Herb took up half a foot of grass and did not overtake Rogerson, whose ball was several club lengths farther on. Herb swore. Rogerson now noticed that it was a lovely day, the sky blue and cloudless, and birds sang somewhere. Herb's next shot was extremely good, too good; it carried over the green and into some trees. With two strokes of his seven iron, Rogerson was not only on the green, but four inches from the hole. Herb was still detained by the woods, out of sight, though several times Rogerson heard what seemed to be a hit and then the sound of a ball caroming and ricocheting among the trees. The sound of Herb's cursing seemed to confirm that unsuccessful efforts were being made there in the woods. When the ball did come out, preceded by no sound of a hit, it landed in a sand trap. Herb got out of the sand in one, but the ball rolled off the green. After getting on, he three-putted.

"You owe me a dollar," Rogerson said.

"What did you get?"

"Seven."

Herb snorted. "I had a six."

"You have to count those before you came out of the woods too."

"That does it." Herb threw down his putter. "I won't golf with a man who doubts my word."

"Then you won't golf with me."

"You can bet on that."

"Herb, I wouldn't bet with you on anything."

"So you're quitting."

"No, I'm not quitting. I am going to finish my game."

"That may take till Sunday."

"I'll finish if it takes till doomsday."

"I won't play with you."

160

"You're goddam right you won't."

They stood glaring at one another. Sweat ran down Herb's face. His polo shirt was wet with perspiration. His ridiculous shorts were twisted around his middle so that the side pocket was in front. Herb shook his head slowly. He picked up his putter and put it into his bag. He grasped the handle of his cart, turned smartly on one heel and marched away over the fairways in the direction of the clubhouse.

"Cheater," Rogerson yelled after him.

Herb's shoulders lifted and his back stiffened, but he continued on his way. Rogerson picked up his bag and went morosely in search of the next tee. There he sat on a bench, brooding. He had lost all interest in golf. He would give Herb time to get clear of the clubhouse, then go in himself. There was a map of the course on the back of the score card. Rogerson located the ninth tee. He would head for that and play in on nine. Laplace would certainly be gone when he came off the ninth green.

Sylvia Wood stood on the ninth tee, alone, swinging a club with an expertness that would have commanded attention even if she had not been wearing a single-piece terry-cloth suit, armless, shorts, that zipped up the front. The bill of her white cap jutted out over her eyes.

"Where on earth did you come from?" she asked when Rogerson came through the spirea onto the tee.

"Are you going in nine?"

"Of course. I didn't see you on eight."

"I didn't see you either."

"Are you alone?"

"Are you?"

"I always golf alone."

"I started out with Herb Laplace. We argued."

"How could you go out golfing with him after what he did to you?"

"What do you have in mind?"

"Taking away your Milton course. Grundtvig is seething."

"How reassuring to have Grundtvig as my champion."

"It isn't just the faculty who are angry. A girl named Hopper stopped by my office today. She has dropped the course now that Keane is taking over. You made quite an impression on her."

161

"Maybe we should drive off."

Sylvia agreed and addressed her ball. She shifted her hips several times while the toes of her white golf shoes went nervously up and down. Her backswing was almost slow motion, she came through the ball as if illustrating the proper way to swing, her ball zinged out straight and true, never rising higher than five feet off the ground. It came to rest at the small juniper tree which marked two hundred yards.

"Very good."

"Thank you."

Rogerson hit a three iron one hundred and fifty yards and by the time they had holed out he had taken twice as many strokes as Sylvia. Losing to her was not as depressing as losing to Herb, if he had indeed done that. Sylvia was young, she seemed a natural athlete, and besides, playing with her he found it possible to entertain the thought that there was something faintly undesirable about being good at golf. A gentleman's game, that is all he wished to play. Sylvia herself took no excessive pleasure in her manifest skill.

"Going to play the back nine?" she asked.

"I don't think so."

"Let's have a Coke."

They had their drinks on the porch of the clubhouse overlooking the eighteenth green. Rogerson found the cool glass soothing to his sore hands. Blisters had formed on his palms. When he got home he intended to put the clubs away, in the attic, basement or garage, and forget them forever. Golf, it was now clear, is a bourgeois pastime, not the way he intended to spend his summer.

"I suppose you'll be joining your family now."

"No."

"You're going to fight Laplace?"

"In order to teach Milton?" Rogerson laughed. "Sylvia, the story Grundtvig is passing around is completely false."

"But he says you are his source."

"I was pulling his leg. I told him as much, but he didn't seem to grasp the point."

"He is arousing the campus."

"Has he talked to Keane yet?"

"It isn't Keane's fault."

"There isn't any fault at all. I wanted out of the course. Over ninety students signed up for it. Keane needed a course. I was happy to deliver it into his hands. All Laplace did was agree to the transfer."

"You're serious?"

"That is all that happened. Grundtvig is an ass. Apparently he is in the process of proving that fact to the one or two people still unaware of it."

"He'll make trouble."

"Only for himself. Laplace will demolish him."

"That is a cruel thing to do to him."

"I know. But not cruel enough. Anyone who is active in the AAUP deserves whatever he gets."

"But we all benefit from the AAUP's efforts."

"Do we? If you're prepared to argue that the present situation on this campus is beneficial to us or anyone, you could have a point. The AAUP, for all its vaunted opposition to the administration, is its mirror image. They have succeeded in making teaching into a mere job; our function has become a commodity. I loathe this life. My secret dream is to become a day laborer, digging ditches, paving streets, some simple task which accomplishes an observable goal."

"You're a romantic."

"Of course I'm a romantic. When I came into teaching one had to be a romantic, particularly about things like eating, paying rent, raising children. I had no idea what professors were paid until I signed my first contract. I'm sure you knew what the salary schedules were before you completed a semester of graduate work."

"There's nothing wrong with wanting to earn a living."

Rogerson finished his Coke. He had no wish to argue the meaning of life with Sylvia. His own thoughts on the matter were muddled and obscure. How lovely the course looked in the late morning sunlight. Perhaps he would sit on here awhile when Sylvia resumed her round. He suggested that she would be wanting to head for the tenth tee.

"To tell you the truth, I've lost interest."

"Don't be silly."

"You certainly made an impression on Miss Hopper."

"Perhaps she discerned in me a contrary spirit. You and she have much in common."

"She's a brazen little witch. Do you know she asked me where she could get pot on the campus?"

"What did you tell her?"

"I said, I wish I knew."

"Very shrewd."

"It's true. All the sources seem to have dried up."

"What a pity."

"Yes."

She gazed out over the course, rocking her golf shoes on the concrete floor so that the spikes made a rhythmic sound.

"Come to dinner tonight, Matt."

He did not answer. Her words were like a reply to his imaginary ad in the personals column of the *New York Review of Books*. Dangerous thoughts stirred in his breast. A night of dalliance with a comely lass who lived beyond good and evil? What harm could he do? Surely there was no question of corrupting her. The times, the general dissolution, had already accomplished that. His own moral principles aside, why shouldn't he take advantage of her invitation? Sylvia had stood. She seemed to be making a point of not looking at him.

"Don't decide now. I'll get in touch with you later."

"All right."

"You'll be at home?"

"Yes."

He watched her walk down the asphalt path toward the tenth tee, pulling her cart, the leather flaps on her shoes flopping up and down, the spikes making an oddly attractive sound. He felt in the grip of some strange perversion, a footnote in Krafft-Ebing. Subject impotent save in the presence of nude girls wearing golf shoes with giant spikes.

"Eric? This is Matthew Rogerson. I have an unusual request to make."

"I'm no longer in the bicycle business."

"So I heard."

"From your friend Chief Ketchum?"

164

"Your mother told me."

A derisive laugh came over the wire. Rogerson was having second thoughts about the wisdom of this call. His pulse galloped. He was sweating. A lifetime as a more or less law-abiding citizen was in the balance.

"I'd like some . . . grass." He decided on the slang word, hoping this would sound less like a first offense.

"You're kidding."

"I am perfectly serious. I have been told that you can supply me."

"Who told you that?"

"Is it necessary to give names?"

"Unless you want me to hang up."

"Gilbert Plummet-Finch."

"Aha."

"Can you help me?"

"Where do you usually get it?"

"The usual sources have dried up."

"Well, it's summer, you know. The amateur suppliers have gone."

"Can I pick it up this evening?"

"Assuming I had any, how much do you want?"

Rogerson had no idea of the quantities in which marijuana is sold. Indeed, he had no idea of the condition in which it might come. He said, "Ten should be enough."

"Ten ounces?"

"If you have it." Rogerson had meant ten cigarettes. Ten ounces did not seem much.

"That's a pretty big order. And expensive."

"How much?"

Eric named a price. Rogerson was astounded.

"Will you take a check?"

"Why not a credit card? No, cash on the barrelhead."

"Very well. I'll drop by at five. Before your mother comes home."

"Don't hurry. She'll be delighted to see you."

"As I would be to see her, normally. I don't think she need know of this transaction. Surely you agree?"

"So it's a secret?"

"Of course it's a secret."

"From Norah Vlach as well?"

"From everyone," Rogerson said angrily.

"I mention her because she is here with me now. You interrupted us while we were in prayer."

Rogerson hung up. He sat staring at the phone. It had been a mistake to call Eric. This sort of thing should be done anonymously, a furtive exchange on a street corner, buyer and seller strangers. But he had no idea how he could do that, what corner he should go to, what sign he might give to indicate his intention. If he was going to surprise Sylvia with the wherewithal for an interesting evening, he would have to do business with Eric. He tried to think of this as on a level with bringing wine, marijuana as aphrodisiac, but the undeniable difference was that wine was not against the law. The note of danger, of the illicit, added zest to the evening. Rogerson went upstairs to shower. It was scarcely noon and he was atremble with anticipation.

"Are you down there?"

It was Sylvia, calling at the head of the stairs. Rogerson, having showered and eaten lunch, had descended to his basement study the better to escape the heat of the day. He rose from his desk.

"I'll come up."

But Sylvia came thundering down the stairs. A skirt of minimal dimensions had been wrapped around the outfit in which she had been golfing. She was barefoot and came gingerly across the basement floor to the carpet whose borders were the boundaries of Rogerson's study.

"What a neat place to work. I did knock, by the way. The door was open, so I came in. I heard you typing."

She went directly to the desk, quite shamelessly bent over to look at the sheet in the machine. Rogerson had been transcribing a fragment of verse, hoping that the lines he had written would when typed suggest their sequel.

"Whose is that?"

"I didn't think you'd recognize it." Rogerson could not think of a ploy to get her away from the desk that would not involve touching her. His heated thoughts about the coming evening conferred on her an additional attractiveness which rendered him shy. "Please sit down."

166

She did, at the desk, though he had pointed to the easy chair. He himself now sat in it.

"Are you coming to dinner?"

"Yes."

"Wonderful. What's your favorite food?"

He said he had none. She persisted. He really did not have a thing to suggest.

"All right," she said. "I'll surprise you."

She had placed her hand on the box containing Heep's manuscript. Rogerson half rose from his chair. What must have been an apprehensive expression on his face brought a smile to hers. She drew the box toward her.

"More poems?"

"No."

He willed her to leave that box alone. In less than a minute he had disproved ESP, or perhaps had proved it. She had the top of the box off and with what now seemed terrible inevitability brought forth the envelope containing the Polaroid photographs of the genitalia of Heep's patients.

"Don't open that."

"Didn't I tell you? I'm terribly nosy."

She dumped the pictures onto the desk and for a moment there was an awful silence. She gathered them up, made a pile of them, looked about to shuffle them like playing cards. She was studying the top photograph without visible reaction.

"This is a side of you I didn't expect," she said clinically.

"That is someone else's side, I'm afraid."

"Well, you couldn't prove it by me."

She went on to several other photographs, then put them all back in the envelope. "They get rather repetitious."

"Reproductive is the word."

She giggled. "What on earth are you doing with those?"

"It's a research project."

She tipped her head to one side and looked at him through narrowed eyes, a strange smile on her face.

"Not mine. My urologist hopes to write a book. The manuscript is in that box. Those are his proposed illustrations."

"But what are you going to do with it?"

"He wanted editorial advice."

"I should think you would have suggested Gilbert."

"Good idea."

He found it oddly exciting that she should so casually mention Gilbert's presumed penchant. The promise of the evening no longer seemed merely a matter of his imagination. He realized that this frightened him. Would she be a connoisseur who would find him sadly wanting, hopelessly straightforward in his approach? He dismissed the thought. Sylvia had stood.

"Well, I wanted to find out if you were coming tonight. Now I have things to do."

"Don't go to any bother."

"But I want to."

"Now you are surprising me. I had no idea you would be so domestic."

She came to the chair and smiled down at him. Reaching out, she ruffled his hair. "Matthew, I am one hundred and ten pounds of surprises. Come at seven. Don't get up. Unless you want to lock your door. Anyone is likely to walk right in."

"So far I have no complaints."

Her smile of pleasure seemed utterly unliberated. Rogerson felt his apprehensions about the night ahead dissolve. All he had to do was remember that Sylvia was a woman.

"Write me a poem."

"I already have."

"Come on."

" 'Who is Sylvia and what is she that all . . .' "

She snorted and tiptoed to the stairs, then ran up them, her one hundred and ten pounds sounding substantial indeed as she did so. A moment later, he heard her pad through the house to the front door. Rogerson got up and put Heep's manuscript in a drawer of his desk.

Sylvia had an apartment in one of the student residence buildings on campus, though she did not fulfill the function of prefect. Rather she was a faculty presence meant, so went the permissive theory of the administration, to inhibit the more *outré* behavior of young people made frisky by living away from home and feeling that peculiar insistence of the flesh which afflicts those a year or so shy of twenty. That someone like Sylvia, not much older than the students, should exercise any repressive effect on their behavior was a thought only an ass could entertain, or an administrator who wished to make a gesture in the direction of conventional moral comportment and then not bother himself further. As a result, though orgies were infrequent, the residence hall had the general air of a bordello, male visitors coming in at all hours, staying the night, as frequent of a morning in the showers as the female residents. Counseling on contraception and sexual technique was available at the student health center, but for all that, students, as they had from time immemorial, relied generally on the more satisfying if also more demanding mentor of direct experience. Pregnancies were not unheard of, but thanks to the leniency of local physicians, in league with the student health service, this came to little more than an easily corrigible inconvenience. In this situation, if influence ran in any direction, it was from the students to Sylvia. Perhaps she felt a moral obligation to show the students that she was every bit as profligate as they. Is it not a senior's duty to give good example? As Rogerson suspected, Sylvia Wood accepted the absence of moral restraint as itself a moral code with its own exigencies, sanctions and supererogations.

He had scarcely knocked when she opened the door and pulled him inside. She peeked out, closed the door and breathed a sigh of relief.

"What's the matter?"

"Julia Hopper. I didn't want her to see you coming here."

"Oh?"

"Matt, she is perfectly capable of dropping in and staying till all hours. That girl is a menace. She has read everything. She makes me feel like a complete dope."

"Speaking of which."

Rogerson handed Sylvia the plastic bag he had purchased from Eric some hours earlier. In the interim he had felt its presence on his person like a leaden weight, accusatory, subversive. He was glad to get rid of it. Sylvia smiled naughtily.

"Is that what I think it is?"

"Yes."

"Why, you old pusher. Good grief, why did you bring so much?"

"It is a lot, isn't it?"

He had been surprised at the size of the bag Eric pulled from under his couch after Rogerson handed over the money.

"Will you need papers?" Eric had asked.

"Papers?"

"To roll it in." Eric looked disappointed. "Have you ever done this before?"

"No."

"I didn't think so."

"It's not for me."

"Hey, you're not going into business, are you?"

Rogerson had not answered. Let Eric wonder. He was anxious to get out of the house. His flesh tingled at the thought that Brenda might come home and find him here, furthering her son's life of crime. If she should ever find out, Rogerson was certain he would never hear the end of it. And of course the same was true of Norah Vlach.

"Was Norah really here when I phoned?"

"What difference would that make?"

"None. Unless you were stupid enough to tell her who called and why."

"I told her who it was. I think she thought you were showing concern for my spiritual welfare."

Leaving the house, Rogerson felt that he had betrayed the ideals of a lifetime. He belonged on the other side of the line, with Norah Vlach, no matter how flaky she had become. Better to be a religious fanatic than a new recruit to the drug culture. Rogerson was assailed by memories of his past caustic comments on drug use, comments made over the years and with complete sincerity. Did he really want to try pot? Surely he felt no overwhelming compulsion to do so. As he walked away, taking a route that he hoped would ensure avoidance of the returning Brenda, he had nowhere on his person to adequately conceal the bulky plastic bag he had bought from Eric. He imagined Marge watching him skulk down the street. She was joined in his imagination by his children, who pointed at him with shame, calling out his name. Rogerson the junkie. Not wanting to return to his own home and it still being too early to go to Sylvia's, Rogerson went to his campus office, locked the door, put the bag in his desk and locked the drawer. Sitting motionless in the chair behind his desk, he listened to the sound of his own breathing. His respiration seemed to convey the message that he was a traitor to his own code. What will a man not do for a chance to roll in the hay? It was humiliating. He felt governed by his genitals, numb and maimed though they were by Heep's ineptitude. He began to fear that he would be unequal to any opportunity that came his way, rendered impotent by Heep's scalpel.

He let himself out of his office, locking the door behind him, and went silently down the hall to the men's room. At the urinal he verified to his alarm that there was no feeling in his organ of reproduction, the flaccid flesh felt but not feeling. He put it away, groaning inwardly. He would sue Heep. He imagined the case coming to court. University professor charges urologist with impairing his sex life. Can you tell the court your symptoms, Professor? The judge leaned toward Rogerson, white eyebrows dancing lasciviously, the jury snickered, there were ribald exchanges in the press corps. Marge and the children sat in a pewlike bench, eyes cast down, bitterly ashamed. Heep, at the defendant's table, pared his nails with a scalpel, trading insouciant glances with his attorney.

Rogerson remained in his office until five to seven and then, with the plastic bag inside his seersucker jacket, pressed against his arm and side, walked rapidly to Sylvia's apartment, certain that unseen pursuers watched his every move.

"I don't have any papers," he said to Sylvia.

She looked crestfallen. "Neither do I."

Rogerson felt a quick elation. They would be unable to use the stuff. He would have made the gesture with impunity. He would leave the bag with Sylvia and go and sin no more. He felt almost light-headed with the return of innocence.

"I know. My pipe."

"You have a pipe?"

"Of course. Don't look so shocked."

She brought out the pipe, a delicate little thing with a bowl the size of a thimble. Would she fill it immediately and light up? But she put the pipe and plastic bag away, in the other room, the bedroom. Rogerson's throat was dry. Sylvia gave him a martini and went to look after things in the compact kitchen along one wall of the room.

171

It was an ingeniously designed all-purpose room: kitchen, sitting room, study, all in one, these different uses of space flowing into one another without clashing. Rogerson went to the window behind Sylvia's desk and looked out at the campus in summer twilight.

"I keep my raunchy photographs locked up."

Rogerson turned to look at the cleared rectangle of her desk.

"Good idea."

"It's nearly ready."

Whatever it was, it smelled good. Sylvia was wearing a white linen dress which accentuated her tanned limbs and sun-streaked hair. She seemed a paragon of health, good living and now easy domesticity. The table was attractive: flowers, candles, a bottle of rosé she asked Rogerson to open. He did. She served: pork chops, rice, sweet potatoes, salad and glass after glass of wine. The food was the best Rogerson had had in weeks. He said so.

"Ready for coffee?"

They drank it in chairs pulled up to the screen door leading onto the diminutive balcony. Sylvia vetoed going outside. Julia Hopper again. Rogerson began to think that the Hopper girl represented the outside world in general. They had not turned on lights, and as dinner progressed, the glow from the candles seemed to intensify as night fell. The room was all but dark now, but since their eyes had adjusted to the failing light it was possible to think of the gloaming as merely intimate.

"Mmmm," Sylvia said, apropos of nothing.

"Yes."

Silence. It occurred to Rogerson that a first move would have to be made sooner or later, undoubtedly by him. He had no idea what the first move might consist of. For the moment it did not matter. He wanted to sit here and allow his dinner to settle, to sip coffee and look out at the shadowy campus. Sylvia brought her chair closer to his, got up and went across the room, blew out the candles, sat again. Her bare arm on his. Rogerson felt the hair on his forearm tingle. Sylvia's hand closed over his.

"Nice," she said.

"Yes."

He turned his hand over so that their contact was palm to palm. Ah, the metaphor of any bodily contact, signifying the ultimate conjugation. Rogerson felt euphoric with the certainty that this night was aimed at a sensuous peak and would arrive there no matter what he did or did not do. It was fated. Aware of Sylvia's breath on his cheek, he turned his head and their lips met. They necked—this was the word that kept running through Rogerson's mind, a silly word, a word from his childhood, but somehow the only appropriate word and one which regained the excitement it had had when he was seventeen—for a quarter of an hour. His mouth on hers, his cheek laid on hers, a bump of foreheads, an awareness of sockets for eyes, of nares, of bone and flesh, give and resistance, dreamlike, unhurried.

"I'll get my pipe," Sylvia said.

Rogerson had forgotten the bag he had brought. What need did they have for it? Their contact had been completely above the shoulders, his body was not yet engaged, but that was all for the best; he imagined they would make slow and certain progress, as in classical pornography, allowing each tip and surface of the body to play its part before the main act was even broached. Sylvia was all the aphrodisiac he needed, aided by the dark and his imagination. Still, he had brought the bag as one bearing gifts and if they were ever going to try the stuff this was as appropriate a time as any, no matter that his curiosity had dropped to zero.

"If you'd like."

She withdrew, stood, went into the bedroom. The sound of movements, a drawer opening, closing, then another. She was talking to herself. Perhaps she could not find it. He did not care. But she found it. Again she sat beside him. He heard the rustle of the plastic bag.

"Should I do the honors?" she asked.

"Yes."

"Do you have a match?"

He had a match. He handed the packet to her. A moment later one flared into life, bright, blinding, applied to the bowl of the pipe. Sylvia's profile, the pipe in her mouth, her eyes intent on her task, drawing so that her cheeks hollowed. Powerfully exciting. The smell of the smoke was wholly unlike tobacco, sharp, somehow exotic. Rogerson could already feel the effects of it. The match was out, but the pipe glowed in the dark. She passed it to him.

"Inhale and hold it down," she said.

He followed her instructions. His first impression was that he was a boy again, smoking dry hollyhock stalks. The smoke entered his lungs like flame, and holding it there, he felt tears pop into his eyes. His head began to inflate, he felt that he would be lifted from his chair and float helplessly about the room. He had had no idea that the effect would be so immediate. He let the smoke out and took another, deeper drag on the pipe before handing it to Sylvia. He closed his eyes. He seemed invaded by a benevolent spirit which tried each nook and cranny of his body, making him extremely aware of his own borders. Sylvia's hand in his again. He turned to her and pressed his mouth to hers. Smoke, his, hers, theirs, escaped from their nostrils, mingled in their mouths. Their kiss became deeper, more passionate. A moment later, the pipe in one hand, Rogerson's hand in the other, Sylvia led him into the bedroom.

Half an hour later, Rogerson lay staring at the bedroom ceiling. Beside him, facing him, Sylvia splayed a hand on his stomach. She seemed resigned. Nothing had happened. Rogerson's gloomy preoccupied expression was for public consumption; Sylvia must imagine him brooding on the darker aspects of sexual pathology. He had failed. Rogerson also rises, but not tonight. The polar icecap had nothing on his supposed erogenous zones. Heep had jumbled his geography. It was amazing that he had left him a north pole at all. As an illicit lover, Rogerson was a failure. Make a clean breast of it, Mae, you're a bust. Joking? Why not? Rogerson had seldom felt better. He had not banged Sylvia. He was still *coniunx intactus*. What his character had lacked, Heep's scalpel had supplied. Is this how the old ascetics had felt, their disciplined bodies totally subservient to soul?

Beside him, Sylvia sighed as if bidding farewell to romance.

He said, "It must have been the pot."

"I guess."

Whatever the explanation—a vestigial moral sense, numbed nerve ends, what they had smoked—the attempt had been like one of those experiments with radioactive materials conducted with mechanical extensions of hands. Or trying to pick up a prize instead of a gum ball with the claw of the machine. Rogerson's head was still light from the smoke. He mentioned this lingering effect to Sylvia.

174

"I didn't feel a thing."

"That's not possible."

"That was the strangest stuff I ever smoked, Matt."

"Care for some more?"

"Okay. Maybe this time I'll feel something."

Her words seemed a coded chiding of his ineffectiveness in bed. Surely she must have felt the effects of the pot.

Rogerson went naked into the other room. He had taken the pipe from the bedside table. The bag of marijuana lay on Sylvia's chair. Filling the pipe, Rogerson looked out at the campus. Lights twinkled through the trees. He had been initiated into the campus immorality against which he had railed for years. He had smoked marijuana; he had, at least in his heart, committed adultery with a girl almost half his age. Half ass, as it were. This second pipeful was a kind of expiation. He could hear people in the hallway. He filled the pipe and groped for matches. He put the pipe between his teeth. The voices seemed to be right outside the door.

"Matt." It was Sylvia, a significant catch in her voice.

Before he could answer, the door from the hallway burst open and the light went on. At the same time, Ketchum plunged into the room, merely a silhouette at first, as were the two Keystone cops who followed him. Another man then entered the room and finally a real patrolman, a city cop. Behind them all, framed in the doorway, Julia Hopper stared wide-eyed at the discovered Rogerson. The pipe fell from his mouth, he let the bag drop to the floor. Instinctively his hand formed a clutching protective cage over his inert, scarcely healed and far from rampant genital digit.

8

Recusant Rogerson recumbent on a cot in his jail cell, its single occupant, he segregated from the rabble in the tank, they visible to him if he cared to look through the mesh of intervening cells, audible if he did not. His eyes are closed, but mimicked sleep will not put in a real appearance. He is not surprised. His head is a riot of remembered scenes of all too recent shame, his throat is dry, his chest and stomach constricted with angry sadness. His being here is unfair, unjust, a travesty. He opens his eyes and stares at the burning bulb encaged above him, illuminating the seams of the concrete ceiling. Mesh, bars, concrete, an abstract scene. Dear God, get me out of this.

But it was disbelief that had gotten him here without a howl of protest or outburst of rage. This could not be happening to Matthew Rogerson, forty-seven, husband and father, professor of humanities, heretofore the impassioned spokesman for old-fashioned virtues if not always their best exemplar. If he has transgressed the law, he has also been betrayed. The police had been set on him, there was little doubt of that. By whom? Julia Hopper, perhaps. Perhaps by Eric Mapes. Turnabout is unfair play. And he had been betrayed by Sylvia too.

"It doesn't belong to me," she had screamed, emerging from her bedroom. She was fully clothed or seemed to be; perhaps she had on only her dress. In any case, it admitted her to polite company, while Rogerson had only a towel the contemptuously compassionate Ketchum had flung at him.

"I want my clothes."

"You'll get your clothes," Gresham, the plainclothesman from downtown, growled. He seemed to resent Ketchum's presence.

"Close the door," Rogerson pleaded. He was turned to the window, but could still see the little-boy face of Julia Hopper looking at him over the heads of the invading police. And what had been the expression on her face? A recycled Eve pointing Adam out of the garden? A mutant glorious Milton in semi-drag turning the cosmos upside down?

"The door is closed, Professor Rogerson," Ketchum said.

"Professor?" Gresham came closer and glared at Rogerson. "Are you a professor?"

"I want a lawyer," Rogerson bleated, the words popping into his head from hundreds of televised episodes.

"You have no right to break in here like this," Sylvia cried.

The detective turned on her, brandishing the plastic bag he had snatched from Rogerson.

"What's this?" he demanded.

"It's not mine," Sylvia protested. "Tell him, Matt."

"Is this your room?" Gresham persisted.

"I brought that stuff," Rogerson said. "It isn't hers. It's mine."

Sylvia was stopped from leaving the room by one of the police. Gresham sniffed the air. "I don't suppose you even tried it."

"No!"

"How about you, Professor? Did you have some?"

"Leave him alone," Ketchum said. All triumph was gone from the chief of campus security. He seemed to derive no pleasure from the sight of a towel-draped Rogerson surprised in a young lady's room.

"You admit this is your stuff?" Gresham asked Rogerson.

"Yes."

Gresham turned on his heel. "I want pictures of this place."

The deed was father to the thought. Several policemen had been snapping away with Polaroid cameras for several minutes and were now comparing results. They seemed to have concentrated on Sylvia, but Rogerson saw that one of the photographs was of himself, a back shot in the buff. Shades of Heep's projected volume.

"Ketchum," Rogerson said. "Please give me my clothes."

"Where are they?"

Rogerson cleared his throat, but was unable to speak matter-of-factly. "In the bedroom."

"Tell them to leave me alone," Sylvia begged Ketchum.

Ketchum sent one of his men for Rogerson's clothes. How twisted they looked. His shorts and socks were inside out. These signs of hasty disrobing brought a lump of self-pity to Rogerson's throat. How little he had suspected, when he got undressed, that he was but minutes away from the ultimate ignominy. The police ringed him while he dressed; they might have been screening him from Sylvia.

"Leave her out of this," Rogerson whispered to Ketchum.

"It's not up to me. Not anymore."

"But I brought that stuff."

"It's her room, isn't it?"

"What difference does that make? Every other room on campus . . ."

"Shhh," Ketchum said. "I don't want these guys tearing the campus apart."

"Who called them?"

"I didn't. One of the gate guards phoned me when they drove in. I caught up with them in the hall outside."

"Order them out of here."

"I can't. He has the stuff."

"At least get Miss Wood out of here."

Ketchum took the detective into a corner, where a heated discussion took place. The chief of campus security tried to make a point about jurisdiction, but Gresham shook the plastic bag under his chin as though it were a thurible. Sylvia avoided Rogerson's eyes. She went into the bedroom. When the conference broke up, she was summoned.

"I didn't do anything," Sylvia said, bursting into tears. "Please, you can't do anything to me. It's not my fault."

"All I want from you is a statement. You're not under arrest."

"What kind of a statement?"

"Just tell us what happened."

Defiance flickered in Sylvia's tear-filled eyes, then died. She looked to Rogerson for sympathy, for understanding, then nodded assent to Gresham.

Rogerson rode downtown in the back seat of a squad car, Gresham and Ketchum on either side of him. Ketchum professed indignation at this treatment of Rogerson, though his grievance seemed to be that Gresham had trespassed on his territory.

"You should have phoned first."

"Your line was busy."

"You never tried and you know it. You'll regret this, Gresham."

Gresham, lighting a cigarette, looked free of regret. His words emerged on exhaled smoke. "The narcotic laws include the university campus, Ketchum. Calling you is only a courtesy and you know it."

"And you know we have an agreement."

"We? I have no agreement."

"City police don't just roam about the campus."

"Until you want us to put down a riot?"

"Who called you?" Rogerson asked Gresham.

"She didn't say."

She? Was Gresham being facetious? The elfin face of Julia Elpis Hopper formed in his mind. But why? How? Shame gave way to a sense of being unjustly used. He did not want to think of the perfidious Sylvia, eager to withdraw from the consequences of the grand experiment she had urged upon him. Briefly, very briefly, the role of the aggrieved and betrayed innocent appealed to Rogerson. But he was not innocent. He wanted to escape from this every bit as much as Sylvia did. Seated between Gresham and Ketchum, he felt already restrained, chained, locked up, though neither man paid much attention to him. The car whisked through the night streets. Headlights, street lamps, the windows of stores, a whole world of freedom slid past as Rogerson was borne off to a precinct station whose existence came as a surprise to him. It was located on a street he knew well. He must have driven past it hundreds of times and never noticed it. Tonight it seemed the very navel of the universe, his unacknowledged destiny, his fate.

"I'll tell the dean," Ketchum said, as they crossed the room to the desk.

"Why not the chancellor too?" Rogerson said. Ketchum's ineffectual protests had begun to annoy him. Sylvia was already there, seated at a table in a corner of the room, speaking hurriedly to a policewoman, who, Rogerson thought, was nodding with altogether too much understanding. He himself gave perfunctory answers to the questions directed his way by an extremely fat cop behind a type-writer.

"On TV they always get one phone call."

"I mean it," Ketchum said beside him. "The dean is going to hear of this. He won't sit still for it, believe me."

The cop at the typewriter pushed a telephone toward Rogerson. "Make a call, if you want to."

Rogerson stared at the instrument. There was nobody he wanted to call. There was nobody he wanted to inform of his plight. He still hoped that this was a scare, that they would scold him and send him chastened home. He could not believe that someone would actually lead him away and put him in a cell. Some minutes later he was led away and put in a cell.

It would have been convenient, lying on his bunk, to direct his wrath at Sylvia. She had behaved with complete selfishness. Her impulse had been to shift the entire burden to him. What had she said in her statement? He would have preferred to choose the path of gallantry unprompted, but in any case he had made the gallant choice. During the first hour on the bunk he imagined that he had reclaimed his soul from an alien occupant. What had gotten into him, for the love of God? Buying pot, succumbing to Sylvia's allurements, betraying Marge and the kids. Imagined infidelity had its charms, but the real article was ashes in the mouth. It required distraction, forget-fulness, the suppression of one's better self. Shame on you, he said half aloud. Shame on you, you silly sonofabitch.

How nice it would have been to compare himself with Socrates, Boethius, Saint Paul, but they had all been innocent. They had a right to wonder why the ways of the wicked prospered. Rogerson could only ask why the stupid are punished. He searched for some middle ground between guilt and innocence. He was not unjustly accused, but neither had he flaunted his defiance of the law. He had not, as one or two of his colleagues allegedly had, smoked marijuana in the classroom, the deed a gesture of protest however conveniently buf-fered from the outside world. Nonetheless, public transgression. He

180

on the other hand had been furtive, skulking from Eric's, darting from his office, his wrong done rightly behind closed doors in the privacy of Sylvia's apartment. How in hell had Gresham heard and known exactly where to find him?

A phone call. "She didn't say." His suspicion of Julia Hopper seemed both right and wrong. Sylvia had feared the girl might be lurking in the hall and see him arrive. Okay. But how could she know that there was reason to call in Gresham? If she had wanted simply to break up the party—and what motive could she have? a woman scorned? he hardly knew the girl—she was, according to Sylvia, perfectly capable of bursting into the room herself, unaccompanied by the boys in blue. Only Sylvia knew that he was there and why.

What would happen to him now? He was a first offender, hustled off to the hoosegow like Public Enemy Number One while, if rumor and gossip were correct, the campus fairly crawled with addicts gone unapprehended for years. There was motive for feeling unjustly put upon, but his head echoed with old pronunciamentos of his own. Lock the bastards up, throw away the key, stamp out crime and drug abuse. My God. How bloodthirsty he had been. The objects of his wrath still went scot-free while he lay broken-hearted on his jail-house bunk. Self-pity drew attention to his loins, to his ruined man-hood, and Heep appeared in the accusing crowd of oppressors shuffling on the edges of Rogerson's imagination. The summer was a disaster. Olson dead. Marge and the kids gone. That damnable operation and now this. Rogerson sat on the edge of the bunk. He felt a crazy impulse to throw himself against the mesh walls of the cell, to stand at the door and grip the bars and indulge in a Cagney wail. He got up and walked to the door of the cell. Bars are an impediment only if one desires to be free, will conferring a restrictive power on steel, the coefficient of adversity. Sartre. Madness. Roger-son got out his keys and began to bang on the cell door.

In the tank the jangling sound was taken up. The drunks and deadbeats began to bang with things metallic on the confining steel. The scene in the prison mess hall when Cagney gets the news that Mom is dead. Rogerson stepped up the intensity of his banging and so did those in the tank. He felt like the leader of a prison riot. A door opened and a guard began subduing those in the tank. Rogerson continued to bang his car keys against the bars.

"What the hell do you want?"

"I have to use the phone."

"Go to sleep. This isn't a hotel."

"Let me make a phone call. Please. The sergeant offered to let me call and I didn't. I want to now."

"Sobering up, eh?"

"I am not drunk."

"Coming down out of the clouds?"

"I want to make a phone call."

The guard, a short, slouching man in his late twenties, his dim view of the human race apparent in his indifferent stare, thought a moment. "Wait," he said.

Rogerson waited. Would Sartre admit that as a choice? Five minutes later the guard returned. The sound of his key in the cell door was like the first robin of spring and Rogerson's heart leaped within him. Once outside this cell, he would do anything to avoid returning to it. An hour of incarceration had made him stir-crazy. He would confess to the use of nerve gas, of dropping napalm on the police pistol range, anything. It was all he could do not to run out of the cell area. From the tank several bleary pairs of eyes watched him go by. Rogerson felt no fellowship at all with his oppressed brethren who had floated down a stream of muscatel into this dreary drydock.

The first time he dialed Gilbert's number he got a busy signal. He was amazed to see that it was only a little after eleven on the clock behind the desk. How little time had passed since he had set out for Eric's and the fateful purchase. How swiftly the fabric of a lifetime is undone. Of course, that was not true. He had been preparing for months to do the stupid deed he had done tonight. The overt act was merely the upshot of a thousand minor betrayals enacted in heart and imagination. He should have sensed the hollowness of his supposed rectitude when his voice grew strident in defense of the moral code. He had been attracted by a minority point of view. And had he not been divorcing Marge subtly over the years, the sundering concealed until her physical distance allowed it to show itself? The sergeant's quizzical stare interrupted this meditation.

"The line is busy."

The sergeant shrugged. The guard was somewhere behind Rogerson in the room. It was mad but inevitable that he imagine a dash for freedom. Humanities professor stages jailbreak. Posse formed. Police delayed by conflicting and perhaps bogus reports. Suspect professor of phoning police himself. Rogerson once more dialed Gilbert's number.

"Yes?" There was something aloof and off-putting in Plummet-Finch's tone.

"Gilbert, this is Matt Rogerson. I've been arrested."

"Dear God."

"It's a very long story. They have let me make one phone call. Can you come down here? I really don't know what to do."

"You're downtown?"

"No." He gave Gilbert the address of the precinct station.

"Oh, yes. I know the place. Matt, I will come immediately. Should I contact a lawyer?"

"I don't know. Can't we talk about that here?"

"Very well. Sit tight."

It was an exhortation worthy of Heep. The sergeant drew the phone back toward him across the desk.

"He'll be right down."

"Your lawyer?"

"He wants me to wait for him right here," Rogerson said boldly.

"Is he going to post bail?"

"Yes."

Lying came easily here. Bail. Had that been mentioned earlier? Rogerson found it difficult to remember in detail what had transpired. The table where Sylvia had sat an hour ago was empty. She was free, no doubt home again. He imagined Julia Hopper commiserating with her on the embarrassing contretemps. Rogerson felt that he had been thrown to the wolves. The street door opened and Ketchum came in, followed by Herb Laplace. Herb's entrance was reminiscent of the way he had burst through the bushes flanking the second fairway to follow the flight of his ball. He saw Rogerson, but continued his bustling progress toward the desk.

"What's this about one of my faculty?" he demanded, and it was difficult to know what his voice was meant to convey: indignation, delight, conspiratorial glee, anger that he had been routed out at this hour.

"Mr. Rogerson? He's over there."

Herb ignored the sergeant's pointing finger. Ketchum, who had detoured to Rogerson, now joined Laplace at the desk.

"What's the charge?" the dean asked.

"Possession of marijuana."

"I was afraid of this." Herb shook his head. "I suppose you'll have to hold him?"

"He's under arrest, yes."

"What about the young lady?"

"We let her go."

"You found Rogerson in her room?"

The sergeant consulted a report. Rogerson watched the scene as he might have a sequence in a very bad dream indeed. The sergeant leaned forward and spoke in a low voice.

"Naked!" Laplace bellowed. He turned to Rogerson and could no longer suppress the delight he felt. The villain's revenge. Rogerson felt trod upon by a fiend in golf shoes. Was he to pay for every folly of recent days? But he could not bring himself to wish that he had overlooked Herb's cheating on the links. Laplace turned back to the sergeant.

Ketchum said, "I called Chancellor Wooley too."

"You what!" Laplace turned on the chief as if he might bite his nose.

"Professor Rogerson suggested it."

Laplace's wrath traveled across the room to Rogerson. He followed it with a bouncing stride.

"What the hell is this, Matt? Are you proud of what you've done? Have you telephoned the newspapers too?"

"One favor, Herb."

"Favor? You're crazy. What is it?"

"Go to hell."

"I don't think I'd like the company. I can't get you out of this, Matt. You're lucky they haven't got you down as a pusher. Ten ounces. My God."

Rogerson tried to sit tall in his chair, but there was little point in pretending that he had not granted Laplace, and everyone else, moral superiority. He had been arrested on a narcotics charge, Herb had not. Herb had only cheated at golf and there are no punitive sanctions attached to that. His cavalier execution of his duties as dean were likewise beyond the reach of the law, except that of litigation, which was a buzzing annoyance and not a personal threat.

"What's this about Wooley?"

"I was kidding."

Herb cackled in disbelief. "You're going to die laughing, do you know that? But I'll tell you one thing, it's not going to be in Fort Elbow."

Chancellor Wooley came in from the street, smiled an unctuous, anonymous smile until he saw subordinates before him, then directed his stomach across the room to where Laplace and Rogerson stood.

"What in the world is going on, Herbert?" Wooley had the ability of some actors to speak while smiling. There was no merry glint in his eye.

"Do you want to tell him, Matt?"

"Let Ketchum do it."

Wooley inclined his head while Ketchum, half turned away from Rogerson, brought the chancellor up to date. Wooley's fleshy lips pursed, his brow rose, knit, then flattened into a single snowy line. His eyes darted from time to time to Rogerson.

"Very good, Chief. You were wise to call me."

"That was Professor Rogerson's suggestion."

"Indeed? Quite right, Matthew. You are in trouble. By the same token, you are in luck. I cannot afford to have a member of the faculty figure in a scandalous news story, particularly when campus buildings are involved."

"You can't just let him off," Laplace protested. "Don't ask them to let him go."

"Do you suggest that I permit a full-blown scandal to develop? Can you imagine what our enemies in the legislature would do with something like this? Drugs?" His moist eyes went wistfully to Rogerson. "Women?"

"Wooley, Rogerson was caught in the nude in a woman's apartment by the city police. He had ten ounces of marijuana on him."

"Ten ounces!"

"It was my first purchase," Rogerson explained.

"Is that a lot?" Wooley asked Ketchum.

The chief assured him that it was. "Dr. Wooley, Gresham's squad had no right to come onto campus like that and search a residence hall. If you let them get away with this, they'll be out there every other night. You know what that could mean."

"This is not rare?" Wooley asked ingenuously.

"It's never happened before. We have an agreement with the city police."

"*I* have an agreement," Wooley corrected him. "I meant, is there much marijuana on campus."

Ketchum consulted his shoe tops. "I get rumors all the time."

"Have you ever turned up any?"

"Not yet."

"Then there is certainly no reason for the city police to be invading the campus."

"That isn't the point," Laplace said urgently. "Look, Wooley, you can't keep this quiet. Too many people know about it. What effect do you think it will have if you walk in here and get a known user freed without so much as spending a night in the can? The campus will be wide open within a week."

Wooley considered this. He turned to Rogerson. "Who was the young lady?"

"That isn't important."

"Is it not? Who was she, Herb?"

"Sylvia Wood. The new instructor."

"The redhead?" Wooley's eyes rounded in admiration. In slightly different circumstances he might have smiled benevolently at Rogerson. "Was she too in the nude?"

"I wasn't there."

"The lady was clothed," Ketchum reported, bringing a frown of disappointment to the chancellor's pudgy face.

"What were you doing in her rooms, Matthew?"

"She invited me to dinner."

"And he brought along ten ounces of marijuana," Herb said in shocked tones.

Wooley said, "That is not inconsiderable. I do not mean the amount," he added. Ketchum was having trouble with the double negative.

A familiar voice became audible behind Rogerson's unofficial jury and Gilbert Plummet-Finch joined them. He was accompanied by a pale, thin man wearing a very outdated straw hat.

"This is Mr. Snerkin," Gilbert announced. "Chancellor Wooley, Dean Laplace." Gilbert hesitated at Ketchum, but the chief too shook the thin man's hand. Meanwhile Gilbert got between Rogerson and his accusers.

"Is everything all right?"

"No."

"What is *he* doing here?" He meant Wooley.

"It's a long story. Who is Snerkin?"

"He is a bail bondsman. Liberation is always the first order of business. He is quite reliable."

"Thank you, Gilbert."

"I too have known moments of embarrassment, Matthew."

A fellow outcast with Gilbert? Well, why not? Plummet-Finch took his arm and led him away from Wooley and Laplace, who continued to argue Rogerson's fate.

"Matthew, what on earth happened?"

"I was arrested in Sylvia Wood's apartment with ten ounces of marijuana."

"You! And with Sylvia?"

"Thanks, Gilbert."

"How am I to take that?"

"You are the first one to find me out of character here. Or to show any genuine concern."

Gilbert almost blushed. "So Sylvia talked you into trying it?"

"No. It wasn't that way. I brought the stuff. She didn't know I had it."

"Where did you get it?"

"Eric."

"Aha."

"I used your name, incidentally. He demanded a reference."

Gilbert dismissed this with a wave of his hand. "But why on earth did the police show up?"

"Good question. Apparently someone phoned them. A woman."

"A woman." It was not the sex that puzzled Gilbert, but the identity of its perfidious member.

"Don't ask me who. I haven't any idea." There seemed no point

187

in mentioning Julia Hopper. What difference did it make anyway?

"You're sure it was a woman?"

"That is what the detective said. Why?"

"Eric. I would not put it past him to sell it to you and then put the police on you. He is a very reckless person."

"Matthew." It was Wooley, beckoning imperiously. Gilbert started toward the chancellor and Laplace, but Wooley indicated that this was to be between the culprit and the administration. "Sit down, Matthew."

Rogerson sat where Sylvia had sat when she gave her statement. Herb was already seated, scribbling on a piece of paper.

"We have arrived at a compromise," Wooley said. "I have already made it clear that the university simply cannot afford a scandal now, not with the composition of the legislature what it is. I shall shortly make a phone call which will enable you to walk out of here a free man."

"Thank you," Rogerson said humbly. He would take anything— a scolding, a fine, fifteen hours of teaching a week—he would become assistant to the fencing coach, anything, to walk out that door and into the night.

"Don't thank me, Matthew. There is more. Dean Laplace is quite right that while it is beneficial to the university, on the state level, that you should be gotten out of this, locally, on the campus itself, it presents an entirely different face. Matthew, I must ask for your resignation."

"My resignation!"

"It is much less unpleasant this way."

"Sign this," Herb said, shoving the paper he had been writing on toward Rogerson.

"You want me to quit my job?" Rogerson asked Wooley.

"I am sorry, Matthew. Surely that is preferable to the alternative."

"I have taught here twenty years."

"I know. I know. Matthew, I shall be glad to give you a letter of recommendation."

Rogerson thought of the form letter he himself had been using for years. He suspected that Wooley's would be even more Delphic than his. Nor did he have any illusions as to what his prospects for another teaching job were at his age and coming from this campus. Marge's mention of a community college in Wisconsin came back to him. He had sneered at it then. Perhaps he would be begging for it soon.

"That is a tough bargain," he said.

"Rogerson, you're lucky and you know it. I'm for leaving you here to face the music. You've been getting away with murder for years, thumbing your nose at the administration and the students. Okay, big shot, here's your chance." Again Herb pushed the paper toward Rogerson.

"Give me that pen." Rogerson scrawled his name, large and bold, on the paper. He read it before giving it back to Herb. The dean had no doubt taken delight in being explicit. "In recognition of the embarrassment my arrest for possession of narcotics might be for the university, I hereby resign my position as professor of humanities and absolve the university of all obligations accruing to me as a member of its faculty." That was the legend to which he had boldly signed his name. Bravura came less easily when he saw what he had done. But it was almost worth it to watch Herb scramble as the paper, shoved back by Rogerson, skimmed across the table and then continued on its way, fluttering to the floor.

Snerkin joined them at the table. He too carried papers. "I'll need your signature on these," he said to Rogerson.

"What is that?" Wooley inquired.

"Contract for a bail loan."

"That won't be necessary."

"You don't want out?" Snerkin asked Rogerson. "You intend to stay?"

"Gilbert," Rogerson called. Wooley and Laplace were now huddled with the sergeant. "I won't be needing bail, Gilbert."

"Wooley?"

Rogerson nodded.

"I am sorry, Reginald," Gilbert said to Snerkin. "Truly."

Snerkin shrugged and left them.

"Well, this is decent of old Wooley. I wouldn't have thought it possible."

The possibility was delayed while the sergeant called the captain and the captain phoned his superior, to whom Wooley spoke for some time in inaudible confiding tones. Gilbert, Ketchum and Rogerson waited at the table for developments.

"That goddam Gresham," Ketchum moaned. "He is trouble, that guy. He always was."

"Have you any idea who telephoned him?" Gilbert asked.

"I don't even believe he got a call."

"Then what brought him to campus?"

"Gresham? You don't know that guy."

"No, I don't," Gilbert agreed. "Is this likely to be a frequent occurrence?"

"It better not be."

"If so, it would only be fair to announce it. After all, things have been going along so nicely. But if the police are likely to pop in at any moment, well . . ."

Ketchum found little to console him in Gilbert's remarks. He went to study the Wanted posters on a far wall.

"You must have something on the chancellor, Matthew. Imagine him hopping right down here like this."

"I resigned from the faculty."

"Belonging to the faculty requires resignation. Surely you're not serious."

"That was the deal."

"What deal?"

"I quit and they get me off. It seemed a good bargain."

"But that is blackmail."

"I'm not sure I give a damn. Twenty years."

Rogerson looked around the precinct station. It was a dreary official room. The sight of Wooley and Laplace at the desk, the chancellor with a phone to his ear, connected the scene with his two decades on the faculty. Was it fitting or unfitting that it should end here? Dear God, what would he tell Marge? And would she even care?

"Well, I give a damn," Gilbert said. "Tell them you have changed your mind."

"I signed it."

"They had a resignation written out?"

"Herb drew it up."

Gilbert glared at the dean. "This time they have overstepped themselves, I promise you. Whatever you have done shall be undone. They cannot hold you to such an agreement."

"There is nothing I can do. I don't want the publicity any more than they do."

"Oh, dear. Your family."

"At least they're out of town."

"Yes."

Wooley hung up the phone. He turned toward the room, a smile of satisfaction on his ruddy face. Herb seemed only half satisfied. On his way out of the station, Wooley said to Rogerson, "You may go, Matthew. Everything is taken care of."

"So long, Rogerson," Laplace said with a grim smile.

"Cheater," Rogerson called after him. Laplace stopped, turned, furious, but helpless too. He could not attack Rogerson in the precinct station. Grinding his teeth, he hurried to catch up to Wooley.

"Cheater?" Gilbert asked.

"At golf."

"No doubt. And at life. Well, then, where shall it be?"

"Gilbert, what I need is a very tall drink."

"The faculty club."

"No!"

"It was merely a suggestion."

"I want to go home. Come along."

"I'd be delighted."

Stepping into the night, Rogerson did not feel the elation he had imagined, lying on his bunk. Freedom is too normal a condition to sting one with surprise. A car went by in the street. It might have been himself once, blithely indifferent to the existence of the precinct station.

He could not get drunk. He had had three very stiff drinks with Gilbert and two more after Plummet-Finch had gone. Rogerson remained on his front porch, buzzed by bugs, watching fireflies turn on and off in the yard. Nature is a marvel. Rogerson unemployed. That upshot of the night was the most incredible of all. He was almost surprised that Herb should have exacted so extreme a revenge for what had happened on the golf course. How could he at forty-seven move out of the groove his life had known for twenty years? The dream of escape is sweet when one can reawaken into the comfort of one's putative prison. Rogerson, middle-aged, a critic not a creator, disenchanted with himself and blaming the world, his work, his wife, was not a good bet as a potential employee. There are no second acts in American lives. But he had long since ceased thinking of his life as drama. It was episodic, random, an unintelligible mixture of the intended and adventitious. If it had meaning, that lay around some corner he would never get to.

God loomed like the night sky, behind the twinkle of stars, his heaven beyond the inky dark of space, needing the impediment of wills and persons to become visible in reflected light. Rogerson chased the tortured metaphor from his head. It was both simpler and more complex than that. The contingency of the cosmos was only a crude image of the helplessness of men. Invisible stress and pull, the needed radiance of the sun, the atmosphere wrapped round the clod of earth, so many things and laws to hold it all together, yet it is only the stage on which our dreams and deeds and wishes are worked out. Conjunctions and collisions all intended, marionettes without strings? Again Rogerson shook his head.

The mind was better off without such contrived thoughts. Philosophy has been reduced to minutiae, puzzles over mirror images, the shape of coins, the reality of color and sound. Let the big questions go, get lost in detail. That turned out to be a sterner task than it seemed. Sitting on his porch, his now iceless drink in his hand, Rogerson longed for cosmic theory to crowd his mind. His forced resignation from the faculty might become tolerable if viewed as one of the major joints in human history. Oh, the hell with it. I am free, he mumbled. I am free.

Bullshit. This was his house, his city, his life. Marge and the kids were temporarily out of their natural habitat. He could not leave Fort Elbow. He had no place to go. Unlike Felix Freeman, he had no pension to support him in the Arizona desert, defeated on the Avenida de los Conquistadores. He had signed that promised pittance away in the precinct station when he resigned his job. But what if Marge refused to join him here? What after all was the point? He had no job, there was no longer any anchoring reason. She could stay at Lake Walleye, invest in land with Wadley, support the kids.

They had no need of him. The possibility sent a chill through him, as if in signing Herb's hastily drawn up resignation he had resigned from his family too.

"It can't be legally binding," Plummet-Finch had insisted, sitting beside him only an hour ago.

"Why not? I signed it."

"You were under duress."

"Herb didn't get me arrested. I was already boxed in and he simply took advantage of it."

"Why does he hate you so?"

"I don't think he does, not really."

"What more could he do if he did?"

"Appoint me chairman of the department?"

"They'll wipe out the humanities department for sure now."

"After me the deluge."

"For what comfort that brings."

Rogerson had sipped his drink. Good old Gilbert. He was a decent sort of fairy. Years ago he might have been accepted by the Old Bastards. In those days the standards of mediocrity had been stringently applied, honest mediocrity, the task tailored to the talent and no misdescription of either.

"Matthew, I intend to tell Grundtvig about what has happened."

"After the line I gave him the other day?"

"He still doesn't realize that. In any case, you seem to have had a premonition."

"As I told Grundtvig, I've known Herb longer than the rest of you."

"Sylvia rather let you down."

"It doesn't matter. I made a damned fool of myself."

"We all do. Including Sylvia."

"She's still young."

"Yes."

Eventually Gilbert left, not having retracted his threat to enlist the dubious aid of Grundtvig. Rogerson no longer cared. Any help Grundtvig might give would fall short of the mark. He would make a lot of noise, no doubt, roar and shout and garble the facts and finally subside. Rogerson would remain what he was on this June night, one of the unemployed. Perhaps he would go on welfare and up his standard of living.

A baby's cry rode the night air, piercingly, bringing swiftly back the anxieties of earlier times when Rogerson had been awakened by one of the children. Rogerson stood and as he did so the full force of the drinks he had had struck him, along with the whole clobbering sequence of events since he had set off for Eric's to make that stupid purchase. He was weary in body and dazed in mind, but the cry of the infant struck a dutiful chord and he went around the corner of the house to the porch steps and down to the driveway. The sound came from the back yard. Why would a baby be crying in his back yard? Rogerson canted his head and listened. It was not a baby, or babies. Cats. The mewling mating sound of cats.

Rogerson lurched up the steps and into the house, groped for and found Marge's water pistol. Goddam cats. He hated cats. So did Marge. They both hated cats. When he came outside again the sound from the back yard was continuous. Brazen beasts. Sounded more like a fight than a joyous encounter. Rogerson went through the gate and into the back yard, the water pistol held out before him, his body crouched. Rogerson the hunter. The grass was wet, condensation, dew, all is water, Thales, where were those goddam cats? The noise seemed everywhere and nowhere, a shameless bawling in the night. Rogerson gave a testing tug on the trigger of his pistol. Had anything happened? He had had no sensation of it. But then a whiff of ammonia filled his nostrils.

"Here, kitty," Rogerson called, moving through the wet uncut grass. "Here, kitty kitty."

The cats ignored him. Their noise had become a guttural gargling indication of pleasure.

"Hey!" Rogerson shouted. "Hey!"

The noise stopped. Rogerson cocked his ear, listening for sounds of movement. It was ridiculous to expect to hear cats move in the dark. Metaphysics has been cynically defined as the search in a dark room for a black cat that is not there. It occurred to Rogerson that the scientific approach would consist of running in circles of ever diminishing diameter until he cornered the cats in the center of the final circle. He began to execute this reasonable plan, calling out as he did so, "Kitty, here, kitty. Here, kitty kitty." From time to time, he sent a spurt of ammonia into the night. The sounds he made canceled any sound of the cats, but now that he had embarked on his encirclement it was fixed in his mind that the cats were immobilized at the term of his centripetal movement.

"Here, kitty, here, kitty," he chanted, the words pumping from him with his labored breathing. A light went on in the yard next door, illumining the hedge separating that yard from Rogerson's, throwing odd beams into the night. Rogerson stopped. A door slammed. He heard a woman's urgent voice and a man's reluctant grunt.

Rogerson, frozen, waited. His neighbor went out into his yard, came into the light, moved toward the separating hedge. The beam of a flashlight joined those cast by the yard light. Rogerson sat down in the grass. It was very wet. A beam of light swept over his lawn. He fell on his side before it reached him. It passed over him. Rogerson rolled onto his stomach and clutched at the grass. With his eyes closed, he was nearly overcome by dizziness. He could feel the earth spin beneath him. He might have been hanging on.

"Nothing," his neighbor's voice said disgustedly.

"Are you sure?"

"Do you want to come look?"

"But I heard a man. It sounded like you-know-who."

"Cats I heard," came the surly reply.

Rogerson, listening, felt that he was overhearing normalcy. A man with a job, in bed at night with his wife, roused by her fears, inspecting his property. Who but an outlaw would lie in the wet grass alone and drunk? He had been chasing himself. It was he who lay at the point from which the concentric circles swirled. Metaphysics indeed. He was going to be sick. The yard light went out next door. Rogerson, on hands and knees, retched. When he was done, he backed away. He felt like crawling to the door, crawling to his bed, crawling under it. He got up and stumbled across the lawn to the back steps, where he sat and tried to focus on the sky. All clarity was gone now. He was drunk, exhausted, defeated. What in the name of God was he going to do? He lifted his face to the stars and addressed that bewildered interrogative to the universe.

"I am ashamed of you, Matthew," Norah Vlach said. "I can see that you are ashamed of yourself."

"Who told you?"

"What difference does that make? This is a blessing."

"It certainly is."

"You have but one hope now."

Rogerson looked at her. They sat in the kitchen. It was twelve-thirty the following day. Norah had knocked and entered and found him seeking in a cup of instant coffee some purchase on reality. Norah's expression was belligerently complacent.

"Jesus," she explained.

Rogerson tried to drink more coffee. Norah watched him until he put his cup down again.

"It is your way," she said. "You had to go to the bottom first, all the way to the bottom. I know."

"What do you know?"

"Everything."

"Herb couldn't wait to spread the news?"

"The dean is not my informant, Matthew. You know now that you are helpless, that left to yourself there is only weakness. And sin. She is not half your age."

"Who?"

"You know who I mean."

"I thought Herb wasn't your informant."

Norah looked wise. "Your intentions have been obvious for weeks to those with eyes to see."

"What big eyes you have."

"Not only me. Of course, I knew her reputation. That girl is trouble. Fortunately that is now clear to all. I doubt that she has a future on this campus."

"Neither do I."

"What do you mean?"

"I resigned, haven't you heard? That was the price. Resign my job or spend who knows how long in the poky."

"You can't resign. What would you do?"

"Good question."

"Are you serious?"

"Ask Herb. Ask Wooley. Ask me."

"I don't believe it. You've been here twenty years. You have tenure. You are not the first member of the faculty to commit adultery." She paused. "Was it because of the drugs?"

"How did you know about that?"

Norah looked knowing. Why was she enjoying this so much? Still, she had seemed genuinely incredulous when he told her he was out of a job. All she wanted was a convert, a confession of sins, a decision for Christ.

"Was it in the paper?"

"No."

"Thank God."

"I wish you meant that."

"I do, Norah. I do."

"Then I too thank God. Have you eaten?"

"I don't want to. Not yet."

Norah considered the hand that she had placed on the table. "Whatever you told the dean last night can scarcely be held against you. No doubt you were out of your head."

"I signed a resignation, Norah. You can probably find it in my file in Herb's office."

"You dreamed that. It was an hallucination."

"Wooley witnessed it."

"Where?"

"At the precinct station."

She closed her eyes and shook her head slowly. "You imagined that."

How he wished that she was right. A light began to glow in his mind.

."Eric told you, didn't he, Norah?"

"What do you mean?"

"He told you I bought that stuff from him."

"Why would he tell me such a thing?"

"What did you do, follow me to Sylvia's?"

Norah stood, pushing back her chair, causing it to scrape on the kitchen floor. The sound ripped through Rogerson's head.

"If you have learned a lesson, this can do you no permanent harm."

"I lost my job."

"Stop saying that!"

"You called the police, didn't you, Norah? It has to be you. They told me it was a woman."

She looked down at him, aloof, unashamed, saved. "I see no reason to answer that."

"You don't have to."

"Will you pray with me?"

"No. No, I don't think so."

"As you wish."

She hesitated a moment, then came toward him. He felt her hand on his head, a biblical blessing, consolation, a show of affection.

"Poor Matthew."

She left her hand where it was. Did her fingers move slightly? How pleasant it would be to have her, someone, massage his aching head.

"Why did you do it, Norah?"

"You mustn't think about it."

"I was dragged off to the police station!"

"It was you who broke the Lord's commandment, not I."

He looked up at her, sighting along her arm to her face. She mentioned transgression in a wistful voice. It was said that Norah read the entire Bible twice a year. How her mind must teem with Old Testament hanky-panky. Those few fragments of Jewish folklore the Church chooses to regard as inspired. Belloc. Norah, flustered, removed her hand.

"I must go." She said it as if he might protest.

"Goodbye, Norah."

"You're going to Wisconsin?"

"Probably. I have to find a job somewhere."

"You have a job," she insisted.

Rogerson sighed. "Better check with Herb Laplace, Norah."

She drew herself erect. "I shall."

Plummet-Finch put Grundtvig and the lawyer on the porch before coming inside to tell Rogerson that they were there.

"What lawyer?"

"Grundtvig has hired him. He intends to make yours a *cause célèbre.*"

"Exactly what I don't want."

"So I assured him."

198

"Get rid of them."

"If that were possible, do you think they would now be seated on your porch?"

Gilbert had stirred him from a nap. After Norah left, Rogerson had adjourned to bed. The coffee had not sobered or wakened him and he wondered why he had wanted either result. He felt much better now. Or at least he had until Gilbert told him who was waiting for him on the porch below.

Rogerson sat on the edge of his bed. Gilbert was looking around the room. It seemed more Marge's room than his, than theirs. Marge. He had to call her. No, he would go up there. Norah's assumption that he would head for Wisconsin and the cottage seemed founded in his present disposition.

"Tell them I'll be down."

"I suppose you'll want to offer them a drink."

"Meaning you want one? In the kitchen. The cupboard above the refrigerator."

"Don't keep them waiting, Matthew. I presume you want me to stay?"

"Of course."

When Gilbert was gone, Rogerson remained seated on the edge of his bed. He could hear Grundtvig's whining voice on the porch below as well as another, querulous, clipped, unconvincing. What sort of lawyer would accept a case from the local chapter of the AAUP?

The lawyer's name was W. C. Privett. He wore a washable suit, had three oily bands of hair stretched across his bald pate, his brown shoes were scuffed and his tie hung askew from a rumpled collar. His gnarled hand gripped Rogerson's and he breathed commiseration while he shook the hand of the latest victim of institutional oppression. The phrase was Grundtvig's. Grundtvig seemed to regard the retaining of Privett as a watershed in the history of academic civil rights.

"He represented the Fort Elbow Five," Grundtvig explained.

"Weren't they convicted?"

"Of course." Grundtvig sneered. "The courts are the running dogs of the establishment."

Privett sat back in a wicker chair. Mention of his recent and locally famous defeat brought a flush of half-embarrassed pride to Privett's face. The Fort Elbow Five were a band of degenerates who had been arrested for broadcasting obscene records on the campus radio station. Rogerson had followed the case in the *Tribune.* The defendants had one day appeared in court wearing trench coats. Only trench coats, it had transpired. At a crucial moment they divested themselves of these impedimenta and cavorted about in the nude while the judge gaveled helplessly and the bailiff wrestled with their greased bodies. Rogerson, himself recently apprehended in the nude, did not like the possible implication that he was a typical Privett client.

"Grundtvig, I have no desire for any publicity."

"Drinkie-poos," Gilbert cried, coming out with a tray. The drinks, gin and tonic, were distributed. Rogerson first refused, then gratefully took a glass. He was glad Gilbert was there. Still logy from his nap and frazzled from his experiences of the night before, he felt at a disadvantage.

"Tell us what happened," Grundtvig said.

Rogerson told them, a very brief version. How ordinary the events of the previous evening were beginning to seem.

"There was nothing in the paper," Privett said. Rogerson had a vision of the barrister spending his office hours reading newspapers, working crossword puzzles, hoping for the phone to ring.

"Of course not," Gilbert said. "That was the point. Wooley wants no publicity."

"Nor do I," Rogerson repeated.

"What exactly was the paper you signed?" Grundtvig demanded.

"It was a resignation."

"But what did it say? I resign from the faculty, signed Matthew Rogerson?"

Rogerson reconstructed as best he could the legend Herb had composed.

"Narcotics?" Privett said. "I thought you said pot."

"I did. Marijuana."

"Narcotics is not very specific," Privett said with a show of shrewdness.

"The police confiscated the marijuana. What difference does the word make? They can produce the stuff."

200

"But how could they prove it's yours?"

"Do you expect me to deny it?"

Privett screwed up his face. "Grass in a plastic bag. How could you be sure it's the same bag, the same contents?"

Rogerson could imagine him at work in court. As a member of the jury, he would instinctively distrust Privett. In that, apparently, he was typical. No doubt Grundtvig and Privett were less interested in winning a case than in losing with wide publicity. Privett certainly had eminent models. The great defenders plunged from courtroom to courtroom, leaving behind a trail of incarcerated clients, themselves puffed up with righteousness and the certainty of failure which Grundtvig had already suggested was a sign of grace.

Privett said, "Now let me get this straight. You were arrested. You were actually in a cell. Then the dean and the chancellor showed up and traded your resignation for what?"

"For hushing the matter up."

"With whom?"

"Wooley made some phone calls."

Privett fell into thought. An impressed Grundtvig hunched forward, watching the lawyer. "You've got an idea."

Privett nodded.

"What is it?"

"I have to run now," Privett said abruptly. He stood and put his glass on the ledge of the porch. Thinking better of such abnegation, he picked it up again and drained it. "I'll be in touch."

"Wait," Grundtvig cried, scrambling to his feet. "I'll come with you."

Privett had already rounded the corner of the house and was skipping down the steps to the driveway.

"We'll be in touch," Grundtvig called over his shoulder, and then he too was gone.

In the driveway the sound of a starter ground for half a minute before a motor coughed and choked into life. Through the bushes, Rogerson saw an elderly automobile back out the driveway to the street. He turned to Gilbert.

"How do you suppose they'll publicize me?"

"Ineptly."

201

"No doubt. But I must have a numerical designation. I shall suggest The Maimed Digit."

"An odd thing, Matt. I got in touch with Eric Mapes."

"That sonofabitch."

"Precisely. He is also an extremely whimsical person. He said a strange thing when I chided him for putting the constabulary on your trail."

"Did he admit that?"

"No-o-o."

"I think I know who made the phone call, Gilbert. Norah Vlach. She as much as admitted it. The better to save my soul."

"Good heavens."

"Eric must have told her I had bought the stuff. She could have been lurking about when I came for it and followed me to Sylvia's. I had the feeling I was being watched and told myself it was imagination. Apparently it wasn't. My going to Sylvia's was my downfall. Otherwise, why wasn't I arrested in my office?"

"I don't follow you."

"What was the strange thing Eric said?"

"He kept insisting that he had sold you grass. Of course you know the slang term. He used it with curious insistence."

"What's curious about that?"

"I don't know."

They knew forty-five minutes later, when Privett telephoned from the precinct station. He spoke with the unaccustomed air of being on the winnable side of a suit.

"That plastic bag," he said. "It held ten ounces of grass."

"Grass," Rogerson repeated.

"Kentucky blue, they think. It was laced with Latakia, maybe a proportion of nine to one. Who sold you that stuff?"

"It wasn't marijuana at all?"

Rogerson recalled his ballooning head, the lilt of euphoria he had felt in Sylvia's apartment. Had his own mad expectations conferred such power on dry grass and Latakia? It was not impossible. Once he had taken what he supposed was one of Marge's tranquilizers and gone immediately limp and pacific. The pill had been prescribed to dry up Marge's milk when she put Tommy on the bottle.

"False arrest," Privett cried.

"I'll sue."

"You can't."

"Why not?"

"There's no record of your arrest. Not a thing. Whoever Wooley got to had everything destroyed. Do you have witnesses?"

"Witnesses? Certainly. Sylvia Wood."

"The girl?"

"Yes."

"Won't do. It would look like conspiracy. Two people claim they were arrested. The police deny it. No record. You need a disinterested witness."

"Ketchum."

"Who's he?"

"The chief of campus security."

"Another cop? Don't be crazy."

"He was madder than I was that the city police came on campus."

"I doubt that he would stay mad enough to testify in court."

"Why don't you find out?"

"Grundtvig wants to talk to you."

"Matthew? Isn't it great?"

Rogerson agreed that it was.

"Meet us at Laplace's office in fifteen, twenty minutes."

"What for?"

"We're going to get you reinstated. We are going to have Laplace tear up that paper you signed. You might just as well have admitted to murder; it doesn't matter. No body. You didn't do anything. There was no pot. Of course you'll want to sue the university for damages." Grundtvig was swept along by the litigious possibilities. He managed to check himself. "We're leaving now. See you at the dean's office."

"What is it?" Gilbert asked.

"The Ohio One is vindicated. Come along."

Privett and Grundtvig had gotten as far as Norah Vlach, who was holding them at bay. Rogerson heard her explain with infuriating patience that they would need an appointment to see the dean. He took Norah's arm and led her aside.

"Did Laplace tell you I resigned?"

"I still can't believe it."

"Where is that paper?"

"Matthew, what do these men want?"

"Herb's in his office, isn't he?"

Norah could not think of a circumlocution quickly enough. Rogerson let go of her arm and headed for the closed door of Herb's office. His entourage closed quickly behind him. Herb pushed back from his desk when Rogerson burst into the room. He looked trapped. Apparently he had been tuned in to the altercation at Norah's desk via the intercom. He looked at Rogerson with wary anger.

"What the hell is this? You have no business on this campus, Rogerson. You don't work here anymore."

"I believe you know Plummet-Finch and Grundtvig. This gentleman is W. C. Privett, the noted attorney."

Herb snarled with recognition. "Breaking and entering," he bleated.

Privett hooked his thumbs in his belt and stood with widespread legs in front of Laplace's desk. "Dean Laplace, I shall soon be slamming you with a suit for damages that will make your head spin. Defamation of character, acquiring a signature under duress, a breach of a tenured professor's contract, insult, inconvenience, conspiracy." Privett paused to inhale.

"Don't forget cheating at golf," Rogerson said.

"That is not an indictable offense."

"At a dollar a hole?"

"Aha," Privett said, swinging back to Laplace. "Gambling on state property. This will cost the university a million, Laplace. Conservatively speaking."

Herb, reconciled to this barbarian invasion, rocked back in his chair and returned Privett's sneer.

"Privett, you haven't won a case in ten years. You haven't even got a case here and you know it. I didn't arrest Rogerson; the police did. The idiot had a bag full of marijuana in his possession."

"Wrong," Privett said, lifting an index finger.

"He was apprehended in a woman's apartment, in a campus residence, without a stitch on."

"Unproved," Privett said, stabbing the air again.

"Ask the police."

"I have. They have no record of such an arrest."

"They know they arrested this clown last night."

"How can they know it? An arrest would have been recorded. They have no record."

"They have the marijuana."

"They have a plastic bag containing grass, ordinary grass, and some tobacco. There is no indication whose it might be."

"You switched it."

"Ha. In league with the police?"

Laplace looked around Privett at the seated Rogerson. "You were high as a kite."

"Next," Privett continued, "you will tell us that there was a record which you and the chancellor arranged to have destroyed in order to protect the university."

Herb glared at the lawyer.

"You will also claim to have a signed resignation from Professor Rogerson."

"I have, by God!"

"Let me see it."

"Go to hell."

"Dean Laplace, it is a worthless piece of paper. Even you must realize that."

"I don't realize anything."

Herb got to his feet and strode across the office to the door. When he had opened it, he turned. "All of you stay right here."

"Don't worry," Privett assured him. "We are not going anywhere."

The door slammed. Grundtvig struck Privett on the back, nearly toppling the attorney over Laplace's desk.

"Bravo. We've got him."

"First he will have to speak to the chancellor. That is what he is doing now. Gentlemen, I smell the scent of victory."

Despite himself, Rogerson felt admiration for Privett's performance. No man who had ensured that the Fort Elbow Five spend from two to five years in the state penitentiary could be an enemy of his.

"Good work," he said.

Privett nodded and lit a cigarette. He exhaled as if he wished to cloud the room with disdainful smoke. Grundtvig prowled about the office, emitting proletarian grunts at the comfort of Herb's lair.

"I've never even been in here before," he whined. "Look how the bastard lives." He kicked the corner of Herb's massive desk and indicated the leather desk pad, the array of pens, the ship's clock, the great brass ashtray filled with half-smoked filter tips.

In fifteen minutes Herb was back, his manner surly, his face dark with anger.

"All right, get out of here."

"I gather that you have spoken to your superior."

"I said get out."

"Not until you surrender Professor Rogerson's alleged resignation."

"Go to hell."

Privett sat down and gripped the arms of his chair. He stared defiantly at Herb. "The resignation."

"What the hell's the difference? It's worthless."

"I want it."

Herb stared at the lawyer for a minute, then punched a button. Norah Vlach came in. "Get me Rogerson's dossier."

"Yes, sir."

It seemed a remarkably slim record of twenty years when she placed a folder on Herb's desk some minutes later. Herb flipped it open and began to examine the contents. He sat forward. Now he leafed through the folder rapidly. He was agitated.

"Norah!"

"Yes, sir."

"Where the hell is the paper I put in here this morning? It was handwritten, by me. Signed by Rogerson."

"You put it in there?"

"It's not here."

"I see," Norah said, her face expressionless.

"Where is it?"

"If you put it in there, it is your responsibility. You did not show it to me."

Laplace looked around wildly. His eyes settled on Rogerson.

"Have you been rifling my files?"

"Stop," Privett cried. "You are all witnesses to this despicable accusation. Miss Vlach, Professor Grundtvig, Professor French."

"Plummet-Finch," Gilbert corrected coldly.

206

"Cut this out," Herb cried. "The paper isn't here. I don't know where it is. What does it matter?"

"You are saying that Professor Rogerson is a member in good standing of the faculty of this university?"

Herb seemed to huddle into himself. "Yes," he growled.

"I will have to have that in writing."

Privett, drunk with success, proceeded to dictate a memorandum to Norah, who dutifully took it down. It was an insufferable paean to Professor Rogerson, the facts supplied by the latter and his colleagues as Privett constructed the document. When he was done he told Norah to type it up immediately.

"Two carbons," he added.

"Don't you type that," Herb roared.

Norah hesitated. Finally she said, "I think I should."

"I won't sign it."

"In any case, I'll type it."

Norah left. Privett strutted about the office while the sound of Norah's machine drifted through the open door. When she came back, Privett read the ribbon copy, moving his lips as he did so.

"Very good." He slapped the copies on Herb's desk. "Your signature, please."

"No."

"Very well. The chancellor's will be every bit as valid."

Before Privett could pick up the pages, Herb whipped a pen from its socket and began to scrawl his signature. His face had grown purplish. When he was done, he stood, the papers half crumpled in his hand. He thrust them at Privett, who took them and began to smooth them.

"Now get the hell out of my office! Get out or I'll have you thrown out."

His rage was genuine and uncontrolled. They were all on their feet in an instant and moving toward the door. Privett's cockiness was dimmed before this outburst.

"Naturally I reserve the right to bring a civil suit against the university. . . ."

"Out! Get out!"

Rogerson was the last through the door. As he pulled the door closed, he looked back at the defeated dean. Laplace had slumped into his chair and stared in unseeing rage before him. Rogerson was moved to pity. Poor Herb.

And then Laplace saw Rogerson standing there and he leaped to his feet. Rogerson skipped out and pulled the door shut. Something struck the inner panels with a resounding bang. Herb's ashtray?

Norah came up to him and touched his arm. "Brenda Mapes just telephoned."

"Oh?"

"Eric has been arrested. A detective named Gresham."

"Fancy that."

"Yes."

"Professor Rogerson," Privett said. "I am quite serious about a suit for damages. When can we get together to discuss that?"

"I'm going to be out of town."

"You will get hundreds of thousands. That's a promise." Avarice swarmed in the attorney's near-sighted eyes. What percentage would he keep of an amount like that?

"I don't think so."

"Don't decide now," Privett cried. "Think about it."

Rogerson agreed to think about it.

"Call me when you get back to town, at my office, at my home."

"Thank you for today."

Privett made a dismissing gesture. "Of course I will bill Grundtvig and the AAUP for that."

9

Rogerson went by Greyhound to Chicago, wanting to talk with Jimmy Bastable, *son semblable, son frère.* His remembered wrath in Detroit when Bastable had told him of his intent to leave wife and children was now an indictment of himself. How well he understood now Bastable's desire to redefine the moral universe so that his own deeds might meet the revised standards. It is a hard thing to admit to wrongdoing, weakness, error, sin. Rogerson had not confessed to the old Polish priest, whose knowledge of English was imperfect and whose absolution was swift and automatic, given after a sentence or two of encouragement. It was to Merlin, the chaplain of the Newman Club, that he had gone, against his grain, against his better judgment, the deed doubly penitential. It had been a long session and he doubted that he had managed to convince Merlin that he had done anything wrong.

"She is not my wife, Father."

"You had intercourse?"

"I meant to."

"As an expression of love?"

"We tried to make love, yes."

He should have known that this was the magic word. Nothing involving love, however defined, was deserving of censure in Merlin's moral code. The priest was more concerned to get into the matter of Rogerson's marriage and discover the source of his search for love outside his home. To his discredit, Rogerson mentioned that Marge was away for the summer.

"You're separated from your wife?"

"Geographically, yes."

With an effort, Rogerson weaned Merlin from this tempting tangent. The Newman chaplain was far more interested in psychological counseling than in giving Rogerson the sacramental forgiveness he had come for. Merlin agreed to give him conditional absolution. He was unconvinced that Rogerson's quest for love was displeasing to God. For a penance, he asked Rogerson to be especially kind to those with whom he came into contact that day.

Rogerson assigned himself the penance of visiting Jimmy Bastable. Not that he meant to condone what Jimmy had done; the point was that he had had no authority, moral or otherwise, to chide Bastable. There was also a morbid fascination to see how things were going with Jimmy and his child bride. Were they happy, were they sad, were they pretty much as they had been before? He wanted to know. There but for a police raid went Matthew Rogerson.

He suspected that the number given for James Bastable in the directory was not that of his old friend's new domicile. He dreaded talking with Theresa. He stood in a phone booth in the bus station in Chicago while something like Walpurgisnacht reigned in the waiting room. Travel by bus, he was learning, is an introduction to the underside of the nation. He dialed the listed number and was surprised and relieved when Jimmy Bastable himself answered.

"Jimmy, this is Matt Rogerson. I wasn't sure I would reach you at this number."

"Hi, Matt." Bastable sounded drained. Listless, enervated, worn out from prodigious feats of connubial karate? The dog.

"I'm in Chicago."

"What for?"

"I want to see you."

Jimmy did not seem anxious to see him. Where was his ebullience of the spring? Had he become a jealous husband, fearful to show his beloved in public, Chaucerian? Rogerson asked about Jimmy's wife.

"Theresa's fine."

"I don't mean Theresa."

"Where are you?"

Rogerson told him and Bastable said he would be downtown in half an hour. They could have a drink together. So much for the thought that he would get a glimpse of Bastable's new ménage. He checked his bag and walked to the bar where Bastable had said he would meet him.

Bastable slid onto the stool next to Rogerson's without a greeting. He ordered beer. His eyes seemed to avoid Rogerson's. A look of pain appeared on his drawn face when Rogerson asked about his new marriage.

"About that, Matt. Things didn't quite turn out."

With thumb and finger Bastable turned his glass as he talked. He told Rogerson how grateful he was for the chewing out he had given him in Detroit and later on the phone.

"Jimmy, I'm sorry for that."

"No. You were right. I think I knew it at the time."

Dear God, had he actually convinced Jimmy Bastable when his words had seemed to bounce ineffectually off their target like spit-balls? And all the while he was condemning Bastable, his own moral foundations were being subtly undermined. Morose delectation, the fascination of failure, man's disobedience. He told Bastable of Milton; he felt he owed him that.

"I didn't get a divorce, Matt. I'm back with Theresa."

Rogerson stared at him. Suddenly Bastable seemed menacing, an improbable tower of strength, a man who had with who knew what enormous effort turned his back on the beckoning path of dalliance. The ironic possibility that he had played some small part in such a moral victory depressed Rogerson. He had come to Bastable as one less wise, certainly as one no more wise, intent on abandoning the bully pulpit he had occupied last spring in Detroit. And there sat Bastable, dejected, dressed in a style befitting his age, old and defeated, but an ethical hero. Rogerson wished that he had not telephoned his old friend.

"That's good news, Jimmy." His voice was hollow.

Bastable nodded joylessly. He looked as if he might cry.

"She turned me down, Matt. Dolores. Her goddam brother, the ex-priest, suggested that she go on retreat and pray for light. She saw that what we were doing was wrong. She was right."

211

"And you're back with Theresa?"

"I'm lucky she didn't enter the convent."

"Theresa!"

"No, no. Dolores." Bastable looked wondrously at Rogerson. "You met her, Matt. You know how beautiful she is."

"She'd make a lovely nun."

"Wouldn't that serve her brother right?"

Bastable sipped his beer and smiled. Rogerson's questions about Theresa did not interest him. He did not seem to find it odd that his wife had taken him back. But had not Rogerson taken Marge back after her transgressions with Dowlet? What else could he have done that would not have been more ridiculous, as ridiculous as lecturing Bastable on the ins and outs of marriage last spring in Detroit. He might have told Bastable of Sylvia, but he doubted that Bastable would be interested. He was murmuring how fitting it would be if Dolores actually became a nun. He made it sound as if such a vocation would amount to a kind of spiritual marriage between them. Tell it to Theresa. Rogerson said that he had to get going. He knew now where he was going. Bastable remained in the bar.

Rogerson set out in a rented car for Lake Walleye, taking the Eisenhower through Chicago and the Interstate north to Milwaukee. He was glad now that he had seen Bastable. Falling apart in the forties was not something that happened only to others. That we do not do more harm than we do is in part a matter of luck and ineptitude. Bastable's appeal to religion to cloak his infidelity had, in the end, saved him and his marriage, however willy-nilly. What passed for virtue in his own case was due to Heep's scalpel and Eric's practical joke rather than to character. Self-esteem demands a willed blindness. *Miserere nobis.* And did he not owe his reinstatement to Grundtvig and the goddam AAUP? He would not sue the university. That triumph would be denied Privett. Perhaps, like Rogerson, he would welcome a return to the more familiar terrain of defeat. For what did his own victory mean if not defeat, back to the treadmill of his dreary vocation as professor of humanities in a less than humane world? The indefinite continuation of the Department of Humanities, last gasp of a failed educational dream, was one of the stipulations Herb had put his signature to, that and Miss Ortmund's ascendancy to the chairmanship. She would be no worse in the job than anyone else. She might even make the mail trains run on time.

His professional life provided for, Rogerson confronted the problem of his marriage. Would Marge, when he had given her his sordid and silly news, want him to share her inherited cottage? He stirred in the driver's seat, seeking a comfortable position. He should have engaged Privett to sue Heep. Forty-seven years old. In a very few years he would be fifty. It seemed an incredible age. Denied youthful success, was he to be cursed with a hale and hearty longevity, lurching eventually into retirement and an adobe house on the Avenida de los Conquistadores? Unlikely. His golden years would be reflected in the loathed Lake Walleye. If Marge would have him. When he left Chicago, magnetic north seemed to pull the car toward Wisconsin.

He had trouble finding the cottage and became lost in the wooded acreage that promised to propel Marge into riches and power in the tourist industry. Finally he was on the right road, rutted, unpaved, strolled by sunburned urbanites bent on an enjoyable week or two if it killed them. Rogerson was stiff of neck and crotchety when he pulled into the diminutive driveway of the cottage.

A hammock slung between cottonwoods beside the cottage held no human burden. There were voices audible from the lake and Rogerson saw his children cavorting there. Barbara sunned herself on the boat dock, Tommy sailed, Bobby played in the sand. Rogerson started down the path toward them.

"Matt!"

It was Marge, calling from the sleeping porch. He turned like a condemned man and went to the cottage and pulled open the door. Marge looked up at him as from the depths.

"Why didn't you let me know you were coming?"

"I wasn't sure that I was."

Marge tried to hold his gaze, then looked away. "I don't know what she told you, Matt, but it isn't true."

"What isn't true?"

"Did Helen Wadley telephone you?"

"Why should she?"

Marge's shoulders shook with an impatient shiver. "She's crazy. And after all the trouble I went through to get that fifteen thousand dollars!"

Rogerson sat on the day bed. The smell of the lake was strong. Marge's eyes were red from tears. "Tell me about it," Rogerson said, trying to keep confusion from his voice. Come a penitent, he was being pressed into the role of confessor.

"There's nothing to tell. The deal is off."

"I see."

"She won't believe that it is only a business deal."

"You and Wadley?"

"You sound like Helen."

"I'm sorry."

"Fifteen thousand dollars," Marge said angrily, and then began to cry.

"Is there any beer?"

"I don't know," Marge wailed.

Rogerson went into the kitchen. What the hell was going on? He had assumed that his own troubles were the navel of the universe. It was not right that Marge should be on the defensive with him. He was as lucky as Bastable. Husbands love your wives. Back on the porch, he looked out at his children, still unaware of his arrival. Pines, sand, a lake in summer, children: it seemed a rebus signifying peace.

"What about the fifteen thousand dollars?"

"Matt, it isn't even mine."

"I'm not surprised."

"I borrowed it. I mortgaged this place. Everything was all set until Helen Wadley . . . Oh, Matt, she is such a twit. We have the money, but she threatens to leave Frank if I am his investment partner. He's fifty-five years old!"

"Can't you act on your own?"

"I'm not a lawyer. I need a lawyer."

Wadley was a lawyer. Marge got to her feet and looked around, unseeing, angry, disappointed, lost. Rogerson felt a sudden over-whelming tenderness for her. He even sympathized with her desire to do something on her own. No matter that he did not himself aspire to be a real estate tycoon. There are worse ideals. What after all were his own? Whatever they were, they became flesh in this lovely wet-eyed woman, were given voice by those children playing beside the lake. He took Marge's hand and she permitted herself to be drawn to a seat beside him on the day bed.

"Helen Wadley called Mother and she wants the cottage back."

"Let her sue you." Land, lawyers, mortgages: Rogerson felt that he had driven to Bleak House. He resolved to die intestate. Perhaps Heep had already arranged that.

"She says she can take this place away from us."

Us? Rogerson looked around. It wasn't a bad cottage. Mrs. Olson had not wanted it. He put his hand on Marge's.

"Stop worrying."

Marge sat erect and pushed her shoulders back. A wisp of a smile appeared at the corners of her mouth.

"There's really not much she can do. The bank has a mortgage and I have the money."

"How is everything else?"

The smile went. "The kids are bored."

"They don't look it."

"They nag me all the time. There's nothing to do, nobody to play with. They want to go home." Her expression became wistful.

"It might be a good idea. For a week or two."

"And then come back?"

"After a few weeks in Fort Elbow they'll be dying to come back."

"You may be right. Who's taking your classes?"

"I got out of summer school after all."

"And drove up here for a vacation? Oh, Matt." She leaned her head on his shoulder. "Matt, about Frank Wadley."

"Later." Later they could trade confessions. He took her in his arms. It was a crazy summer. Conscious of his wounds, he remembered three years ago when Marge had come home from the hospital after her hysterectomy. She had felt old then, destroyed, deprived of biological significance, unsexed. Perhaps his own fear of being *hors de combat* was unfounded too. The last time he had seen Heep, the urologist had spoken vaguely of an eighty percent recovery. Rogerson would settle for fifty percent. Companionship, friendship, a partner in the daily disaster of life, would more than make up for the rest. Marge in his arms was warm, defeated too, dreams of a financial coup dashed. Well, it would make a man of her. None of that now. Down with ideology, to hell with male or female or neuter mystiques. He had need of Marge and, her clinging suggested, vice versa too. From the lake came the sound of their children at play. Tomorrow or the next day they would all head back to Fort Elbow.

"How do you feel, Matt?" Marge spoke against his chest. "I mean your operation."

Her familiar body in his arms, silver threads among the gold, she was still the prettiest woman he knew. Prettier than some younger women he did not care to mention. He preferred older women. Forty-seven is a good age. He would not willingly be one day younger than he was.

"That," he said, "remains to be seen."